DEADLY TURN:
A DEACON BISHOP NOVEL

Michael Paulson

BooksForABuck.com

2008

**Deadly Turn:
A Deacon Bishop Novel
Michael Paulson**

Published by BooksForABuck.com

ISBN: 978-1-60215-080-5

CHAPTER ONE

I stopped at a rest area on my way back from McAllen, Texas. It was nearly midnight. I had a complaining bladder due to what an optimistic waitress had described as coffee an hour before. Had I known the trouble a potty-break would bring I would have skipped its promised relief, and pissed my pants. As it was, I came out of the restroom to find her waiting beside the Buick.

"I need your help," she pleaded.

She was under thirty, tall and slender. Just the type a dirty old man like me prefers. "Are we talking love or money? The pixie in me hopes for the former."

I took a pack of cigarettes from my pocket and sloughed one out. She grabbed it before I could stuff it in my mouth. That's when I noticed her hands were shaking like church bells on a Sunday morning. I took out another smoke and gripped it between my lips, then put the pack away, brought out the Zippo and gave each cigarette some fire.

"I must get to Austin." She blew smoke toward the stars. "My car broke down." She paused a beat, giving the wrinkles in my suit a brief scan. "I don't have any money."

From the I-35 Freeway came the sound of humming tires. In the distance I saw approaching headlights. The woman's head twisted on her neck to look in the same direction. Then she grabbed my free hand and pressed it against one of her breasts.

"Please?" she begged, her eyes pulling tight at the corners, with fear. "I'll do anything you want—anything."

I liked the sound of the offer. I also enjoyed the feel of firm flesh beneath fingertips. I didn't trust it, though. Young women rarely bed old men unless cash is in the offing. Reluctantly, I pulled my hand from its heart-thumping perch.

"What's your name?" I asked.

"Helen. Helen Martinis. Please help me?"

Helen was not what I would consider pretty. But she had a good face. Her hair cuddled into a bun at the back of her head, like an overripe apple. Her eyes were wide-set below a high forehead. Her mouth was full-lipped above a squarish chin. Below her slender neck, was a nice clean wrapping of blue denim —shirt and pants. The belt buckle on her jeans looked to be silver. There were reddish boots on her feet. Under the sulfurous lights dotting the rest area she looked like a kid scared white-faced, by the boogeyman; a kid without purse, or pocketbook.

"If you're running from your pimp," I warned, "don't count on me for financing. I'm so cheap I squeak."

"I just need a ride!"

"Who's after you?"

Helen glanced at the approaching headlights, moved close and wrapped her arms about my waist. "Anything you want. Just name it."

If the terror in Helen's face was genuine, someone with a bad case of nasty was after her.

The hum of the approaching tires dropped in tenor as the car slowed to enter the rest area and Helen stiffened.

I gave her a nod.

She let go of me and we climbed into the Buick. Fifteen seconds later we were heading back onto I-35 as fast as I could make the tired V-8 move. Helen sat in the front seat staring out the rear window as if expecting to see demons.

"I asked you a question." I glanced between the road and my passenger. "You got your ride. An honest answer is the price."

When the lights from the rest area disappeared from the rearview mirror and nothing with headlights followed, Helen twisted in the seat, let go a relieved sigh and leaned back.

"Nobody's after me," she murmured; her tongue snaked dryly over her lips. "I'm a little on edge."

"Where's your handbag?"

She glanced down as if expecting to see it, then took a deep drag on the cigarette. "I don't carry one."

"I must be Mother Teresa." I eased up on the throttle. "Helen, you're so scared your ribs are rattling. Somebody's after you. Somebody who's got the handbag you don't carry. If there's trouble coming from your quarter, I have a right to know."

She snuffed out her smoke in the Buick's ashtray. "You've got nothing to worry about."

"When I hear 'nothing to worry about,' I think the opposite. Are the police after you? Did you escape from San Antonio's holding-tank?"

"Of course not."

"That leaves bad people with guns that go bang in the night."

She tossed another glance out the rear window. "If driving me is a problem pull over, and let me out."

My lips curled back in a grin. If the quake in her voice was an indicator, Helen was bluffing. Still, she had guts. That made her more interesting.

"Okay. You've got no problems. I've got nothing to worry about. And the sun might rise in the morning. Where in Austin are you headed?"

"Anyplace with people."

"By the time we arrive night will be fading to dawn."

She looked over at me, her eyes going cold and her jaw muscles rippling. "If you want sex, pull off to a dark spot."

Her harsh voice wiped the grin from my puss. "I was thinking along the lines of breakfast."

Her stare took a sheepish drop to her lap.

From the corner of my eye I saw Helen drag her palms across her face. When they fell away, her mouth opened. She started to say something. But her lips sealed off the words. In silence, Helen turned and stared out of the side window, at the passing black blur.

I was tempted to make another start, but I decided to wait. If Helen needed help once we reached Austin, she could ask. Maybe I would get my question answered. Maybe I would not.

Fast following headlights appeared in the rearview mirror. As they drew close the high-beams flicked on, flooding the Buick's interior with a bluish glow. Helen slouched as if trying to become invisible.

The car lowered its beams and flew past.

Instantly, she jerked upright and tilted toward the windshield; staring after it, as if the receding red Dodge belonged to a long lost friend—or a terrifying enemy.

It continued onward catching the next off-ramp a quarter of a mile ahead, its taillights quickly disappearing below a rise. I made a mental note of the plate number.

"It must be them."

"Friend or foe?" I asked.

Helen bent over, covering her eyes with her hands. "Please, hurry!"

Five miles further on, we passed a dark sedan parked on the shoulder.

Seconds later my rearview mirror trapped its headlights pulling onto the Freeway. The vehicle quickly accelerated; taking up a tailing position about thirty yards, behind. I snuffed out my cigarette in the ashtray, and my palms went wet on the steering wheel.

"Company," I warned. "It's the sedan we passed."

Helen twisted to look out the rear window. "Who's in it? A big guy? Blond hair?"

"Too dark. Now would be a good time to fill me in on those worries I don't have. In particular, about the big blond who might be in the car tailing us."

She twisted back to face forward, crouching low, her arms wrapped around her middle, as if her stomach ached.

The sounds she made were like mewings coming from a frightened kitten.

"It's time for straight talk, Helen."

Red and blue lights suddenly flashed from behind the tailing sedan's grill. The colors danced inside the Buick like fluorescent gumballs.

Helen let go a sobbing curse.

"Police cruiser," I muttered, taking my foot from the accelerator.

Her chest heaved, making one terrified gasp after another. "Don't stop! Dear God, don't stop!"

"No choice."

I touched the brakes lightly, casually slowing the Buick until I could nose it onto an off-ramp. At a stop sign I parked and rolled down the side window.

The sedan stopped directly behind me, turning on its spotlight to illuminate the Buick's interior.

In the side mirrors I spotted two uniformed men climbing out of the sedan.

The passenger remained behind the rider's door, poised to shoot. The driver approached me, one of his hands casually riding the butt of his pistol.

I draped my wrists over top of the steering wheel to keep my hands in view, and waited.

"Going a little fast weren't you?" the uniform asked.

"Not according to my speedometer."

He squatted to peer inside the car, his eyes on my passenger. "Driver's license and proof of insurance." His stare remained upon Helen.

I leaned across her, opened the glove box, and took out the Buick's insurance card. Then I dragged out my wallet and removed my driving license from behind its clear, plastic covering. I handed him both documents. He stood erect, examining each. Then without a word he returned to the cruiser, and climbed inside.

"He's not a cop."

"I know his uniform isn't much to brag about," I said, "but it has that certain air of legitimacy."

She tilted toward me, her voice frantic. "He works for them!"

"Who's 'them'?" I asked.

She gulped as if trying to avoid revisiting her stomach-contents. "The Portellos."

I have never been one for prayers. But I said one. Trouble from the Portello Crime-Family was like acid dripping into a fresh wound: there was no escaping the pain.

"You should have told me right away."

She gave me a surprised look. "You know them?"

I nodded. "Dom and Sal go way back with me—none of it pleasant. How do you fit into their fun and games?"

One hand went to her throat, her fingers coiling to grasp something. "Dominic has the key."

"Key?"

"I meant to say, I'm an agent with the F.B.I. Somebody blew my cover."

My stomach knotted as if I had been kicked. The Portellos would leave no witnesses to a Fed's murder. "Did you make your case?"

"No."

"Does anybody from your side know you're in trouble?"

"No."

"Do you know who recognized you?"

Her hands went to her eyes and she wiped her cheeks. "Jacob Tandem."

The nausea spread like a sickness until I felt stomach acid gurgling in my larynx. Jacob Tandem was the alias used by an infamous Chicago mobster.

"Jacob Tandem aka Agosto De Credico?" I choked.

Helen nodded.

"The bastard's in Texas?"

"I'm not playing games with you, Mister."

I squirmed in the seat wishing I could run. "Didn't your mother tell you that keeping secrets is a sin? Whether those fake cops are owned by the Portellos or Tandem's mob, you and I will soon be getting our wings—you, anyway. I'm scheduled for that hot, little out-of-the-way spot where horns and a tail are in fashion. What in hell kind of an investigation are you working on that involves two crime families that operate a thousand miles apart?"

"I can't tell you anything."

"I'll probably take that little bit of reassurance to my grave."

I took another look into the side mirror. The sedan's driver was speaking on a cellular phone.

She glanced behind. "He's coming back. Please! Get us out of here."

"There are two of them. They'd both shoot as we drove off."

I reached inside my coat and jerked out the Mauser and stuffed it beneath my right hip. The uniform took his time coming back. In one hand, he held my documents. The other firmly gripped the butt of his holstered pistol. I let my eyes dart to the other side-mirror. The sedan's passenger-door was closed. The second man was inside the cruiser fumbling to release the scattergun mounted to the dash.

The driver squatted beside my door to look at Helen. "Who is she, Mr. Bishop?"

"Fiancée," I lied. "Which means she's taken, pal."

He returned my driving license and insurance card. "I won't cite you this time. But watch your speed in the future. You were in a construction zone."

He was lying. "I'll be more careful, officer."

He turned and headed back to the sedan. I put the Buick into gear and barreled up the next ramp back onto I-35, the sedan following at a distance.

I set the cruise-control to sixty and shoved the Mauser back into its holster. Something didn't ring true. If he wanted to get Helen alone, all he had to do was detain me for questioning—I was always suspected in something. Once separated from me, Helen would have made an easy target. What bothered me most was the case of nerves the cruiser's passenger got after the driver returned with my documents. My reputation was far from sterling. However none of its damage came from armed interaction between me, and members of law-enforcement. A Highway Patrolman should not have been frightened enough to grab the scattergun.

"You worried for nothing." I hoped to get Helen talking.

"Only the dead don't worry."

I took out my cell-phone and handed it to her. "Call your people. Let them know you're in trouble. I'll deliver you any place they specify."

She snatched the phone from my hand and punched numbers. Seconds later she spoke in a muffled voice. The conversation was short and emotional, with curses and pleas on her end. For a Federal Agent, Helen was a bundle of nerves.

When she handed the phone back, Helen gave me a weak smile.

"Good news?" I asked.

She said, "There's a café just off exit 311. It's called Pedro's."

"I know the place. They serve-up a pretty good stack of hot-cakes."

"You can drop me there."

"Okay. We can eat while waiting for your people."

Helen gave me a worried look. "It's safer if you keep going—for you, I mean."

In the space of one emotional phone call, she had gone from terrified bobbysoxer to concerned law-officer. Something was rotten in her part of Norway, and it had nothing to do with the Nokkelost.

I glanced in the rearview mirror. No headlights. "Those cops must've found someone else to nudge. But the driver seemed to know you. Somebody you've worked with, before?"

"All I know is he's not on the straight."

I eased back in the seat, giving the kinks in my legs a stretch. "Next exit is Pedro's," I said, offering her a plastic grin. "Feeling better?"

Helen started to say something, but the words never came out. Something red and running without its headlights pulled alongside. I glanced over to see the other vehicle's right front fender line up with the Buick's left. A split second later I heard the screech of rubber on pavement, followed by the shriek of tearing sheet metal.

The Buick lurched onto the shoulder. I jerked the wheel trying to regain control, but the other car rammed, again.

This time there was nothing I could do but hang on, and hope. The Buick went airborne after smashing through a bridge-railing.

Helen let go a scream.

I uttered a low-level exaltation.

Gravity has a grim way with all things. What leaves the ground must return. According to Father Drapula, even angels find a safe perch upon which to rest, and reflect—something each of us should in times of trouble. Unfortunately, I was no angel and there was not a single perch in sight. I held my breath as the Buick toppled.

Luckily, depending upon one's viewpoint, it was a short flight. No food or beverage served. No flaps to drop. No seats to put in their locked, upright position. There were only the constant vocalizations of the passenger for entertainment.

Four seconds later, grass and shrubs reflected greenly in the Buick's headlamps.

The car-springs shrieked and the tires squealed as the heavy hardtop bounced, only to go airborne again.

I heard Helen cry out a prayer but there was no time to offer assurances or apologies.

The second attempt at landing was a bit more dramatic. Not only did the impact spring the trunk-lid open, the Buick's hood danced upon the windshield.

Steel screamed as it buckled. A second later, my seatbelt had all it could do to keep me pinned behind the steering wheel—during a half-dozen nose-to-tail roll-overs.

When the noise stopped, the Buick was wheels-down with steam billowing from its radiator.

Deadly Turn

I released the seatbelt, forced open the door and crawled out.

Blood ran from my skull into one eye. The air stank of gasoline.

I looked back.

Helen lay curled on the floor, not moving.

I crawled back into the Buick, grabbed her by the shirt-collar, and dragged her out.

I was backing away as fast as I could when the Buick burst into flames. A moment later the gas-tank exploded, the blast blowing the trunk-lid toward the stars, and knocking me to the ground.

I'd just managed to get to my knees, intending to pull Helen farther away, when I heard shouts.

I turned toward the voices.

A moment later, a dot of fire winked in the darkness and something pinged the ground a few feet away.

I dropped flat and jerked out the Mauser.

Another ping. This time the bullet sent a spray of dirt onto my cheek.

I took aim at the wink and squeezed off a round.

The lead hit its mark, echoing back a dull thup followed by a cry of pain.

There were two more dots of fire and two more pings, originating from a different spot.

Again I fired. Again I hit my mark.

There was a series of obscene outcries from the distant blackness, followed by dead-silence.

After many seconds of heart-thudding nothingness, I crawled over to Helen and touched her throat.

There was no pulse.

I got to my feet, but something rapped the side of my skull.

I did not notice who hit me. I did not even feel my hands or chin hit the ground. My knees simply buckled as everything went black—very, very black.

CHAPTER TWO

My eyes opened to blazing lights. For a few seconds I saw nothing but a white blur. Then I saw fuzzy shadows.

I blinked and the shadows faded into line-drawings—like cartoon sketches.

I blinked again and colors began to appear within the lines: browns, pinks, blues. Then I heard a voice.

"Bishop! Can you hear me?"

I blinked again. Sgt. Leon Martin from Homicide came into focus. He was nearly forty, but look much older. He was tall and had dark, wavy hair with little sprouts of gray at the temples. His fine brown hands ended with surprisingly delicate fingers. His eyes were gray, his nose classic Grecian. A strong cleft dented his chin and his jaw line was sharp.

Leon looked pretty nifty in his green off-the-rack number with its gravy-spotted paisley tie. He leaned over the bed staring at me like he was not sure who I was.

"Back off," I grunted. "You've been eating corned beef."

He grinned and stood erect. "Thought we'd lost you."

"Then how come I don't hear any celebrating?"

A crooked smile played on his face as fleeting as a humming bird's shadow. "It's going on downstairs. Sgt. Wells is leading the cheering section. He and the Mayor are making out the guest-list for your post-cremation parade."

"It's nice to be loved."

Martin took out his notebook and pen. "What happened out there, Deke?"

"The girl's dead. Her name was Helen Martinis."

His face hardened. "I know she's dead. Shot."

"Huh? Must've happened before the rollover."

"No. Afterward."

"She had no pulse when I got her out of the car—just before it exploded."

He made scrawls. "Better tell me all of it."

A blank uneasy feeling crawled over me. I talked while Martin took notes. Everything seemed clear enough—especially my memory of checking Helen's pulse.

"What about the two I plugged?" I asked.

He folded up the notebook and stuffed it into his suit. "No bodies other than hers. You're certain you hit your targets?"

"Positive."

"Why did she want you to leave her at the café if she was unarmed? Common sense would be to keep you nearby or demand possession of your weapon."

"Probably because she wasn't a Fed and I might recognize the playmate she'd phoned."

"You didn't hear the conversation?" He compressed his lips, as if doubting all I had said.

"Helen turned away, cloaked her voice with one hand. Check the last outgoing-call on my cell-phone."

"There was no phone."

For a moment I pondered why whoever shot her corpse had taken my cell-phone. Then a more likely scenario came to mind. "It must've bounced from my pocket during the rollovers."

"Which means it melted to oblivion," remarked Martin, "along with the rest of your heap."

He asked for the name of my cell-phone service provider. I gave it to him.

"Why didn't you believe she was a Fed?" he asked.

"I'm not saying those clowns turn out heroes. Everybody gets scared. But Helen was terrified to the point of panic. Federal Agents are too well-trained for that. Has anybody been around asking about her?"

Martin shrugged. "Not as far as I know. But you being involved might drop me from the loop. The Feds and the Mayor don't take kindly to our less-than-antagonistic relationship."

"Stop talking like we're engaged. Your wife'll get jealous. Who reported the wreck?"

He laughed, and showed a line of uneven, yellowed teeth. "Tourist. When I got to the scene, dozens of them were rushing around taking snapshots. Did you recognize the patrolman?"

I started to shake my head but stopped when the pain blurred my vision. "The one I spoke with is young, blond and clean-cut," I replied. "I'd never seen him before. I've never met a blond Sicilian, which is why I suspected Helen lied about him being with the Portello mob. But it's possible he bleached his hair. His uniform looked new. The other man was also in uniform. But he was too far away to get a look at his face. Based upon the second man's position behind the cruiser's door, I would estimate his height to be about five-nine. His hair is dark. If his narrow shoulders are an indicator, he's thin."

A skinny, short man in a white coat hurried in, rushed over to my bed, nudged Martin out of the way and dragged out a stethoscope. His eyes rolled back in his head as he put the listening device against my chest. After a few seconds, his eyes dropped to mine and he waved a finger in front of my face. He told me to follow its movement with my eyes, without turning my head.

I did.

He did not seem impressed.

"What's the damage, Doc?" I asked.

He clucked his tongue. "You'll live. For how long I dare not guess. You've got a concussion, and three cracked ribs. Not to mention a pair of lungs overdue for transplants. Don't you know smoking can be fatal?"

"So can hospitals. When do I get out of here?"

"They couldn't find an insurance card when you were brought in, Mr. Bishop." His brows furrowed suspiciously.

"I don't carry any."

With his gasp of despair one hand went to his eyes, the other clutched the stethoscope to his chest. "Dear God!" When his mitts dropped away the doctor's face had blanched, making him look like a man listening to a bank-teller explaining why his paycheck bounced. "You can leave any time, Mr. Bishop. But I would recommend several days of bed-rest followed by a life-long recuperation *away* from my hospital. No insurance? What is this world coming to?" With that, the doctor hurried out.

I looked over at Martin. "What aren't you telling me?"

There was an airy silence. "It looks like your Mauser was the murder-weapon. It was in your hand. Forensics did an acid-wash on your mitts. They found fresh nitrates."

"I told you I fired it. I also told you Helen was dead when I dragged her out of the car."

"The round entered the back of her skull and blew away most of her face on exit," he said with a trace of asperity. "Forensics dug the round from the ground beneath her head. It came from your gun. The striations on the round were caked with her blood and tissue. There's no doubt your weapon fired it. There's no doubt it went through her head."

"You think I'm stupid enough to kill someone with my own gun and then knock myself unconscious to await hospitalization with the weapon still in my hand?"

Martin gave me a level stare and said, "We go back lots of years, Bishop. For my money you are as slick as they come. Even unconscious you're capable of anything—including murder."

"When was the last time I capped somebody without justification?"

"Never—as far as the evidence goes." He waggled an accusing finger at me. "But from years of personal experience, I know how easily evidence can be manipulated. Admit it, Bishop. With you around, only the dead don't have something to worry about."

His words stirred a memory. "Almost exactly what Helen Martinis told me."

He gave me a cool stare. "I've always played it straight with you, Bishop. It's no different now. Were I you, I'd get myself a lawyer."

"When will Helen be autopsied?"

Martin checked his wristwatch. "Right about now."

"I'll give you any odds my weapon didn't kill her."

He paused a moment as if tempted to take the wager before saying, "I hope you're right."

"How long have I been here?"

Martin shrugged. "Twelve hours."

"Did forensics find blood on the grass out there?"

"There was plenty around her and you."

"I mean about a hundred feet from the Buick. That's approximately where I dropped the two who were shooting at us."

He scowled thoughtfully. "I'm not sure anybody looked—considering the trampling that area got by the tourists. I'll have it checked."

He started to leave but stopped when the door burst open and Lt. Herby Mann strode into the room. Mann gave Martin a nod of recognition without slowing his angry stride toward my bed.

"What in hell are you playing at, Bishop?" demanded Mann. "First I'm told you're dead. Then I'm told you're alive. Jesus Christ…"

"Nice to hear you're worried about me, Herby."

Leon Martin chuckled. Mann gave him a warning look. Martin took it as an order to leave. Mann waited until the door shut on Martin's departure before returning his attention to me.

"We found no identification on the woman's body and everything in your car is ashes. Did that woman tell you who she was before you shot her?"

"Is this official, Herby?" I asked. "If so, I've got nothing to say until my lawyer's present."

His teeth gritted. "Your shyster is under lock and key for drunken driving—again."

"It is the weekend, Herby."

Herby squinted at me. "For the time being, Bishop, my questions are between you and me."

I gave Lt. Mann a complete statement, covering the same ground as with Leon Martin. When I finished, Herby's hands were in his pockets and he stared grimly at the floor.

"That's all I needed to hear," he muttered. "Jacob Tandem's in town and either he or the Portellos did a hit on a Fed. Sweet Jesus!"

"Don't jump to conclusions, Herby. I'm going on Helen's claims. Have the Feds contacted you?"

His head lifted a little and then settled down again. "Not yet."

"Then they're overdue. Save yourself some aggravation. Call them."

Mann dragged over a chair and sat down. Then he said, "Why should I? What have they ever done for me? Until I have proof to the contrary, this is a local matter."

"Have you release her description to the public?"

"The mayor told me to hold off. He wants to make sure you're in the morgue. That way he can mollify the bad news of her death, with the good news of yours." Herby made a disgusted face. "The mayor's reelection bid is iffy. You being boxed and burned to ashes would be a boost for him."

"Tell the bastard I'll be voting against him, per usual."

"Hell! When he finds out you're still alive he'll go suicidal. With a little luck he'll have to back out of the mayoral race." Herby put out his under lip and gave me suspicious look. "Did Helen Martinis mention who she contacted using your phone?"

"I didn't ask. When Helen returned it I didn't look at the number."

"Can you identify the people who ran your car off the road?"

"The other car is a red Dodge. We were passed by one a few minutes earlier. It might be the same one. It might not. The Texas plate on it is, 'HJK-641'."

He took out his notebook and wrote down the number. "I'll check on that."

"I got a good look at the Patrolman. I'll be able to identify him. Is the autopsy on Helen finished?"

He shook his head. "But with most of her face gone it's a clear bet that damn Mauser you carry did the job."

"Fifty against your ten Helen was dead when she was shot."

"Done!" he shouted with delight. "When I come to collect, don't try to squirm out of it just because I'm rattling handcuffs for your wrists."

I dragged out my *pleased-as-punch* grin. "Have you told Wells I'm alive?"

"I thought I'd wait until tomorrow. The man just got out of therapy."

"He's still trying to figure out his own stupidity?"

Lt. Mann's features molded themselves into an expression reflecting his past miseries. "No. His wife left him. As a parting gesture she gave Wells a blow by blow account of her affairs with you. News like you pulling through would likely put him in the nuthouse—not that the State of Texas wouldn't benefit."

Mann watched me with a worried look on his round, brown face for many seconds. "Is there any chance you were the target? Maybe the killers thought you were dead and Helen Martinis was killed to keep her from being a witness?"

I noticed the hopeful lilt in his voice. "Admittedly I had enough blood on my face to make me look anemic. But somebody thumped me unconscious. Maybe he thought he'd done me in. It's more likely he left me alive to frame me for Helen's killing."

Mann's stubby fingers raked through his curly black hair. "None of this follows Portello style."

"I agree. The job was sloppy—even by Dom's standards. But good help is hard to find, these days—as you know."

"Don't remind me about Wells." Mann leaned back in the chair. "Salvator would not risk a hit on a Fed using anybody except the Sicilian Brothers. Dominic—God, that's a whole new ballgame. As for Jacob Tandem…"

"I don't think Dom would risk it, Herby—not, on his own. He'd run to Salvator, hoping big-brother could fix things."

Mann waggled a finger in front of my nose. "Have you irritated the Portellos lately?"

"I haven't had dealings with Salvator or Dominic in months—good, or bad. But I'll have a chat with Sal."

He jumped up. "Like hell, you will! You're staying out of this, Bishop."

Looking back, Herby's instruction was a chance for me to back out, and stay out. But my pain made me angry. That, in turn, made me stupid.

"You've had time to run her prints," I said.

Mann's hands went to his pockmarked face as if he were trying to blot out something ugly. "The name we got from the database is Helen Martinis—same as she told you. Small timer. Shoplifting, one charge. Arrested once for prostitution. If she's a Fed, the name and record are meaningless."

"What's Dom up to?" I asked.

"According to my sources, the gifted-nifty of the Portello clan went legitimate." He sighed, letting his hands fall away. "Retail-furniture. High-class stuff—probably without provenance. Salvator financed the enterprise, doubtlessly hoping it'll keep his idiot brother out of the family action." Mann paused as his eyes searched my face. "You're sure Helen Martinis was dead when you got her out of the car?"

"I never make sucker-bets, Herby."

"Shit! I should've known your wager was too easy. You've got my cell-phone number. If you think of anything else, call me."

I called to his back, "Can you get me Helen's address?"

Lt. Mann stopped and looked over one shoulder, his hand on the doorknob. "Emerson Avenue; 1911. I've been through it. Nothing there. Any messages for the mayor?"

"You can tell the bastard he can kiss my…"

"With pleasure, Bishop." Lt. Herby Mann shot me a wry grin, and left.

CHAPTER THREE

After checking out of the hospital, I hailed a passing taxi. In parting, the doctor had urged me to spend the next several days in bed—after purchasing health insurance. I lived alone and the prospect of cold sheets held little interest.

My ribs and skull ached as if gremlins were using them for timpani practice. I had been in McAllen for three weeks. Three weeks with the office air-conditioner turned off, and the office sealed shut. Three week's of coffee grounds putrefying in the trash basket next to the desk. Three weeks of envelopes collecting below the mail-slot. Instead of sleeping alone, I made the trek to my home away-from-home.

My office was in Austin's Nordstrom Building, fourth floor. The setup wasn't plush. It offered two unfurnished rooms and a toilet. The room at the front served as a reception area in case I was blessed with more than one client at a time. The other was my private office. The décor was two straight-back chairs and a swivel-number, an oak desk, five oak filing cases—three of them full of Austin smog—a calendar and a framed private investigator's license on one wall, a phone, a coat-rack, two windows sans curtains, and black-and white check linoleum covering the floor. It was the same office and furnishings I had last year. It was the same as the year before and the five years before that. Not beautiful. But paid-for.

As I unlocked the door to my office and stepped into the waiting room, its thick, vaporous atmosphere hit my face like a dirty diaper covered in rancid coffee-grounds. My throat clenched shut as if I had inhaled a blast of phosgene gas.

Desperate for oxygen, I staggered back out into the hall where I coughed up most of one lung. Then I glanced around, wondering if any of my neighbors might have a gasmask for rent.

Deciding that was an unlikely option I turned once more and faced my office door. In my current physical state, running was out of the question. I leaned against the wall adjacent to the door and hyperventilated. The brief entry into the no-man's land of private-detection disclosed a stack of envelopes nearly a foot high beneath the mail-slot. For the most part, the pile amounted to bills. But several of my clients were overdue with payments, so the prospect of a cash-influx stirred my perseverance and stiffened my spine. I held a deep breath. Then, with eyes bulging, face red and cheeks puffed I attempted another sojourn into the gaseous coffee-hell that had become my office.

By the time I grabbed up the mail and rushed into my private office, I was hallucinating. Whoever described coffee as the elixir of life had never ventured into its netherworld. With lungs aching, I elbowed the wall switch to activate the overhead fan. Then I staggered over to my desk and dropped the envelopes onto its top. My ears rang, as if warning me that forgoing oxygen any longer would be terminal. So as quickly as my rubbery legs and flailing arms could manage, I stumbled from window to window, flinging them all open. As the warm afternoon breeze hit my face, I exhaled—before choking in several frantic breaths. Austin's smog did not rest easily in my throat. But it was a big step up from the nearly-explosive atmosphere still hovering at my back.

Several desperate minutes of office-cleanup later I removed my suitcoat, draped it over the back of the swivel chair and settled behind the desk. It was blistery—even for July. I squirmed in my chair with discomfort. The exertion expended during the cleanout had plastered my shirt to my back with a layer of syrupy sweat, and left my bandages in salt-soaked disarray. With financial hope fading, I thumbed through the mail, tossing the advertisements into the wastebasket unopened, and groaning over the rest.

There were utility bills and a warning letter from my auto-insurance agent. From the building-owner came a past-due rent notice, along with the usual threat of a hex being placed upon my soul by his gypsy-wife. At the bottom of the stack, I found an I-O-U from the grass-widow for whom I had nearly died while locating her wandering-eyed husband.

I cursed my luck and tried to remember my bank balance. As best as I could recall, I had enough to cover the office-rent and the utilities until my pension arrived—provided I did not eat, drink, pay the hospital bill, or attempt any familiarity with the opposite sex. My injuries kept me from feeling disappointed about the latter. The possibility of not eating for several days, made me wish I had hung onto those fermented coffee-grounds.

I took off my watch, intending to take it to the pawnshop. It would get me enough for groceries—if I avoided meat and most vegetables. Before I could rise from the chair, the vaguely familiar face of Hamilton Blake appeared in the doorway. A moment later another face, this one completely unfamiliar, tilted into view.

The stranger's skin was sun-flushed. His reddish hair seemed to be glued back against the sides and top of a narrow skull. The thin line of mustache under his big, carrot nose was much darker than his hair, and his ears stuck out from the side of his head like handles from a Toby Jug. The stranger looked me over without haste—and without pleasure.

Hamilton gave me a toothy, intoxicated grin. "How's tricks, Deke?" He meandered his bulky, seven-foot form over to my desk. "Just got in town from Dallas."

Hamilton Blake had the pulpy face of a boxer—one who'd never won a bout. His chest and belly billowed out like a rum-keg. He had the hips of a runner and the hands of *The Creeper*, a villainous character from an old Sherlock Holmes film.

I'd first met Hamilton Blake two years earlier at a Dallas party thrown in celebration of my returning the wayward daughter of a wealthy physician. Hamilton had not changed much since then. He was still the fifty-something twelve-year-old burning both ends of the candle on money received from his father's estate.

"I hope you weren't driving, Ham," I chided.

His shaved head wagged, sending his bulldog jowls into fan-mode. "Did you know some airlines have limits on the number of drinks they'll serve?"

"It looks like you got more than your share." I shoved the envelopes off to one side.

He tilted toward me, looking at the bandage on my head. "Who slugged you?"

"Friends of friends. What brings you to Austin, Ham?"

He jabbed a thumb at the other guy. "This is my new buddy, Benny Jacobson. Benny owns a string of muffler shops."

Jacobson was short and slightly built. What I had assumed was thickly gelled hair was actually a toupee. His eyes were green and watery.

"Pleased to know you, Mr. Bishop," the little man gurgled, in a distinctly Chicago-voice. The toupee bounced when he spoke, like a leaf on a head of lettuce in a high wind. "Ham's told me all kinds of things about you—I half expected you'd be in jail when we got here."

Both men wore the latest business-fashion—silk shirts, vests with gold chains, pinstripes on the coat and pants, and shiny leather shoes. All were the custom-made-type men in my income-bracket only dream about.

I stood and shook hands with Jacobson. His small paw was wet. His grip was weak. His eyes darted away from my stare, guiltily.

"My buddy's got trouble, Deke," Hamilton slurred. "He thinks he needs a private dick. So I told Benny you could handle this thing."

I pointed to the customer chairs fronting my desk, and then resumed my seat. "Suppose you tell me all about it, Mr. Jacobson."

They sat down, Hamilton licking his lips like a very thirsty man.

I dragged out the bottle of Jack Daniels and two glasses I kept in the desk's bottom drawer, then shoved the lot across the desktop toward him.

With another grin, Ham poured two drinks and handed one to Jacobson.

"The wife's disappeared!" Jacobson bleated before tasting the aged bourbon.

Hamilton threw back the booze with a snort and poured another. "Come right out of the blue, Deke. Me and Benny was up in Alaska doin' a little fishing. We come back. Elsa was gone."

"Elsa's your wife, Mr. Jacobson?" I asked.

The little man slurped on the edge of the glass before offering a tearful nod.

"I assume you called relatives and friends looking for her?"

Jacobson took another slurp, gave another nod.

"It's like she went invisible, Deke," Ham chimed. "No note. No nothing. When broads dump *me* I always get a note—one was a hundred pages long."

"Sounds like that woman really didn't want to leave you, Ham," I remarked.

"Oh, she wanted out. Them hundred pages listed the things she was gonna' do to me with her new filleting knife should I ever show up on her doorstep." He gave his head a dismal wag. "I never knew a knife could do stuff like that."

"Did you report Elsa's disappearance to the police, Mr. Jacobson?" I asked.

"Of course." Then Jacobson broke down into sobs, his eyes as dry as a popcorn fart.

I looked over at Hamilton.

"Emotional type, Deke." Ham refreshed his drink. "Not like you and me. We take the broads, or leave 'em."

After some coaxing on my part Jacobson went on to say he had been married nearly five months without so much as a single argument between him, and his bride. He claimed his wife's work often took her away from home for weeks at a time, but Elsa always returned to their little Leander love-nest.

"Not one argument in five months?"

The little man's mouth began to quiver and his eyes went blank as if I had tossed out a coded question.

"They don't believe in it, Deke. Some psychological thingy about arguing." A dreamy look came into Ham's eyes. "Personally, I think a good shout does wonders for a relationship. Clears the air. 'Specially if you have the bitch chained to the bed."

"What type of work does Elsa do, Mr. Jacobson?" I asked.

Benny shrugged. "Not sure."

"Elsa used to work at the Stork Club in Chicago," Ham interjected.

Jacobson gave him a dirty look. "She never!" Then he offered me a nervous smile. "Elsa did work in Chicago. I don't recall where. But it was a place of noted respectability."

I looked at Ham.

A wide grin stretched across his enormous teeth. Then he rolled his bloodshot eyes.

"We moved to Leander," Jacobson continued, "to improve Elsa's chances of promotion. She's very keen on promotion."

"Sales is what Elsa's doin' here," added Ham. "Fertilizer, I think. Or is it laundry detergent?"

"Elsa knew when I was expected back," Jacobson whimpered. "She should've called. She always calls. I don't know what I'll do if something's happened to Elsa."

"How long ago was this fishing trip, Ham?" I asked.

"Hell," he said. "We've been back over a month. I've been engaged twice, since."

"Your wife has been gone for at least a month and you're just getting around to worrying?"

He licked his lips nervously. "Elsa travels a lot."

I gave Ham a questioning look.

"She's always on the road doin' that sales thingy." Hamilton gave a vague wave of one hand.

"What did her boss say when your wife didn't show for work?" I asked Jacobson.

Hamilton leaned toward me as if about to confide something private. "This is where it gets a bit tricky, Deke," he whispered. "But don't let it put you off. Benny has the bucks to pay."

"I don't know the name of her employer," Jacobson wailed, still dry-eyed.

"You've been married five months, and you don't know where your wife works?"

"Elsa never told me."

"Why hell didn't you ask?"

Jacobson's pretty mouth puckered for a moment as if he were giving in-depth consideration to my question. "I didn't think it right to question Elsa."

I gave Ham another disbelieving look.

"It gets trickier, Deke," he confided. "But hang in there, buddy."

"Does your wife own a car?" I asked Jacobson.

He nodded. "It's white."

"And the make?"

Jacobson shrugged. "I don't know anything about cars."

"Benny's not much for anything mechanical, Deke," Hamilton explained.

"You told me he owns muffler shops," I protested.

"Owns," Hamilton said. "Benny don't go anywhere near 'em. Too dirty."

"Okay, Mr. Jacobson." I felt that this business opportunity would shortly become something to pass off to a competitor, despite my meager finances. "Do you have anything with her car's license-plate number? An insurance policy, for example."

Jacobson waggled his head, his big ears flapping like bird-wings. "Elsa and I use a money-management service. They pay all our bills."

I took a notepad from my desk and slid it over to Jacobson. "Write down the management company's name, address and phone."

"I can't. Elsa hired them."

Hamilton winked and reloaded his glass.

"Is the car titled in your wife's name?" I asked.

"I don't think so," Jacobson replied with a sob. "Elsa insisted we lease, instead of buy."

"Can I assume the car Elsa's drives is gone, Mr. Jacobson?" I asked, as my frustration billowed.

"Hell yes, Deke." Ham grabbed the bottle of bourbon and replenished his friend's glass. "That's the first thing I looked for. I'm no expert on women, even if I have been married more times than the limit set by the State of Texas —another thing we can thank our former governor, for. He marries a murderer and he thinks the rest of us should settle for one, too."

"The State of Texas limit on marriages is seven, Ham," I said. "I don't like the guy any better than you, but seven spouses sounds like a fair number of chances to get it right."

"Then what about his wife killing her old boyfriend?" demanded Hamilton Blake.

"It was a car accident," I countered, impatiently.

"What was not fully investigated." One of Ham's big fingers tapped the desktop to focus my attention. "Think back to your days in Homicide, Deke. How many times did a couple break up where the woman went ballistic and killed the man?"

"I agree it happens, Ham. But she was in High-School, not married to the kid."

"Ain't no different," Hamilton declared. "That boy dumps her. She goes nut-so and arranges for a final meeting. He agrees. She knows the rout he'll drive to the meet. She picks up a girlfriend to be a witness after timing her approach to where she plans to run the stop-sign, and kill him—which she did. The girlfriend swears on a stack of Bibles it was an accident—which she still claims it was because she thought so at the time. But it wasn't, Deke. That killing was carefully planned and never fully investigated. First it was delayed a whole month due to emotional distress to the killer. She claimed she was too distraught to talk to anyone—which gave her plenty of time to work out any flaws in her statement. Then she spent the next several months at home – still too distraught to attend classes. By then the kid was long-buried and the cops had moved on. If that ain't overplaying a hand to get sympathy, I don't know what is. Proves point blank what I've always said. Never trust a woman."

Jacobson twisted toward Hamilton Blake. "Hamilton, we're here about my poor wife."

Ham leaned back in his chair and crossed his arms. "In my opinion, Elsa is leading a double-life."

"What in hell do you mean by that?" Jacobson demanded.

"Nothin' personal, Benny. I'm sure whatever Elsa's doing is being done with great respectability and without a hint of moral turpitude."

"Let's get back to her job, Mr. Jacobson," I interrupted. "I assume Elsa contributed money to the household income?"

Jacobson dragged out a damp handkerchief and blew his nose. "Of course," he sniffed. "We have a joint bank account."

"Then you must have seen her paychecks," I insisted.

"No," Jacobson replied. His next words choked up from his throat as if carefully rehearsed. "Elsa sent her paychecks to that management service. They deposited the money. Elsa's terribly efficient."

"Efficient?" I echoed in disbelief. "You don't know a damn thing about her or what she does! How do you know she's efficient?"

I got another wink from Hamilton. "Which brings us back to that tricky double-life thingy…"

Jacobson let go a snarl.

"…which is completely respectable in all areas," Ham quickly added.

I leaned back in my chair. If I took this case I would be dealing with extended absences by the missing party. There was no verifiable source of income for the missing woman. There was no money trail because she used some unnamed money management service. There wasn't even a license plate to trace, no auto registration to search, no insurance agent to speak with.

"Did your wife have friends I can speak with?" I asked Jacobson.

He finished his drink and started to set down the empty glass. But Ham quickly refilled it.

"I have no idea." Jacobson's face took on a surly twist. "She could be a real bitch at times."

"I thought you never argued?"

"We don't," Jacobson gurgled. "That's what made her such a bitch."

"So I should forget any hopes of locating her friends, Mr. Jacobson?"

Jacobson nodded his head. Then he resumed a tongue-lapping interest in the liquor.

"How in hell do you expect me to find your wife, Mr. Jacobson?"

"You *have* to find her." He took another emotional slurp from his glass. "Elsa's the only woman for me."

"His one and only in all respects—if you get my drift," Ham remarked, sympathetically.

Despite my doubts, I explained my fees to Jacobson. I emphasized there was a strong possibility I would not be able to locate Elsa, regardless of effort. I further explained the complications should I find her and she did not want to return home. Jacobson had no issue with the cost. He was adamant I search for his wife for as long as it took. He was convinced something terrible must have happened to Elsa. His surmise not only cleared away any doubts about my ability to locate his wife, but it put me back into suspicion-mode.

I was convinced Elsa was already dead—killed by her blubbering husband, and buried someplace where her corpse would never be found.

"Did your wife leave anything behind when she moved out?" I asked.

"That's just it," Hamilton interjected. "Elsa left everything behind—clothes, toiletries the whole nine yards. In my experience, when a woman skips out they strip the entire house—right down to the bed-linen. One of my exes even took the toilet." He gave his big head a sorrowful shake. "That hurt."

"Something's happened to Elsa," Jacobson chimed. "If Elsa wanted to leave, she would have taken her clothes."

"What about former lovers, Mr. Jacobson?" I asked. "Perhaps she…"

Jacobson jumped to his feet shouting, "My Elsa wouldn't do such a thing!"

Hamilton settled his friend back into the chair. "Emotional," he muttered to me. "Terribly emotional. Best move onto another topic, Deke."

"What about you?" I asked Jacobson.

"Me?" he bleated.

"Are there other women in your life?" I asked.

There was a short, lethal silence. Then Hamilton pressed one big hand on his friends shoulder to keep Jacobson seated.

"It ain't that type of marriage, Deke," Ham said, in all seriousness. "Them two are the original members of the Bible-beaters club. Righteous right down to their skivvies."

I pointed at Jacobson who was drunkenly licking the dregs from his glass.

"Medicinal, Deke." Hamilton grabbed the glass from his drunken friend. "Him and her insist that alcohol be limited to medicinal needs." Ham refilled both their glasses. "Fortunately, I am liberal with prescribed doses."

"A photo of your wife would help, Mr. Jacobson," I said.

Hamilton grabbed the Jack Daniels and settled back into his chair. "This is where things take another confusing turn."

"There aren't any pictures." Jacobson gave a weary wave of one hand. "There were. I *know* we had pictures. We took pictures on our honeymoon. But they're all gone."

"Elsa left everything but the pictures?"

"See what I mean about the tricky aspects and that double-life thingy?" Hamilton chimed.

I requested a description of Elsa, hoping I would hear about tattoos, scars and a myriad of physical anomalies. But Jacobson described his wife as beautiful, slender and with either red, or blonde or brown or black hair.

I looked over at Hamilton and got another wink.

"Elsa's a good looking woman, Deke," Ham declared. "Nice from all angles. But she has this weird thing about coloring her hair."

Jacobson gave Hamilton another scathing glare. "What in hell do you mean by that?"

"All done in a very virtuous way," Ham quickly added.

I told Jacobson I would need a substantial retainer. He presented a wad of cash the size of a softball and peeled off five thousand dollars.

Then I asked him to excuse Ham and me, for a few minutes.

Without question, Jacobson set down his glass, got up and staggered out to the waiting room.

"Is this on the level, Ham?" I asked.

"Elsa's for real, Deke. And so is Benny. I know this sounds a bit screwy. But it's just like he told it. Everything was hunky-dory. Then she dropped out of sight."

"Based upon what little he's told me I'm suspicious about Elsa being dead —by his hand."

Hamilton broke into a roar of belly-shaking laughter. "Not a chance, Deke. I had to take the fish off his hook because he didn't want to hurt the damn thing." He pointed to the pile of cash sitting on my desk. "This is legit, Buddy. Hell, I've known them two lovebirds for the better part of two months. Both him and Elsa are nice people. Neither would do anything to hurt the other. I'd swear to it on a stack of Bibles."

"But all the traveling and not knowing where she works or…"

"Elsa goes. She's gone for a few weeks at a time, sure. But she always comes back. Only this time she didn't."

"Ham, in a typical relationship the first thing discussed is what each other does for a living."

He jabbed a finger at me. "After listing any social diseases what might complicate things. I fully agree. But these are not people like you and me, Deke."

"I can't believe he's never asked what type of work she does."

His eyebrows flashed. "If you had a woman pulling down a clean, green fortune, would you ask?"

"Fortune?"

"A few days before me and Benny went fishin' I met him at his house. Elsa was dumping packets of hundred dollar bills into two laundry bags. There's must've been a million in cold cash on the damn floor."

Although Hamilton Blake was prone to exaggeration, he was well-acquainted with what millions looked like, spread out on a floor or otherwise. "She let you watch with that kind of money lying around?" I asked.

"Oh, hell no. I was headin' for the John. I just stopped on my way as I passed the bedroom. She and a friend was in there countin' cash like it was goin' out of style. Funny thing, though. They was on their knees—you know how women get on their knees when there's a lot of money involved."

"No. But I'll abide by your assessment."

"They was tilted forward—like kids playin' jacks. And I'll be damned if both of 'em didn't have a key on a chain dangling around their necks. I could see 'em lookin' down their shirts when they was bendin' over."

My mind darted back to Helen's remark about Dominic having the key. "What kind of key?"

Hamilton Blake shrugged. "Key."

"House key? Locker key?"

"Too small for a house, I'd think. More like a locker or a padlock."

"What friend? Jacobson said he didn't know any of Elsa's friends."

"Well, *he* probably don't know any of 'em, Deke. Women don't exactly take to Benny like they do you, and me."

"Did you get this friend's name, by any chance?"

He nodded. "Helen something – that's what I heard Elsa call her. A redheaded number. Nervous type. Wore tight jeans with a real fancy belt-buckle – you know, the type you win in a rodeo. Solid silver if it was anything. Red western boots—real nice."

I had a vision of Helen Martinis. "Did you talk to this friend?"

"Oh, hell no. That redhead kept to the bedroom. Didn't come out once the whole time me and Benny was there."

I described Helen Martinis to Hamilton. He grinned like a kid with a dirty mind catching a peek up a woman's skirt. "That's her! Hells bells! You damn near got this case solved and it ain't even started! I knew you was the right man for the job."

"Keep that between you and me for the time being," I said. "I don't want Benny to think he's overpaid me."

Hamilton Blake tapped the side of his big nose with a forefinger. "Gotcha', buddy."

"You left on this fishing trip that same day you saw all that money?"

"Oh, hell no. Benny and I got hotel rooms for the night. We flew out the next morning after a liquid breakfast of vodka, and prune juice. Great drink. Gives ya a buzz and fights constipation, all at the same time."

"Jacobson didn't stay at his own house?"

Hamilton shook his head. "He didn't want to wake Elsa up when it was time for us to head up north. Him and her is always considerate like that, Deke. It just breaks my heart to think she might've dumped poor Benny for some slick dude with smooth moves."

"Whose idea was it to bring in a private investigator?" I asked, as my doubts about Jacobson's veracity skyrocketed into orbit.

"Benny's." Then Hamilton thumped his chest and grinned. "But I'm the one what told him to hire you."

"What about the Stork Club business? Did Elsa really work there?"

He chuckled. "Benny and her both deny it. But I was in Chicago for a long weekend—I mean, a l-o-n-g weekend. I seen her. Waitressin'. No mistake." Then he reached out with both hands and patted my shoulders. "Trust me, Deke. Benny is devoted to Elsa. And Elsa feels the same about him—at least I hope so. I don't think my little buddy is up to findin' another woman: not a real one, anyway."

"Are Elsa's comings and goings on any type of cycle?"

Hamilton set down his empty glass and with an agreeable belch and nodded. "Three weeks—not like clockwork, but pretty close to it."

"You've seen her return home?"

"Oh, hell no. I only been to their place twice. But after listenin' to Benny, these past two months, I feel like I know her as well as anybody."

"All right, let's get to your double-life theory."

He tilted close. "I heard her on the phone, later that same evening—the one where she and the redhead were countin' all that money. Elsa was talkin' to somebody on the horn. I was in the John takin' a crap. It got pretty hot between her and the other end of the line."

"Who was she speaking with?"

"Never heard no names."

I put a few things together in my mind. "What about anything concerning a new furniture store Austin, or anything about Chicago?"

"I couldn't really hear her words through the wall. The toilet needed a new ball-cock and kept runnin'. But from the sound of her voice, Elsa was steamed about somethin'—and I mean steamed big-time."

"Was the redhead kibitzing while Elsa was on the phone?"

His head wagged. "Not that I heard. Elsa and him talked back and forth on the phone for a good twenty minutes. When she finished, I heard her say to the redhead about how they'd never shake him—or something like that."

"Him? How do you know she was on the phone with a man?"

"She called him Joel."

"You told me you hadn't heard any names."

He shrugged his massive shoulders. "Just the one. I suppose it could've been a woman. But I'm inclined to think otherwise by the sound of her voice." Hamilton Blake stopped with a sudden intake of breath. "What are you thinking? She's a hooker and the guy was a customer?"

"I'm thinking about a dead-woman."

He jerked his back upright and looked toward the waiting room, his big hands fanning the air. "Don't even suggest such a thing, Deke. Elsa ain't dead. She's just pissed about something and waitin' for Benny to come lookin'."

I returned to my chair. "Okay. I'll get on it. Is Benny's address in the Leander phone book?"

Ham took out a slip of folded paper and set it on the desk. "I thought you'd probably want to have a peak at their place. This is the address. There's a key under the mat."

I gave him a disbelieving look. "Under the mat?"

"They're that kind of people, Deke. Trustin' to the point of stupidity. I've tried to talk sense to 'em. But they just tell me the lord will protect." Ham gave another dismal head-wag. "He sure as hell don't protect me. You remember that transvestite I almost married by mistake, don't ya? Dear God, that very strange man still sends me love-letters."

I took the note and stuffed it into my pocket. "If Elsa should get in touch let me know right away."

After they left, I grabbed up the cash and telephoned a taxi to take me to the bank, and then home—to bed.

CHAPTER FOUR

Two days of sleep and pain-pills later I felt strong enough to continue where I had left off. First things first, I needed transportation. So I caught a cab to the nearest Buick dealership. There I signed my life away for something four-wheeled, new and painted forest-green. After a short drive to get the feel for my new wheels, I went to my office. There I discovered an unpleasant surprise. With the exception of my old safe the place had been thoroughly searched. It was the work of someone who knew is or her business. Someone who was looking for something in particular—something quite small. Otherwise the perpetrator would not have taken the time to tear open each of the cigarette packs I kept stored with a bottle of Pinch, in the desk's tall, bottom drawer.

By the time I put everything back into its place it was after noon and I was feeling my injuries. I lit a cigarette, went out to the Buick and let it roll my aching body toward home.

By the time I arrived in the parking lot behind my flop, it was pissing-down rain.

I pulled up the collar of my suitcoat, jumped out of the Buick, hit the electronic lock-button, and hobbled along the rain-flooded sidewalk to my apartment building's front door. It was not until I reached it that I noticed a black sedan parked half a block down the street. Because of the rain, I couldn't see the driver. From the vehicle's plain-Jane appearance, I assumed it belonged to the Feds or the locals. Considering Helen Martinis, it would not be unusual for either to keep an eye on me. I went inside.

I grabbed the day's delivery from the mailbox in the foyer. My landlord, Horace Gibbons, had dutifully collected the previous days posts during my absence. I shuffled through the envelopes while doing a crippled-dance to my flop. Six ads, two bills and a long, handwritten letter from a man named Ambrose Henderson, from Dallas.

Mr. Henderson wanted me to locate his missing son, as cheaply as possible.

I stuffed the mail into a pocket and continued my limping way. From somewhere I smelled bacon frying. I licked my lips, wishing I had some of my own for the cooking. After three weeks out of town, anything in my refrigerator would likely be either disgustingly green or vaporously poisonous.

My stomach was growling and my brain was whirling with confusion over the apparent link between Helen Martinis and Elsa Jacobson, when I stuck the key in the lock. I was too preoccupied to consider my own potential fatality. A door-shove later, my eyes realized all was not well in my little part of hell. Pots, pans, flour, sugar and everything else previously occupying space in cupboards littered the kitchen floor.

I shut the door and moved forward, but the situation was no better in the front room. What had once been a mattress on a Murphy bed was now a pile of springs and shredded batting. What used to be my favorite recliner was more or less a clutter of crushed wood, and shredded nogahide.

I thought the worst was over until a big, blond man come out of the toilet wiping his hands on a piece of a curtain. His name was Joel Kingsley. He was a special agent with the F.B.I.

"Lost?" I glanced around at the damage.

Joel and I had butted heads several times during my years as a Homicide investigator. I did not expect anything better now.

"What took you so long to get home?"

He was about twenty years younger than me, trim and fit with strong Nordic features. From the cut of his blue suit you might infer Joel was a well-heeled business executive. There was not so much as a hint of gun-bulge beneath his coat. But I knew one was there. I also knew he would not hesitate to use it on me.

"Buying a car." I gave one hand the breeze. "I'm glad you kept busy during the wait. Miss anything?"

He tossed the curtain to the floor. "Not my doing, Bishop."

"Silly me for assuming so. I thought this mess had your delicate touch." I pulled a pack of cigarettes out and lit one. If your hobby didn't bring your light and life to the darker corner of my shit-hole, what did?"

Joel focused angry blue eyes upon me. "I've got a personal interest in what happened to Helen Martinis."

I blew smoke into his face. "So do I."

He thumped his chest. "But she was a colleague of mine!"

"A Fed? You're conning me."

He blinked. "You'd better believe it, shamus."

I dragged deep on the cigarette and blew more smoke into his face. "If you thought so highly of Helen, where in hell were you the other night—when she was in trouble? I'm assuming she called you."

Another surprised blink. "I was on a stakeout. By the time I got to the scene, Helen was dead, shot."

I started to shake my head but a lightening-bolt of pain cured that impulse. "Helen talked to somebody, Joel. If not you, who?"

"Her handler, of course. Standard procedure in a crisis."

"Does her handler have a name?"

His blond head jerked. "You know I can't tell you that."

"Sure. Just like I know you left me out in the boonies for the buzzards to browse after checking her corpse."

His forefinger pierced the air between us. "I had my orders, Bishop. I follow orders."

"What orders? From that idiot in the White House, or somebody really stupid?"

He crossed his arms over his chest, his cheeks pinking with irritation. "Were you charged?"

"They don't have laws against being unconsciously stupid. If they did the mayor's office and the Republican Party would be short on players."

"I spoke to the mayor," Kingsley said. "He contends you killed her."

"He's just being hopeful. Helen was dead when I dragged her out of my car. Whoever shot her did so afterward. But don't believe me. Her autopsy will confirm it. Now, if you don't mind I have a little dusting to do."

Joel frowned in confusion. "You're certain Helen was killed in the crash?"

"I checked her pulse as soon as I got her clear of the wreck."

A bolt of brilliance blazed through my bubbling brain. What was the name Hamilton Blake heard Elsa Jacobson say? Joel? Joel Kingsley, perhaps? "How does Elsa Jacobson fit with Helen and that mysterious handler?"

His jaw dropped in shock.

I grinned. "Hit a nerve there, did I? Was Elsa Jacobson Helen's mark? She's disappeared, according to Elsa's husband. Could it be you guys have her stuffed someplace quiet and out of the way?"

"Husband?" he echoed.

Again I had hit a bull's-eye. "Ah, so there really is no Benny Jacobson, tearful worrier of beloved Elsa. Talk to me, Joel. What's this all about?"

"I can't say anything either way." He scratched his broad nose. "How did you find out about Elsa? Did Helen tell you?"

"I was hired by Benny—a guy who claimed to be her husband. I had my doubts at the time, but a pal of mine, Hamilton Blake, reassured me. I don't like being suckered, Joel."

"Neither do I."

Remembering Hamilton's words about money in a laundry bag I asked, "Is it counterfeiting?"

He suddenly moved closer, his face eager. "You saw the money?"

I took a pull on my cigarette, filling my lungs with satisfaction. "So it is counterfeiting."

His face stiffened with impatience. "What happened with Helen, Bishop?"

I gave him the condensed version of the spiel covering Helen Martinis' death. Then I asked, "Is Hamilton Blake in on it?"

"Where can I find Blake?"

"Dallas. He shouldn't be hard to find. Just follow the long line of ex-fiancée's trying to cut his throat. Is there a reward for locating the money?"

"Possibly." His reply was cagey, baiting. "Where did you see it?"

"I didn't. Hamilton Blake told me he'd seen Helen and Elsa loading a laundry-bag with piles of it. Ham isn't the brightest bulb on the Christmas tree. But he's got good eyes—particularly when it comes to women, and money."

"Do you know where Benny is, now?"

"How does he fit in?"

He gave me a crooked grin that made him look obscenely dishonest. "I can only tell you he's a person of interest."

I was used to Joel's evasive tactics, but I was certain there was more to it—something personal, something beyond his professional relationship with Helen Martinis.

Perhaps she had been on the straight about being a Fed. Perhaps her uncontrolled fear was due to inexperience. Counterfeiting would hold little interest to Ham—he was rolling in money. But Benny was another consideration—regardless of how he was linked to Elsa.

Complicating matters with respect to Benny was my lack of background information on him. I had no doubt, however, that Benny was serious in his desire to locate Elsa—his five grand of front money proved that. Unless Joel was leading me down the proverbial garden path, the money angle was the basis for Benny's eagerness.

"Did Helen give you anything?" asked Joel.

"A bad case of nerves. What was she supposed to be handing out? Samples of cash?"

He dragged one hand slowly across his mouth. "Did Helen say anything about her case?"

"Just that it involved the Portellos," I replied. "Something about Dominic having the key."

His eyes brightened with eagerness. "She said that?"

I nodded. How had Hamilton described the key around Helen and Elsa's necks? Small—like for a locker or a padlock? A storage locker, perhaps?

"Which brings me back to the money," I said. "Was Helen referring to the key for the lock where the money is stored?"

Kingsley did a poor job of feigning disinterest. "Possibly."

"Salvator generally doesn't have a ready-market for counterfeit cash. Stolen money, however, he likes to sniff at. Are we talking genuine currency?"

Then a blaze of brilliance raced across my brain. Could the money be the hundred million Jacob Tandem had embezzled from the Chicago Mob? I considered the weight of a hundred million in hundred-dollar bills. For each million there would be ten thousand bills. Each bill is 6.125 inches long and 2.625 inches wide. Each million would weigh about twenty pounds and stack about forty inches high. So a hundred million would bend the scale to the tune of a ton and would fill five large crates. My fingertips itched with greed. A hundred million in untraceable cash could provide a man with a very comfortable retirement. Could it be that the key Hamilton saw and the Key Helen mentioned were one and the same? He did say they each had a key dangling from their necklaces.

"Do you have a lead on Elsa?" he asked.

"Let's talk about Jacob Tandem and the money he was suspected of embezzling."

A frost seemed to cloud Joel's eyes. "What the hell..."

"Is the key related to those millions? Tandem's in Austin. I don't see him fool enough to let a Fed and a couple of losers like Elsa and Benny babysit those hot millions. Not after what Frankie 'The Wop' Gravano did to his lieutenant, Gino Picot. Frankie took over control of the Chicago Mob after that. Personally I didn't think Frankie had the brains to run a big operation. But stranger things have happened. Like Dominic Portello ending up with the bundle. Has he got it?"

Deadly Turn

Joel Kingsley moved off to the side, one hand tugging at his fat lower lip. "How did you get a line on Tandem?"

"The police asked questions. I asked for reasons to give answers," I lied. "You think Helen Martinis sold out to Jacob Tandem. Is that it? Is that why you're worried enough to visit me?" I jabbed a thumb in the direction of my crushed Murphy bed. "Did you think the key was here? Is that why I've got an interior designer's nightmare? Or is somebody else after it? There has to be a link between it and Helen or my place wouldn't have been torn apart."

Joel gave me an impatient, sidelong look. "What are you holding back?"

I offered him a tolerant smile. "What are you willing to trade?"

"Don't play me, Bishop."

"Likewise. They way I figure it, Helen either sold out to Tandem or she conned him out of the cash and made a run for it. I can't blame, her. A hundred million is a big temptation. Maybe she transported it here? Maybe she figured Tandem wouldn't follow. But he got a lead on her. Is that it? Is that what dropped him in Texas and put her in the morgue?"

His mouth thinned as his brain worked. "What I tell you stay's between us. Agreed?"

I nodded.

"You got part of it, Bishop." Kingsley rumpled his blond hair. "Helen Martinis was assigned to an undercover operation at Jacob Tandem's Chicago nightclub—the Stork Club. Her job was to find the embezzled money. She did. But Helen didn't sell out to Tandem. She got greedy. Helen copped the cash Tandem had embezzled. He caught on. She brought the money here with the help of her cohorts—Elsa and Benny Jacobson."

"I don't see two women and a guy the size of a gopher looting a hundred million from Jacob Tandem."

"There were two other players in the action. So far we don't know who they are. But we suspect that one didn't get clear of Tandem when the others took off with the money. That individual talked. As a result, Tandem came to Austin in hopes of reclaiming his missing money."

"How do you fit into it?"

"After we realized Helen was on the run, I was assigned to get the money— and her—before the Chicago mob did. They're probably the ones who tossed your place. I'm sure they're the ones who ran you off the road."

I nodded, but was far from being convinced.

"The Chicago Mob," Kingsley continued, "sent someone down here to keep an eye on Tandem after hearing rumors about him losing the embezzled funds. Did Helen say anything to indicate the money's location?"

"No. But I might be induced to look for it."

Kingsley offered me a toothy, appreciative grin. "You locate it and I personally guarantee you a reward."

I had my own idea on what would be an appropriate reward should I find the hundred million. But I kept that to myself.

"Where were you going to drop her off? Did Helen give you an address?"

"She never said," I replied. "If Helen was on the run from you guys and Tandem, why would she suspect the Portellos of being after her?"

"Helen was scamming you," Joel was being smug. "She was scared and needed help. You fell for it."

"There's no connection between Tandem and the Portellos?"

"There is, actually—money-laundering." Kingsley's smile was a condescending, twisted grimace—the sort a judge gives a prisoner before handing down a death-sentence. "But as far as I know it's preliminary—until Tandem gets hold of the missing money."

"How did Helen Martinis hook up with Elsa and Benny?" I asked.

"Elsa was Helen's love-interest. Benny is Elsa's brother."

"Which probably means Elsa has the money?"

"Knowing Helen like I did, I don't think so. She would've kept it under her own control." Joel pointed to the kitchen. "Let's go someplace. I haven't eaten, today."

I fell in behind him more out of curiosity than a desire to feed. Joel was completely out of character. He'd never cooperated with me during our past interactions. He was always tight as a clam about everything. My willingness to assist him in locating the money earned me a small measure of consideration, but he had disclosed a good deal more than I had told him.

We dodged raindrops to a brown sedan across the street from my apartment building. Joel jumped behind the steering wheel. I did a feeble imitation of clamoring-in on the rider's side and glanced out the rear window as we drove off.

The black sedan parked down the block immediately followed.

"Benny," I said. "I take it Helen and Elsa scammed him into helping steal the money, and then left him empty-handed?"

"We know Helen and her pals did a small split of the proceeds shortly after getting the hundred million," said Joel. "Our investigation verified that the brother and sister act immediately went out on a spending spree—which clued Tandem he'd been taken. I think Helen retaliated by cutting Benny and Elsa out of their full split."

"Why would Elsa and Benny have tolerated that?"

"A black sedan's tailing," he said, as we rolled onto I-35.

I jabbed a thumb over one shoulder. "I assumed it was your mob, or the locals."

He gave the mirrors more glances. "It's neither. Are you carrying?"

I shook my head. "What I had is now evidence for the shooting-review board."

He pointed at the dash near the glove box. "Put your hand underneath, and back about six inches."

I did as instructed coming away with an ancient .38 snub-nose Marley revolver. "I'll be dead before I hit anything with this antique."

"Just point and hope it doesn't blow up in your face."

I slipped the pistol into my suitcoat pocket. "If the Frankie Gravano, *Capi de Capo* of the Chicago Mob, knows Tandem has that money, why haven't they grabbed him?"

"Initially, they believed Gino Picot had taken it," said Kingsley. "When they did not recover the money from Picot, they figured it was lost. But after Helen Martinis and her pals grabbed the money from Tandem, he raised waves with his efforts to locate her. Frankie Gravano got curious and did his own digging. I'm sure his first impulse was to put the snatch on Tandem. But after failing with Gino Picot, he probably realized the importance of getting the money before taking revenge. We assume Gravano has someone in town keeping a close watch on Tandem—probably someone in his own organization." He glanced over, smiling wryly. "Did you see Helen before stopping at that rest area?"

"I'd been in McAllen setting up a security system at a bank. If I hadn't stopped to answer nature's call, we wouldn't be talking."

"How did Helen get there?"

"She claimed car-trouble. But at the time I assumed Helen had taken a ride with somebody who wanted more than she was willing to deliver."

"You mentioned a car arriving at the rest area as you and Helen left. Did you see it?"

I shook my head. "Just headlights. We were out of there by the time it pulled in. As I recall Tandem had witnesses against Picot to substantiate his claims."

"The four men who reported directly to Gino claimed he had taken the money. Gino had his own witness—his lady-friend—but the mob didn't believe her."

"I imagine the men who worked for Gino are in hiding."

"All are dead. Nobody knows for sure who did it, but if I were to guess, Frankie Gravano ordered it after discovering they'd framed Picot."

We caught the Leander exit and cut east on some cracked asphalt. After a short tour of soggy gravel, we pulled into the parking lot of *Taqueria del Sol.* The restaurant was a white, low-level, stucco affair with tables on the patio and salsa music emanating from speakers mounted to a red-tile roof. I was not optimistic about the upcoming meal. On the plus side, it was no longer raining.

"The black sedan dropped back," Kingsley warned. "But stay loose."

I got out and casually glanced in the direction from which we had come. No black sedan.

Inside the restaurant, we took a booth near the front windows. Within minutes the black sedan parked at one end of the lot. Joel took out his cell-phone and called Leander P.D. In his best Norwegian yodel he reported a stolen car. When asked for a description and the plate number, he offered up the black sedan.

"Just like the good old days," I commented.

"It won't do much good in the long run of things," he remarked. "But we'll get a free peek at who's interested in us."

A chunky, Hispanic waitress came over and took our orders. After she left, I asked, "Did you see any status-reports from Helen while she was working undercover in Chicago?"

His hands folded on the tabletop. "Only her handler saw those."

"Between you, me and the wall, did you see the reports?"

"I saw what was in her file. I was allowed to go through it this morning. But there's nothing I can share with you."

"How did Tandem fool the mob about the money?"

"We assume Tandem had a number of bank accounts. But we never found any that had anything like a hundred-million dollar balance—not even close. So we guess he had the money physically stashed someplace."

"Helen's fingerprints listed her as a sometime hooker. Why that history rather than something more respectable?" I asked.

"We thought a discolored past would make Tandem more likely to hire Helen. It proved to be true."

"Must've been rough—her being gay."

"Helen was a good agent—before she decided to go independent. She did what was expected to get the job done."

"I'm still having a hard time accepting the terrified woman I was with as actually being one of your kind."

Joel stared at me for a second. "Tandem nearly killed Helen in Chicago. That shook her up."

"She was betrayed to Tandem after the theft?"

Kingsley shrugged. "I heard it third-hand from her handler."

A frown tugged ripples of doubt into my forehead. "You're lying, Joel."

He glanced over growling, "Don't push it, Bishop."

"Tandem must realize the Chicago Mob is onto him. What does he expect to gain by getting back his money? Instead of drawing attention to himself by chasing it, he should've quietly accepted defeat. As it is, he's dead as soon as he gets his hands on what was taken."

"We think he's hoping to get protection from Dominic Portello."

"Dom doesn't have the juice to protect Tandem."

He shrugged. "Salvator does."

"Sal isn't stupid enough to do anything like that."

"For a chunk of a hundred million, I disagree."

"How did Tandem hook up with Dominic Portello in the first place?"

"We don't know who precipitated the initial meeting. But they met several times in Chicago."

"Have you questioned anyone from the Portello camp about Helen's murder?"

"I talked with Salvator and Dominic, this morning. They denied any involvement." He snickered, "Dominic suggested you were the shooter. Salvator agreed. They both offered to supply witnesses to get you convicted."

"Nice to hear they still think badly of me."

The waitress returned with our meals. I gave her a lusty wink.

Not only did she not wink back, but she departed quickly, as if expecting my hands to become expressively familiar with her thighs.

I loaded a tortilla with pulled beef, sweet peppers and a salsa laded with Serrano's. "Was their any connection between Tandem and the Portellos before Dom's trips to Chicago?"

Joel took a bite of chili and chewed thoughtfully. Then his eyes came up to mine as if realization had set in. "Not that I recall."

He was lying, again.

"I'm having a hard time with Dom instigating anything with Tandem. It's like trying to stuff the square peg into the round hole."

"Dom has the intellect of a toad, I agree," Joel said. "Tandem's smart and savvy. So we think Tandem made the first move, hoping to get Salvator's sympathy."

"What brought Dom to Chicago?"

"Furniture sellers' convention. Dominic bought several lines from various jobbers. We were tailing Tandem at the time. His nephew by marriage—Harold Maybe—was murdered. From the way Maybe was tortured it looked like Tandem's work. At the time we did not believe the rumors someone had heisted Tandem for the missing hundred million. But we had information that Tandem had been with Harold Maybe the evening Maybe was murdered."

"Why would you get involved with a local murder?"

"Normally we don't. But Harold Maybe had contacted us seeking protection. That gave us an in. Tandem attended the furniture convention. At the time we did not understand his motives. Then we spotted Dominic Portello. For various reasons of the stupid kind, we lost the pair. We assume they holed up to discuss matters." Joel gave his right ear a nervous tug. "You said Helen told you the Highway Patrolman was Portello's. Did she get a good enough look at him to be certain?"

"I assume so. The guy knew her. I'll try to get a look at the State Police roster-photos. If he is one of them, I'll be able to spot him."

His mouth pursed in thought a moment. "Would you say Dominic is capable of taking control of the Portello family?"

I nodded. "Morally, yes. But Dom doesn't have the balls to kill Salvator—which he would have to do."

"He wouldn't necessarily have to do it himself."

"Sal is surrounded by bodyguards—some you see; most you don't. They're a loyal as a tic on hound and they don't trust anybody. The only people who get anywhere near Sal without being frisked are family. Dom would have to manage the hit, himself."

"I've been working against goons like the Portellos my whole career, Bishop. They all have a price."

"Not Sal's men. But for argument's sake, if Dom somehow did kill his brother, Dom would still have to contend with little-sister Rita, and Momma. Momma would never forgive Dom—something he would not be able to bear.

He's always been a Momma's boy. Rita would kill Dom for it—and I'm not exaggerating."

Joel chuckled. "I heard Rita was temperamental."

"Try death-dealing. That's on good days when she's feeling amiable."

"You were involved with her for a while."

"Unofficially. I'm not on her brothers' approved prospect-list. What are you thinking? That Tandem might be urging Dom to take over the Portello mob?"

He gave me a lazy smile and went back to his meal. "Brothers have killed brothers in the past."

"I'm sure the idea crosses Dom's mind. Sal is always calling him on the carpet—mostly for being an idiot. But take it from me; it's not going to happen. When Sal speaks, Dom cowers. But, again for argument's sake, why would Tandem want Sal out of the way?"

"I've got nothing to base this on, but we think Tandem plans to offer up the Portello holdings to Frankie Gravano in exchange for Frankie Gravano leaving Tandem in peace and with enough money to live out his life in style. Sal is the only obstacle. With him out of the way, Dom will be an easy hit."

A Leander police car pulled into the lot. A second later its light rack came alive in reds and blues. Two uniforms jumped out. With weapons at the ready they went over to the sedan.

I twisted to watch the action. Two black men I did not know climbed from the sedan, with their hands raised. The officers did a frisk on each, confiscating numerous weapons.

"Anybody you know?" asked Joel.

I shook my head.

"The driver is Angel Rico. A small-time pusher. He used to work for Blind Ray as an enforcer—maybe still does. I don't recognize the other one. From the armament those two are carrying, they're real worried about somebody."

"I haven't had dealings with Blind Ray's mob in some time," I said, returning to my meal. "Does Ray have a gripe with you?"

"Could be. I nudged him a bit, last week. I'll drift by the Leander's holding-tank to question those two."

"I can't see Ray ordering a hit on you."

"Ray's got a vindictive streak."

I nodded. "I agree. Especially if the object of hate is white and carries a badge. But a hit on a Fed? Not a chance."

He grinned, then. "Which probably makes you the target."

"That's all I needed to hear to help my digestion."

Joel tapped the window drawing my attention back to the parking lot. One of the police officers was waggling a sawed-off shotgun, apparently taken from the sedan.

"Looks like those clowns had something painful in mind," I remarked.

"Are you in Ray's good graces? Enough to get answers?" asked Joel.

I nodded. "Unless he's gone black-supremacist, again. For an old man, Ray gets real moody."

Joel gave me an amused look. "He's younger than you, Bishop."

"It's not the years, Joel. It's the miles."

"Bishop, you've got more miles on you than a gypsy-cab."

"Where is Tandem staying?"

"He's rented a place on Lake Travis."

"Why would Helen Martinis come to Texas?" I asked. "Does she have family here?"

"None we're aware of."

"What about Elsa and Benny?"

"It's a possibility. Their backgrounds are shady enough to hide a lot of history."

"Anything you want me to tell Salvator when he and I chat about Helen?"

"He already knows my feelings on the matter."

While Joel paid the tab, I telephoned my cleaning woman and explained the situation at my apartment. She vowed to have the debris cleared—assuming I would pay for her extra efforts. I agreed and then told her to fit the place out with replacements for what was irreparable. This led to kibitzing in the background at her end about an unlocked furniture warehouse. I pretended not to hear, and rang off.

"You trust strangers to buy your furniture?" Kingsley scoffed as we climbed back into his car.

I returned the snub-nose pistol to its keep. "How tough can it be to fit-out a place like mine?"

"Based upon the debris I saw, not very."

"Drop me at the Ninth Precinct. I want to chat with Sgt. Leon Martin. I'll catch a cab home."

"You'll let me know if you get a lead on that money?"

I looked over at him and smiled my most honest smile. "You'll know about it as soon as I do."

CHAPTER FIVE

The gray-haired desk-sergeant, Ollie Fish, looked contrite as he watched me limp into the building.

"Bishop," he muttered, "you look like warmed-over death."

"I'm close, Ollie. Is Martin in?"

With a jab of one gnarled thumb toward the door behind him Ollie grunted, "Squad Room."

I hobbled off toward the detention cells, past the "Duty" board, then up a flight of steps and down a hallway. At the open door to the squad-room, I peeked in.

Leon Martin sat at his desk behind a stack of file-folders. He wore a white-on-white shirt, a brown bow tie, and a double-breasted brown suit that had considerably fewer wrinkles than the number I had one. In one hand Leon held a sliced carrot, in the other, a Styrofoam coffee cup. I winced my way over, feeling the eyes of the half-dozen other police officers in the room, then slumped into the chair fronting Martin's desk.

"Looks tasty." I tried not to shudder.

"Wife says I need to lose a few pounds," Martin explained, grimly. "She claims veggies are free calories."

"How's it working?"

He made a sour face. "Ain't nothing free, Bishop. What brings you to me? You don't look healthy enough to be in more trouble."

I crossed my legs and lit a cigarette. "Anything new at your end on Helen Martinis?"

"I followed up with your cell-phone provider. The number Helen dialed was to a cell-phone registered to Carla Smith. The address listed is a phony."

"Then how does Carla Smith keep her phone active if there's no place to receive the monthly bill?"

"It's one of those prepaid phones. When the number of calls prepaid is used up, she had to return to her provider and purchase more phone-time. I went out to the murder scene with a forensic tech and checked the area you described. We found brain tissue in one spot, liver tissue in another. Two hits, definitely. Two terminations, probably. Which means a few months from now some unlucky boater on Lake Travis will come upon the floating remnants of two corpses—with your bullets in them." He sniffed the air. "Is that Salsa on your breath?"

I nodded. "You ought'a try it on your veggies. Did you know Jacob Tandem was in Austin?"

His eyes got big. "Tandem aka Agosto De Credico from Chicago?"

"The same."

"What in hell is he doing in Austin?"

"I had a chat with my least favorite Fed—Joel Kingsley. Joel says is Tandem's hooked up with Dominic Portello."

"Why would Tandem come all the way from Chicago to make friends with the Portello family's idiot son?"

"Two reasons. First, Tandem needs protection from the Chicago Mob. Second, according to Joel, Tandem's trying to reclaim the hundred million he embezzled—from Helen Martins who stole it from him. What about the autopsy report on Helen Martinis?"

"You mean he had her hit?"

I shrugged. "The autopsy report?"

"You were right. Helen *was* dead before she was shot."

"That clears me?"

"Not exactly." Martin's face became suddenly grave. "The Mayor is calling for a special investigation into the possibility you tampered with evidence to make it appear Martinis was dead before you shot her."

"Wells' idea?"

He nodded. "Did Kingsley give you anything on Martinis?"

"Helen Martinis was a Fed. She was also gay. Her lover was Elsa Jacobson. Of course I took it all with a grain of salt. What was the cause of death?"

"Broken neck." His brows furrowed. "Is Elsa Jacobson a name I'm supposed to recognize?"

I shook my head. "According to Joel, she has a brother named Benny. I was hired by Benny Jacobson to find Elsa—who Benny claimed was his wife. I suspect Benny is hoping I'll lead him to the hundred million Tandem is trying to reclaim."

Leon Martin cocked an eye at the ceiling. "But if Tandem embezzled it and then lost it, the Chicago Mob must know Tandem lied to them."

"And they have someone in Austin waiting for orders."

He groaned, "The Mayor is not going to like hearing that."

"Which is why I made a point of stopping off here."

He tapped the desktop. "What if Tandem contracted with Dominic Portello to whack Martinis? That might explain why you were left alive to face the music on her killing."

"Whoever was after her didn't want her dead," I said. "Running me off the road might've been the work of some over-exuberant amateur who didn't plan on her being killed. But I don't think so. According to Kingsley, she had the hundred million. Tandem would've ordered his people to keep her alive at all costs. They would've let me drop Helen off and then made their move."

One of Martin's eyebrows arched. "You said Helen was convinced one of the Highway Patrolmen worked for the Portellos. How would she know that unless she had some tie-in with the Portellos? Maybe Dominic found the money and killed her to keep her from telling Tandem?"

"I don't think so. If Dominic wanted her killed, why let me live? He hates me as much as anyone. Why not kill both Helen and me at the same time? To my mind, it has to be someone else, someone who now has the hundred million; someone like her partners in crime."

His face screwed itself into a maze of wrinkles and lines. "How much storage-space would a hundred million in cash require?"

"If boxed-up neatly, about as much as half a single car garage."

He pushed aside the veggies and took a slurp of coffee. "So your theory is her pals tracked down where the money was stored and then whacked her? Which means Tandem's still looking for it. I could be faced with at least two more murders before that money is put to rest."

"Nothing like job-security, Leon."

"You don't have to do the paperwork, Bishop." Then he slumped back in his chair. "How in hell do you embezzle a hundred million? A million I can understand. But a hundred million? Why would you want to? I mean, how much money does a guy need to live good?"

"It took Tandem over thirty years to do it and he needs that much to keep his bodyguards' payroll covered while he's living the good life."

"But a hundred million…" He licked his lips as if anticipating a piece of warm pie. "I should've gone into crime."

"Not with your nerves. You'd be babbling a confession at every turn."

"For a hundred million I could learn to keep my mouth shut."

"I take it your wife is urging you toward the Lieutenant's exam, again?"

"You don't know the half of it." His lips pressed together tightly as though he was defying a mental image of his wife wedging them open.

"According to what I've gleaned," I said, "that hundred million's probably stored somewhere in Austin. Any chance your people could search the local storage facilities?"

"So you can collect a fat finder's fee?" He looked over at me distrustfully. "No chance, Bishop!"

"I'll split what I get with you."

Leon Martin looked around to make sure we were not being overheard before whispering, "I can't take a gratuity for doing my job and you know it."

"But you can take a cash gift from me."

His eyes became the size of golf-balls. "How much cash are we talking about?"

"Your end would be over two million—give or take."

Martin grinned dreamily. "With that, I could afford to leave my wife and her diet programs. Hell, I could retire from everything."

"What about it? Do we partner on the deal?"

Martin gave another cautionary glance around. "I'll see what I can do. Oh, I ran the plate number you gave me for that red car. They came off a 1958 Edsel. I talked to the Edsel's owner. He has no explanation as to how or when his plates were stolen."

"I'm not surprised. What do you have on Angel Rico?"

"Rico?" he echoed, sitting up straight. "What's he to do with Helen Martinis?"

"Somebody put a tail on me or Joel Kingsley. Joel identified Angel Rico. The locals shook down their car and came up with lots of artillery."

"Rico's got no history as a shooter. He's Blind Ray's legman. He just got out on bail pending trial on a drug bust—narcotics possession and distribution."

"Maybe Rico wants to move up in Ray's organization?"

"As much as Ray might like you or Joel dead, I don't see him encouraging Rico to try it. He'd send someone with lots of experience and a sense of humor about dying."

"Could be Rico is branching out on his own?"

"You mean whacking you on spec in order to induce the mayor to recommend him for a pardon on the drug bust?"

"You think that's impossible?"

His head wagged. "Not considering the mayor, the governor and the fact that this is Texas."

"Who else could he be working for? Rico couldn't cut it as an independent. If he left Ray, he'd need to get himself on the payroll of a big organization." Martin's head made another disbelieving wag. "Not going to happen, Bishop. The Portellos would never touch him."

"Jacob Tandem might."

His eyebrows arched in consideration. "You may have something there. I'd heard Ray cut back on his troops. Rico would've been a good one to let go—lots over overhead with him, or so I've been told. Did you know Ray opened a rib-joint?"

"The big man cooks?"

"And damn good, too!"

"When did Ray sell the Hungry Eye?"

"It's still in business—just barely. Big Momma Lulu's no longer headlining — she's suing Ray for sexual harassment."

"I know the man is blind but…"

Martin stood and stretched the kinks from his back. "Ray says her claims are completely unfounded and in retaliation for him firing her."

"Why in hell would Ray fire Big Momma Lulu? There's nobody like her. Once she gets all she's got in motion on that stage, there's no stopping it, or her. The audience loves it."

"Apparently," continued Martin, as he resumed his seat, "Big Momma Lulu was giving very personal service to some of Ray's preferred clientele."

I shuddered. "That would be a braver man than me."

"Me, too." He frowned reflectively. "Without her at the Hungry Eye, business must be slow."

"Ray has to do something about his vindictive bent," I remarked.

He looked at me doubtfully. "Now who's calling the pot black?"

I offered Martin a Gallic gesture.

"Ray's calling his new joint, *Adam's Rib*," Martin said. "It's over on Highway 183-South." His eyes went misty. "Surprisingly good food. And there's never any trouble getting a table. I usually stop off for a quick snack before heading home—to more veggies. Deke, you should taste the sauce…"

"Stop drooling. We're not taking an impromptu lunch-break." I dug the slip of paper Hamilton Blake had given me embossed with the Jacobson's address, and handed it to Martin. "Tell me what you have on Elsa Jacobson of Leander?"

"This the one paired up with Helen Martinis?"

I nodded.

Martin studied the address, dubiously. "Did Martinis meet her in Austin?"

"Chicago. According to Joel, Helen Martinis worked undercover at Jacob Tandem's nightclub. According to another source, Elsa Jacobson also worked there."

"Did Benny Jacobson just show up at your office out of the blue?"

"Hamilton Blake brought him."

"Big Blake? That rich cowboy from Dallas?" He laughed sardonically. "The one who goes through women like my wife goes through my paycheck?"

I nodded. "I don't see Hamilton being in on the business Helen and the Jacobsons had with Tandem."

Leon Martin waggled a finger at me. "Big Blake's been conned by half the scam-artists in Texas."

"Which is why I don't think he's smart enough for them to need him for anything."

"Smart, hell! Blake dated a transvestite for nearly a month before catching on. The wedding invitations were printed. The reception-hall was rented— Blake went the whole nine yards before realizing their equipment was mismatched." Martin let go a shiver. "God, just thinking about it…"

I jabbed a finger at the CRT on his desk. "Benny Jacobson claimed he reported Elsa missing. Let's take a peek at what Missing Persons has on file."

Martin turned to the computer terminal and began to key. A few seconds later he gave the terminal a turn and tapped its screen. Displayed was a dark-haired woman wearing thick eyeglasses.

"Does she look gay to you?"

I got up and gave the image a close scrutiny. "Gay or not, she looks mean enough to chew nails. Are you sure this is Elsa Jacobson?"

Martin spun the terminal back and took another bite of carrot. "What are you talking about? She's a good-looking woman—without those coke-bottle specs."

"I take it your wife has you on short-rations, again?"

He nodded, grimly. "She wants her mother to move in with us. I refused." He gave the Styrofoam another lick. "Maybe I'd better take a drive to Leander this evening. I've dealt with Rico, before. He might be willing to give up something in exchange for consideration. If there is a connection between him and Helen Martinis I'd rather get it first-hand. You want to come along?"

I shook my head. "These days, my style of interrogation doesn't work well under police-scrutiny."

"It never did."

"Can I get a look at the personnel photos for the State Highway Patrol?"

"What for?"

"I want to see if the patrolman who pulled Helen and I over is among them."

"Forget it." A sound like a hoarse, dry cackle came from Martin's throat. "If I ask for a couple of thousand photos of State-Police troopers, Commander Pulaski will want to know why. "

"I thought Pulaski was forced into retirement."

"Despite the heart attack, he managed to pass his last physical."

"Over a million heart attacks each year, and he has one that heals?"

Martin tilted across the desk in warning, "Last I talked with Pulaski, he vowed to outlive you—even if it means killing you on his death-bed."

"Grudge-holding bastard!"

He flashed me a sharp look. "You arrested his wife. Your testimony earned her a life-sentence behind bars."

"The crazy bitch hired her boyfriend to kill Pulaski, Leon. For Christ's sake, Pulaski took four nine-millimeter slugs and spent ten weeks in intensive care. If it hadn't been for me his wife would've gotten away with it."

"What can I say, Deke? Pulaski and his wife reconciled. He's working on a deal to get her parole. And you can bet she's planning revenge on you."

"Skip it. That patrolman is probably not on their roster, anyway."

Martin lowered his eyes, folded his hands on the desktop and studied his thumbs. I had seen that routine before. It was when he was about to say something he should not. I took a long drag on the cigarette and waited. When he was ready to talk, Martin looked up at me, joining his thumbs against his chin, his fingers laced, his eyes a study in concern.

"I'm going to give you something I overheard. But it's got to stay between us."

"You know I'm not one for idle chatter."

He rolled his eyes. "The Feds met with Lt. Mann a few minutes ago—here. It was the mayor's doing, not Herby's."

"The mayor's hoping the Feds will punch my ticket?"

"Were I you, I'd hire a good friend to watch my back."

"What was said between the suits?"

"The Feds told Herby they had no knowledge of Helen Martinis—which makes me wonder about Joel Kingsley's claims."

"You're certain?"

He raised a hand to silence me. "I said they had no *knowledge* of her. After the meeting with Herby, the Feds went into one of the interrogation rooms. I'd just finished questioning a suspect, and still had the video running. They talked. It was recorded."

"Can I see the tape?"

His head shook. "Mann ordered me to erase it."

"God, I hate people who follow the rules."

"This is where it gets weird. The Feds speculated Helen Martinis might be someone from their own internal investigation unit." Martin's eyelids quivered a trifle. "So it could be Kingsley knew what he was talking about."

"But why would she work undercover—except to nail one of her own? And, if that were the case why would Kingsley know Helen?"

"Kingsley might be her handler."

"He claimed not."

"What makes you so special he'd tell you the truth?" Martin looked at me shrewdly. "Look, Deke, if I were to speculate, I'd say the Portellos bought themselves a Fed. Helen Martinis went looking for proof against that Agent and got hit to silence her. That's how she recognized the patrolman as part of the Portello mob. Further, if Joel isn't her handler, than he must be her target."

"Assuming a lot. Any names bandied while the Feds were chatting?"

"One. But it probably isn't relevant."

"Who?"

"Henrico Romero. Ever heard of him?"

It took me a few seconds to dredge the information from my memory. "The only Henrico Romero I know runs a small café in East Austin."

He grunted with emphasis. "Then it probably isn't him."

"Why not? Romero's in their witness-protection program."

"How would you know that?"

"Joel Kingsley was his handler. Romero used to bitch about how Joel always made Romero toe the line. He complained loud and long enough to get himself reassigned to another Fed. The Feds mention Tandem?"

Martin shrugged. "Not one word. But, then, I didn't know he was in town until you showed up."

I got to my feet. "Let slip there's going to be a gang-war between the Chicago mob, and the Portellos. I'd like to give the mayor something to worry about besides me."

Martin leaned toward me. "Are you crazy? He'll go off the deep end. He'll get the governor to call up the National Guard."

"After which, the mayor will leave town to make certain he does not become a fatality. And by the time he gets back, the mayor will have forgotten all about Helen Martinis."

Martin shook his head. "No way am I starting rumors for you."

"You're not as much fun as you used to be, Leon."

He pointed at the veggies. "How much fun would you be, eating stuff like this?"

Out on the sidewalk I stopped and lit a cigarette. Then I tossed smoke to the hot breeze and glanced around looking for a taxi. The sun peeked through the clouds and a couple of lonely birds were singing to each other. Across the street, a young man with shoulder-length, sandy hair stood in the doorway of a magazine-shop. He wore a tan suit with matching shirt, belt and shoes. Everything on him looked expensive. Everything on him looked new. I started off down the sidewalk, keeping a wary eye on the road in hopes of spotting a taxi. Immediately, Long-Hair and his new clothes followed.

There are five rules for working a tail: Stay behind your subject whenever possible. Never try to hide while in pursuit. Act in a natural manner no matter what happens. No matter what, never make eye-contact. And dress to blend in with the rest of the crowd. Follow those guides, and your mark will not likely know he or she is being followed. Miss one and you're a sitting duck waiting to be shot. Long-hair had four of the five down pat. His penchant for expensive clothes was his downfall.

About mid-block, I stopped. Long-Hair broke another rule by halted in mid-stride, looking like a duck waiting for an invitation to wade. I pretended to check the ash on the end of my smoke. Desperate not to be the focus of my attention, he quickly turned to face a lingerie shop—apparently admiring a bra and panty display. Based upon Long-Hair's clothes and mop, it was a dead-certainty he was neither a Fed nor a police-detective. When the authorities send an overdressed man out on a tail, they have the sense to give him a trim. Based upon his complexion, Long-Hair was not one of Blind Ray's mob. Blind Ray was too much of a racist to send a white man to do a job—unless there was a strong chance the guy would make a fatal mistake. He might be one of the Portello gang, but I doubted it. Lanky blonds in their employ were as rare as transvestites in nunneries. That meant my pursuer was either part of Tandem's consortium, or someone new to play scrape-the-knuckle with.

I flexed my fists. Regardless of his intent or who he worked for, I intended to have a little fun.

I did an about-face and headed back. Long-Hair did likewise. From time to time I glanced in his direction. He was keeping pace, doing a bad job of ignoring me. At the corner I crossed the street to make it easier for us both.

He paused until I walked past, standing by a children's clothing shop pretending to admire a bunch of papier-mâché dummies wearing diapers.

Halfway down the block, I squatted to retie a shoe. From the corner of one eye I watched him following. The only other person in sight was a bag-lady rummaging for aluminum cans.

I stood up and walked on. Before testing his knuckle-busting endurance, I needed to lure Long-Hair to a place where vehicles were few and people even fewer.

At the next corner I turned onto a side street.

He trailed along, now moving more quickly, apparently intending to take the same advantage of this nearly-empty side street.

I continued on for another block. Then, in front of sandwich shop, I stopped.

The shop was squeezed between two fortress-like apartment buildings/ Behind it was a wide blacktop alleyway. After crushing my smoke under heel, I gave my tummy a hunger-man's rub and strode into the sandwich shop.

Instead of taking a stool at the counter and placing my order, I continued on as if heading for the toilet in the back.

I passed that door and slipped into the storage area, intending to use the shop's rear-exit. There I came upon a naked couple, frantically humping atop a lettuce-crate.

Without loosing pace or cadence I offered advice on safe-sex, the value of love-eternal, and the importance of locking doors before taking that first plunge into a extra-marital relationship. Then with an encouraging thumbs-up for their technique, I hurried out the back way into the alley.

A quick but quiet trot down the asphalt brought me back to the sidewalk fronting the shop. Long-Hair was pretending to read the menu on the window and trying to catch sight of me inside.

He was quite young: not yet thirty. His facial features were coarse, his skin ruddy. He was so engrossed in feigning a visual tour the gastronomical delicacies inside that he did not notice my approach until I was two strides away.

Then with a cry of surprise, he turned and jerked out a Makarov pistol. By the time he got the weapon clear, my right fist made contact with the left side of his head.

The Makarov boomed, blowing a chunk of brick from the building.

I returned fire with a hard left hook, solidly catching his liver.

He let go a painful gurgle, dropped the weapon and then let his knees hit the sidewalk.

That is when my knee caught his chin, nearly lifting him off the concrete. As he floated in mid-air, I railed his temple with a right cross that sent him rolling. Not wanting to leave a job half-done I limped over and gave his nether regions a kick with my right shoe. His eyes bugged. His mouth opened. Then he flopped onto his back, unconscious.

I went back and picked up his pistol. After stuffing it into my suit, I strolled over and rummaged through his clothes. He had a pocket full of quarters, a matchbook bearing the Chicago Stork Club logo, a wallet with an Illinois driving license assigned to Joey Fortuna, and a wad of hundred-dollar bills.

I dropped the money in my pocket and stood up. As I turned to leave the romantic pair from the sandwich-shop rushed out.

"We heard a gunshot," the guy exclaimed, zipping up his pants.

I pointed at the unconscious man. "He was planning to rob you." I tried to casually stretch the kinks from my back hoping to give the impression that this was nothing out of the ordinary in my life, for the girl's benefit. But a deep groan slipped past my lips as my adrenalin lost its grip on the frayed nerve-endings from my injuries in the rollover. "I think I changed his mind."

She giggled to her lover, "I told you he was all right for a geezer."

Despite the bruising her remark left upon my ego, I dusted off my suit and went over to the pair. "Better get back inside," I said, and handed him the Makarov. Then I tilted my head toward Long-Hair. "Just in case he tries something else."

Then I hobbled back toward the main street. With a little luck I could flag down a taxi to take me to the nearest emergency-ward where I and my aching body could succumb, in peace.

En route I handed the bag-lady Long-Hair's money, suggesting she enjoy a good meal.

The old gal responded in no uncertain terms. "Meal, hell! This is enough to get a case of Pinch, a steak at the best joint in town, and a damn good chance at getting laid."

I gave her a wink of approval and continued on my limping way. I tried to convince myself that the exercise with Long-Hair had been well worth the pain, screaming across my body. Admittedly, my knuckles felt twenty years younger. But the rest of me was begging for a suicide pill.

After getting repairs to sutures, a scolding from the kid claiming to have a medical degree in the hospital emergency-room and another supply of pain-killers, I arrived back at my flop a few minutes before seven, that evening.

I unlocked the door and went inside to find the place spotless. I also discovered it had been completely refurbished with items of unexpected and enviable quality.

The kitchen table and chairs looked like something out of House Beautiful. The chrome and glass microwave oven on the counter looked like something from the future. The refrigerator seemed to have its own aura, not to mention ice and water dispensing capability. I made my mouth-gaping way into the front room. There I found a new recliner that offered heat and massage in addition to the most comfortable backside-experience of my life.

The table next to the chair had a built-in gooseneck lamp with three crystal globes. The new Murphy bed was made of solid oak and automated for opening and closing. It also had an adjustable mattress that coiled head to foot into a myriad of contortionist-positions in the event the sleeper wanted an out-of-the-ordinary bedtime experience.

Taking up most of the wall facing the bed was a flat-panel television—the first visual entrainment unit to take residence in my flop. Not only was it the latest High-Definition model, a sticker on it claimed the set offered the best in stereophonic surround-sound.

I giggled like a schoolboy. "Dear God, I've died and gone to heaven."

I took off my coat and tie, then my shoulder holster, went through my pockets and put everything in them on the table next to the recliner. Then I stripped off my pants and dropped them on the floor. I was just about to stretch out on the Murphy bed for a few dozen hours of blissful sleep, when my eyes focused upon a slip of paper taped to the television's remote-control.

It was a bill from my cleaning lady. The balance requested for cleaning and furnishing was not what some people would consider astronomical. From my debt-ridden prospective, what she demanded held a close second only to the national-defense budget.

"Where in hell does that woman think I'll get this kind of money?" I croaked.

I retrieved my robe from the front closet and went to the kitchen where I consoled my economic grief by gulping down several shots of Pinch. Then I set about warming my grocer's idea of Tandoori chicken in the shiny microwave— a novel experience for me. In awe I watched as the glass turntable within the microwave turned and the chicken mixture began to steam. It was as close to a miracle as I would ever witness. No blazing fire. No red-hot element. Just invisible rays rendering something frozen into lip-smacking, steamy submission —or so said the microwave's instruction-booklet.

Five minutes later, my taste buds understood the rubberizing effects of microwave cooking. I dumped my meal into the garbage disposal, swallowed several pain pills as my supper and then meandered my whimpering way over to the Murphy bed. What I needed, more than anything, was several days of nonstop sleep accompanied by a quiet demise.

CHAPTER SIX

Twenty-four hours later, I was again confronting the Microwave Oven. This time the promised delicacy within its care was a Salisbury steak, accompanied by mashed potatoes and a pile of something brown that probably should have been green. I waited until I saw smoke rising from within the container before pushing the cancel-button and opening the oven's door. Then I took out what I hoped would be editable and set it on the table.

Much to my relief it was the cardboard covering that had caught fire. The meat beneath still looked worthy of chewing. Although the potatoes had acquired the green that I thought belonged on the pile of brown. I grabbed a fork from a counter-drawer, sat down and took a bite. Much to my disgust the Salisbury steak tasted exactly like the chicken from the night before.

I heard a key scrape in the lock that secured my private domain from nefarious passersby.

If I had not been choking in an effort to swallow a piece of hamburger tough enough to vulcanize a truck-tire, I might have gotten to my feet before the apartment door swung open. As it was, I was just rising when Rita Portello strolled in.

"Bishop, you bastard!" Rita shook one fist. "You were supposed to call me."

I spat out the inedible meat. "I love you, too, Rita."

She slammed the door. "Like hell."

"Forgive my nosiness," I said. "But when did I give you a key to this place?"

Her eyes burned a path across the distance between us, up my body and then locked onto my face. "You didn't." She stuffed a ring of keys into her purse. "I had your landlord make me one."

"I'll have to chat with Horace about his impulsive behavior."

"It won't do any good." Her eyes darted toward the front room as if half-expecting to see someone. "Your landlord's two months behind on the finance-payments for this dump. Sal is not happy."

"So you made Horace an offer he could not refuse?"

Rita grinned. "If he wanted an extension on his late-payments it was either face broken kneecaps, or make me smile. Horace chose to follow the safer path." Then Rita made a disgusted face. "Are you actually eating the stink I smell?"

"I may have warmed it a bit too long." I resumed my seat at the table. "I've never had a microwave before. It does magically terrifying things to food. You should have been here last night when I had Tandoori chicken. That was an eye-opening experience—and for the other end, as well."

Rita strode over to the counter and looked at the gleaming machine. "What button did you push, for God's sake? Death and destroy?"

"I'm not sure. But from the taste of this beef, I think it's likely."

Rita smiled a little mocking smile at me. "You're the only man I know who buys TV dinners but who doesn't have a television," she said. "Don't you think that's an oxymoron?"

I jabbed one thumb toward my sitting room. "I am now the proud possessor of new sixty-five-incher equipped with a cable-box, a remote and promises of entertainment I've merely fantasized about. Tonight I'm planning to watch *Gigi Does It in a Limo*. I think it has something to do with Barbeque Short-Ribs."

Her beautiful face twisted into a revolted glare. "You're disgusting."

"Don't let me keep you from business, *elsewhere*."

While I toyed with the idea of trying another bite of Salisbury steak, Rita went to the cupboards, took down a tumbler, grabbed up the Pinch from the table and poured a stiff drink.

"I heard you were dead," she declared. "Then I heard you'd knocked off some broad—redhead. I thought it had to be your third wife, the bitch. But according to the newspaper the dead broad wasn't. Later I heard you'd damn well better be dead if you knew what was good for you."

"Brother Sal offered that last bit of encouragement?"

Rita nodded. "He blames you for the Feds taking root in his back-pocket." She grinned above the rim of the glass. "God, how my brothers hate you."

"The feeling is mutual."

"I, however, find you deliciously irresistible—in a kinky sort of old-man way."

I winked at her. "Also mutual—the kinky part, anyway."

Rita took a good draw on the glass. Then she set it on the table, slipped off her leather coat and dumped it across the back of a chair to expose a silky red dress, clinging in all the right spots.

I let my eyes wander, enjoying the view. Rita was one of those women who became more beautiful with age.

I am not the type to fall in love. My idea of a romantic relationship hinges on a combination of lust, and my paramour's willingness to lend money to financially strapped P.I. types—an extremely rare combination of virtues. Nevertheless, if I were to settle for one woman it would be Rita. She was past forty, with all the smarts and wit that went with maturity. But she still had the figure of a twenty-year-old.

She stared at me with hard, dark suspicious eyes. "Are you going to tell me what's going on between you and that dead-woman?" she said, sitting down across from me. "Was Helen Martinis your latest cuddle-bunny?"

"Not a chance. I have to save my strength for you."

"Then who was she?"

"According to the F.B.I., Helen Martins was an undercover agent. According to yours truly, she knew your brother Dominic. In fact, she made mention of him having her key."

"Did she say anything else about the key?" Rita asked, cagily.

I shook my head. "But one of her hands went to her throat, as if she had worn it on a necklace—which makes me think it must've been important to her. Maybe important enough to kill for."

Rita grabbed up her glass, her eyes darting away from my stare. "Dom's not stupid enough to do a hit on a Fed."

"I beg to differ."

"There'd be no reason for Dom to kill her," she calmly explained, still not looking at me. "He'd have pumped her full of LSD and dropped her at the nearest asylum." Rita paused and her stare returned to mine. "The Fed would be alive. But she would be incapable of testimony for the rest of her days. Not nice. But it's not murder."

"As usual, your family is a class-act. LSD leaves no trace—therefore no crime was committed. But that doesn't explain Dom's relationship with Helen Martinis. She was a part-time hooker. Is Dom expanding into the fun-flesh business?"

Rita fell oddly silent, nursing her glass, her eyes staring down, looking at nothing.

"What was Dom's angle on Helen?" I asked.

"I don't know and I don't give a damn. Leave it, okay?"

After deciding what remained of my dinner was beyond digestion, I gave Rita my dirtiest leer. "Did you come to brighten my meager existence with a little mattress frolic? Or are you hiding out because Momma is wondering why you're not married—still, yet, again?"

Rita's glass rattled onto the tabletop. Then she leaned back, crossing her arms and tilting her head to look at the ceiling. "It's my damn life, isn't it? Who is she to demand I settled for her idea of womanhood?"

"Momma loves you and wants you happy. Just agree with her and continue on in your own sordid way."

"I'm not going to spend my life barefoot and pregnant."

"You're her only hope for grandchildren. No woman in her right mind would risk matrimony with Dom's kinky streaks."

Rita jumped up like a cat suddenly aware of a vicious dog. "You should talk."

"As for Sal, he's too busy running the family business to get tied down with anyone. You're Momma's only hope for perpetuating the Portello family genes."

Rita flailed the air with frustration. "Happiness does not mean becoming a baby-machine. I'm at my wits end, Bishop. All my mother does is harp on how my clock is ticking and if I'm going to have a kid, I have to have one now—as if I was not aware of it."

I gave Rita a lecherous wink. "You and I could always go through the motions. Then you could report back to Momma how you and I are making every effort to accommodate her desires for grandchildren."

"You make jokes because you think she wouldn't take that as good news, considering we're not married," she snapped. "Actually, nothing would please Momma more than to hear you're interested in me."

I adjusted the lie of my ratty bathrobe. "Which is why you've come to the master of romance?"

"He was busy. I came here thinking it might be fun to get stinking drunk and bed a disgusting old man."

"Despite your less than endearing remarks, I think I can accommodate—providing you do all the work."

Rita giggled. "Do you know what Sal would do to you if he caught us in bed?"

A chill went down my spine. "You're not helping my eagerness, Rita."

"I can get you where you need to be under." She flipped ashes from her cigarette into the ashtray. "When we were kids, my bedroom was directly inline with yours. Sometimes you got undressed without pulling down the shades. I used to sit in the dark, watching out the window into your room—waiting, hoping." Rita picked up her glass. "I'm getting wet just remembering."

"Before you get your motor running too fast, are you sure Dom didn't follow you here?"

"Not a chance." She took another sip. "He's at his warehouse wondering how to explain things to a very nervous insurance agent."

"It caught fire?"

"Not yet. I think that's what Dom's got in mind."

"I don't recall your family trying insurance fraud, before."

She turned her palms up, waved them. "Dom was never this desperate, before."

"What do you mean?"

"Dom's store-manager called. A bunch of assholes overrode the security system at his warehouse, and emptied it. Beds, televisions, recliners, tables…" Rita suddenly gave my new kitchen table a tap with one red, lacquered fingernail. "Dom has one exactly like this in his showroom. Exactly. He planned to give it to my mother on her birthday. If I remember right, this puppy costs a fortune."

Recollections of background-remarks about warehouses heard during the conversation with my cleaning lady came to mind. This was abruptly followed by a new sense of foreboding.

"The little number you're admiring arrived a few weeks ago," I lied.

She tilted back and let her eyes drift from the floor to the tabletop. "I'm surprised you had the bucks, Bishop. This isn't run-of-the-mill. With these six chairs it runs higher than the price of new car."

"The bill was a bit more than I intended to spend. But, I'm thinking I'll be getting more than a slight discount—considering recently acquired provenance information."

"Momma asked about you, last week," she said, tilting forward to rest her elbows on the table. "I told her you were still dodging trouble. She said she'd say a prayer for your soul—as if she isn't saying prayers for you every night, as it is. Why my mother adores you is beyond me."

I got up and dumped the remainder of the Salisbury steak and its accompaniments into the garbage disposal. Then I pulled out a pack of cigarettes and lit two. I handed Rita one and sat back down.

"Momma is simply reacting to my inimitable charm," I declared.

"She loves you like a son and don't make jokes about it." Rita tried to laugh but it came out as a smoky cough. "When we were kids she treated you better than your own mother. Momma would cry when she heard your old man giving you hell and knocking you around."

"I'd have starved if it wasn't for Momma's lasagna."

"You could wrap her around your little finger—my father, too. At least until you took his Lincoln for a joyride. He was steamed about that. But he forgave you."

"His forgiveness did not come easily or without pain."

"The point is he forgave you. Old Frank never forgave anybody else." Her lips thinned. "He wouldn't have if he known you'd become a cop." Then Rita gave the table another visual assessment. "Damn, but this is nice. Where in hell did you get the money?"

I took a deep drag on the cigarette trying to invent some way to switch the topic of discussion away from my new furnishings without making Rita more suspicious than she already was. Failing to do so, I said, "I was just thinking about calling you when you arrived."

Rita put her cigarette between her lips. "Like hell."

"Seriously."

"Bishop, the only times we get together is if I make the effort." She took a lung-full and then blew the smoke into my face. "Do you know how demeaning it is for a woman to do all the chasing?"

"I used to call you every night."

"Yeah," Rita snorted. "To breathe into the phone and make naughty mutterings. Momma picked up the extension, once, and damn near fainted." She blew me a kiss before leaning toward me. "Marry me. It would make me happy. It would make Momma delirious. We could make beautiful babies, together."

"Your brothers would kill me."

Her eyes shut. "Momma would protect you."

"Tandem," I said.

Rita blinked several times in confusion before tilting back, scowling. "I'm talking marriage, and you change the subject to the standard-position for group-gropes?"

"Jacob Tandem AKA Agosto De Credico."

Her eyes almost popped. "Where in hell did you pull his name from?"

I freshened my drink. "Is he trying to arrange protection through Dom?"

"How would I know?" She made a nervous face, suddenly uneasy. "The guy had dinner with us tonight. What's your interest in him?"

"You know how rumors start."

"Yeah. You phone the city-desk at the Chronicle and it ends up on the front page." Her neatly plucked eyebrows arched. "What gives, Bishop? Did you have a run-in with Jacob Tandem?"

"No. But Helen Martinis did."

She rolled her eyes. "I'm done talking about her."

"Helen died trying to steal a hundred million from Tandem."

Rita crossed her legs, and ran her fingers through her long black hair as if trying to gather her thoughts. Her lacquered nails glinted, jerky and nervous, like red dots behind the glimmering dark strands.

"What hundred million? That's all hooey."

"I'm betting my eyes it isn't."

She gave me an uneasy smile. "You bet on anything. That's your biggest fault."

"What's going on, Rita? Was Dom in on running me off the road?"

She stood up and turned away, pretending an interest in her watch. "Dom was with me when you had that trouble. I'll swear to it."

"When you tell me that, it usually means he doesn't have an alibi."

"Go to hell!"

"Rita, the hundred million Tandem embezzled from the Chicago Mob links him, your favorite brother, and Helen Martinis.

The money is missing, Tandem's in Austin looking for it, Helen Martinis robbed Tandem and is dead, and your brother is in the middle. He has to be. He has her key. Did Dom show you a key?"

"Damn you, Bishop! Dom had nothing to do with her death."

"Somebody did."

"I don't want to talk about it." Then she looked over at me. "When I was a kid I couldn't wait for my boobs to start rising. I wanted something for you to stare at."

"I noticed them right off."

"I doubt it." She settled back into her chair. "You were always the gentleman with me, Bishop. Polite, considerate—which was a real pain in the ass. I wanted you to pull me into your arms and hug and kiss me! When I was fourteen I actually fantasized about seducing you. I started stuffing Kleenex in my bra. When the counterfeit boobs failed to garner a grope from your corner, I stopped wearing underwear and pressed against you every chance I got."

"I noticed that, too."

"Still, nothing—although my raging hormones were giving me a great time during each effort."

"What's going down between Dom and Tandem?"

She snuffed out her cigarette in the ashtray. "Jacob is just an old gentleman who loves Momma's lasagna, and likes peeking at my boobs. That's all."

"Did Dom mention Elsa or Benny Jacobson?"

Her mouth gaped in surprise. "You get around for a beat up old man."

"What did you hear?"

"Tandem's looking for them. How did you know about those two? They're from Chicago."

"They're in Texas, now. What about Hamilton Blake?"

"I don't remember that name."

"Was Dom locating Helen Martinis for Tandem?"

Her eyes darted away from mine, as if a revelation had taken place. "Not that I know of."

"What aren't you telling me, Rita?"

She bit her lip and looked away. "Nothing."

"I understand Dom met Tandem in Chicago."

Rita gave a disinterested shrug. "Chicago is a friendly town."

"Did Dom tell you about Tandem's hundred million?"

Her face suddenly became worried. "What if he did? It's just rumor."

"It's fact. I'm looking for a big blond guy."

Rita glanced over and laughed. "That's what happens when you don't get laid often enough."

I gave her a description of the Highway Patrolman. She twisted uncomfortably in the chair, still avoiding my gaze. "Nobody like that is on Sal's payroll. If they were, I'd be humping his eyes out."

"You're playing me, Rita."

She gave me an angry look. "Dom had nothing to do with what happened to that woman."

"You know who that man is. I want his name."

She pushed back a lock of long, dark hair with a lazy hand. "I don't know his name, damn you."

"Where did you see this guy?"

She shrugged. "The furniture store, I guess. I saw him and Dom talking."

"I want his name."

"I don't know it." She rubbed her nose, her angry eyes going soft. "Bishop, I didn't come here to argue. Please don't do this to me—not tonight."

I took a drag on the cigarette and spat out a stream of smoke. It coiled around my glass like a white snake looking for a place to sleep. "Did Dom mention a key to you?"

A frown rippled across her forehead as her head wagged in disappointment. "What's wrong with me, Bishop?"

"Nothing from any angle. Does Dom own the warehouse where he stores his furniture?"

"He bought it from Sal. Why?"

"A hundred million wouldn't take up too much space crated and stacked."

Her eyes widened; her voice became bitter. "You don't believe me, do you? You think Dom actually had that woman killed, don't you? You think he got the money from her and had her whacked."

I shook my head. "Helen told me Dom had the key. Rita, what's Dom up to? Is the stuff he's selling hot? Are the Feds investigating him for interstate trafficking in stolen goods? Is he storing that hundred million after Tandem got it back? What?"

Rita jumped up, reached across the chair to the ashtray and snuffed out her cigarette. Then she grabbed up the pack and plucked another from it. The movement brought back memories of when she was a kid, sitting with me on the back porch of my parent's home. We were sharing caramels, then. But the intimacy of the action was the same. Despite the tense topic of discussion at the time—her upcoming first date—Rita felt a need to be near me. It was the same, now. It was not sex that brought her to my flop. She could get better action— she wanted to be with me. As back then, she was nervous. But this time I did not know what was bothering her, and I suspected I never would. I lit her cigarette. Then I let my eyes drifted from her fingertips to her hand and then up her bare arm, enjoying the melding of firm flesh with soft curves.

Rita sat, took a deep drag and blew smoke at the ceiling. Then she wrapped her hands around her glass, the fingers interlocking, her eyes on its contents.

"Do you want me to stay?" she asked without looking at me.

I reached across, tilted her chin up and gave her my best dirty leer. "What do you think?"

Her face softened into a smile. "I'd do anything for you, Bishop."

"That's my hope for tonight."

"I mean *anything*."

"Did Tandem get that money back? Is that why Helen was killed?"

She glanced at me then held her breath a beat. "Jacob Tandem is still looking for it. What's your plan? To beat him out of it?"

"A hundred million in untraceable cash is nothing to sneeze at."

For a few seconds neither of us spoke. Then Rita said, "If I help you get that money what's the split?"

"Anyway you say."

"I help you get the money and you marry me."

"You're the type of woman who would insist on something like that."

"I've been in love with you since the moment I first saw you."

"The first time you saw me you were in dirty diapers."

"I was two years old."

"Do you know where the money is?"

"I have some ideas." Rita stood. "I'll wait for you in bed."

I watched her walk away out of the corner of one eye, her shadow following on her heels. But I did not get up. Instead I remained where I was thinking about Helen Martinis. Rita was nothing like her, but I imagined Helen saying those same words at some point, making that same walk in some apartment with someone else playing my role. It did not matter what she had done. It did not matter who she loved or who loved her. She deserved better than she got. A nervous impulse sent my fingertips to the ashtray where I poked at butts among ashes.

"I'm cold," Rita called from the other room.

Deadly Turn

I stood, listening to blankets rustle. It was cold—almost as cold as a body-tray in the morgue.

CHAPTER SEVEN

The next morning I left Rita to her dreams, swallowed several pain-killer hoping they would revive my will to live, dug out the old Beretta I kept as a backup-pistol and shoved it into my shoulder holster. Then I went outside and nosed the Buick toward Leander. I did not expect to find much. People on the run from the Mafia and the F. B. I. generally put a great deal of effort into hiding their trail. Especially, if those people have stolen a hundred-million in Mob money. Nevertheless, I wanted to have a look around before I telephoned Hamilton Blake about his best new friend Benny.

The address Ham provided was on the small town's outskirts. It was a solid, cool-looking house with red brick walls, a blue terra cotta tile roof, and a white sandstone trim around the windows. The glass in the front windows was leaded. The sidewalk and the parkway were both very wide, for Texas. A small metal portico offered shade over the front stoop.

I pulled the Buick into the parkway and got out. There was a heavy scent of summer in the breathless air. The leaves from the surrounding pecan trees were perfectly still. It was like the world was waiting for something to happen.

To my surprise, the key was actually under the welcome mat.

I used it to unlock the door, then put it back in its place of foolish concealment.

The front room was large and square, with a sunken area replete with built-in cushioned seating.

I looked around thinking the house had a restful atmosphere. Not unlike what one might find in a funeral chapel. The furnishings surrounding the sunken area were gaudily masculine. They consisted of a massive carved davenport and two matching chairs, all with plush blue cushions and tapestry backs with red tassels. A couple of marble-topped tables with crooked legs took space beneath windows. The fireplace's cherry mantle was decorated by a gilt clock and several pieces of small marble statuary. The carpet was an ugly brown.

As I went from room to room I could not help but wonder who would live in such a place. But it was very clean and orderly. No magazines littered the furniture. No dirty laundry cluttered the floors. No wet towels moldered in the bathrooms. Everything was dust-free and in its place.

There were clothes hanging in one bedroom closet—all female, all the same size. No clothing in the closets of the other two bedrooms. I was not an expert on gay women, by any measure. But I assumed a pair living together would not struggle with a single closet and leave the remaining two empty, even if they were the same size and shared the same bedroom. To my mind, it meant the women had a parting of ways—a parting that coincided with Joel Kingsley's claim that Helen had taken the money.

After finding nothing that would lead me to Elsa or the missing millions, I left the house. The sun danced on the warm lawn and reflected obliquely from the concrete sidewalk. I put on my sunglasses and headed back to the Buick.

Deadly Turn

En route, I spotted an elderly woman with neatly quaffed blue hair pruning rosebushes near the stoop of the adjacent house. She was slim and quite tall. A black and white polka-dotted blouse dangled down like a sheet to her black, linen shorts. Despite Texas's sun, she was quite pale.

Hoping to gather background information, I went over and introduced myself.

In a hard baritone, she said her name was Mrs. Annie Chase. Annie sounded as if she was the type who did not tolerate any nonsense. Up close, I saw that her eyebrows were thin, straight, and a mix of black and gray. Her nostrils flared slightly as she breathed, giving each a whitish ring with every breath. Her chin was small and sharp. She wore no makeup. Her eyes behind thick glasses were large, cobalt blue with large, green irises. Both lids were slightly tilted giving her eyes a vaguely Asian appearance.

After explaining I was looking for Elsa, I asked Annie if she recalled the last time she had seen anyone at the house next door.

"About four days ago," replied Annie, without hesitation.

"You're certain?" I asked, in surprise.

She pushed out her jaw at me causing muscles in her neck to form writhing snakes beneath skin. "I may be old, Mr. Bishop. But I am far from senile."

"I meant no disrespect, Mrs. Chase. What was Elsa doing when last you saw her?"

Annie waggled the pruning sheers within her thick fingers vaguely. "She and that redhead were racing off."

"Redhead?"

"That woman she hangs-out with."

"They were running?"

Her blue hair shook gently. "Driving a car. The wheels squealed terribly. My poor Gerald awoke with an awful start."

"Is your husband here? Perhaps he…"

"Gerald is my budgie." Annie shared a disdainful glare.

I asked if she could describe Elsa.

Annie did so in remarkable detail.

What I heard coincided exactly with Elsa Jacobson's driving license photo.

I then asked for a description of the redhead. Again, I got unexpected detail and it matched Helen Martinis perfectly.

"You should've been a cop," I remarked, in appreciation.

"I did better, income-wise, in the Secret Service."

"Do you hear the redhead's name?"

"I was never introduced." Then she pointed her pruning sheers at the Jacobson house. "She's not very sociable. But I did overhear Mrs. Jacobson refer to the other woman as Helen. No family name was mentioned."

"Would you describe the relationship between the two women as cordial?"

Annie let go a disgusted snort. "I would describe it as licentious."

"Come again?"

"Those women are lovers."

More confirmation of Joel's statements. "How would you describe Mr. and Mrs. Jacobson's relationship? Brother and sister more so than newlyweds?"

"I never met Mr. Jacobson."

"When did the redhead move out?"

"Mrs. Jacobson lived alone."

"What about people other than Helen, in Elsa's life?"

"There were several men. Lately, two would arrive for short visits. There were no overnight stays—at least not among her male visitors."

"Were there other women besides Helen?"

She nodded. "A blonde and a brunette. I think the blonde was Jessie. The brunette was Rita. Again, no family names."

I asked for a description. What I heard sent chills down my back. The brunette was either Rita Portello, or someone who could pass as her twin-sister. The blonde I did not know.

Had Rita ingratiated herself with Helen in order to get the hundred million? And afterward, had she killed Helen—and possibly Elsa Jacobson? As far as I knew, murder was not part of Rita's lifestyle. But she had a vindictive nature and a long family history of homicide, to draw upon. I hoped with all my heart there was another explanation, but murders had been committed for far less than a hundred million. And Rita had said he had ideas about where the hundred million was.

"Were any of the male visitors very tall? With a shaved head?"

She nodded. "Extremely tall—perhaps seven feet. He appeared to be intoxicated, on both visits. I haven't seen him around for several weeks."

"What about the other men?"

"One was a dark-haired fellow in an expensive suit. He was short, slightly built, had big ears and wore a toupee. The third man was blond, handsome, muscular, about forty years of age. Those two were here within the last week."

The descriptions of the other two matched Benny and the Highway Patrolman. "Did you hear any of the men's names?"

"No. With the exception of the bald guy, they were not amicably inclined."

"They argued amongst themselves?"

"No. They never were here together—muscles and Big-Ears."

"So the dispute was always with the women?"

"With Elsa. Helen was there only once when men arrived—Baldy and Big-Ears." She paused a beat. "Curiously, the acrimonious atmosphere desisted completely during Baldy's visits. Elsa actually gave Big-Ears a hug."

"Could you hear what they argued about?"

"Storage. Something of great value must've been stored somewhere and only Elsa knew where."

"The blond man and the bald guy were acquainted?"

She thought for a moment before shaking her head. "I can't say. They were never there together."

"What about the blond woman and the brunette? Were they ever present when the blond man visited?"

Her head wagged. "To the best of my recollection, those two never interfaced with any of the men."

"Did Big-Ears and Baldy always visit together?"

Again, her blue hair wagged. "As I said, Baldy was there only twice. Each time, he was accompanied by Big-Ears—both men arriving in the same car. However, Big-Ears also came on his own. His visits were short—perhaps a few minutes, only. They were extremely vocal. He was angry. He was threatening. Curiously, Elsa did not seem frightened by him. It was as if she knew he was all talk and no action."

"About the storage… Did you ever see any trucks being loaded with crates or the like?"

She nodded. "It was the day after Elsa and the redhead were in the car. The redhead arrived in a big pickup with a long trailer. The kind that is completely enclosed where the rear door serves as a ramp. There were four burly men with her. Two rode in the front seat with her driving. The other two were in the pickup's rear seat. There was a large moving cart in the bed of the pickup – the kind you see being used to move very heavy appliances—straps and whatnot. Helen unlocked the door to the house. The men dragged out the cart and went inside. A few minutes later they came out with the first crate. There were five in total. Each must've been extremely heavy. The four men together—despite the cart - had all they could do to handle each one into the trailer. After loading the last crate the five of them piled into the pickup, and left."

"Were there any markings on the trailer or pickup?"

"A business name you mean?"

I nodded.

"Not that I saw. Both looked quite new."

"I don't suppose you remember the license plate number?"

She chuckled, "My memory is good, but not that good. In any event, neither trailer nor pickup had one." Then she reached out and gave my chest a tap. "Elsa and Helen had a falling out over something."

"What do you mean?"

"Up until that point, the redhead's visits were sociable. She came almost daily. Elsa and Helen would chat like old friends. I would see them out on the yard. I couldn't hear what was said. But Helen always acted very reassuring, consoling. Then just a few days ago, they argued. It was brief and I caught only one word—tandem. Later Helen returned to make amends. But from the way she walked, the way she postured it was clear their relationship had changed."

"Did you see any physical violence?"

"Not as such," replied Mrs. Chase. "But I once heard a scream. By the time I got to the window, Elsa was in the doorway holding a small automatic pistol. The blond man was backing away—not very happy."

"How long ago was that?"

"A day or two before her and Helen drove off, that last time."

"One final thing," I said. "Has anyone been at the house since the day you saw the crates being hauled out?"

Annie nodded. "Two people that I saw. That blond woman came by—Jessie. She went inside and then came out a few minutes later. When she got to her car she took out her cell-phone and called someone. From the way her hands were moving, she was not happy about something. Then the brunette came by—Rita."

She paused a few seconds waggling the clipper as her mind worked. "I know Rita has been at that house before. By before, I mean before Mrs. Jacobson moved in. I can't recall when."

I thanked Mrs. Chase for her time. Then I nosed the Buick back to my office. Last night I had suspected Rita of holding out on me. Now, I was certain my Rita knew a great deal more than she had admitted: about Helen Martinis and about the money. The difficulty would be in getting Rita to disclose what she held back. If Dom had been involved in Helen's death, Rita would never admit it. If she had the missing money or knew where it was, I had a chance at getting that out of her. All I had to do was agree to a marriage contract.

After arriving at my office, it took me about ten minutes of rummaging through my desk to locate Hamilton Blake's business card.

I called the number on it, but I did not make a connection.

I stuffed the card into my shirt pocket and I tried calling Rita at my flop. After getting no answer, I tried her cell-phone. Again, I got no connection.

Finally I rang her house.

Momma Portello answered the phone.

When I identified myself, she told me that Rita was out shopping.

I thanked her and rang off. Then, I went out to the Buick and drove to 1911 Emerson—the address Lt. Herby Mann had given me for Helen Martinis' residence.

As with the house in Leander, I did not expect to discover anything about the crates or Helen's partners in crime. Doubtlessly Joel Kingsley as well as Herby's people had been through Helen's apartment with all the forensic chemistry and artistry available. But there was always a slim chance something might have been missed. With a hundred million in the offing, it was worth checking.

The century-old apartment building on Emerson was three floors of sandstone façade topped by a flat roof. I went in the front door and scrutinized the mailboxes. All but one bore a plastic strip identifying the apartment's resident. None carried Helen Martinis's name. It was possible Herby had bad information, but I doubted it. For him, making mistakes was as unlikely as a virgin offering business in a whorehouse. More likely, the unmarked box had been Helen's. I pushed the button beneath the box labeled: 'superintendent', and waited.

Moments later a voice squawked on the intercom. I identified myself as a Federal Agent wanting information on Helen Martinis. The squawking became a choke, then the intercom fell silent. Moments later, feet made a shuffling approach from beyond the security door.

"The cops said they were done," a worried male voice declared as the door drifted open a few inches. "Your pal said he was done. Now you're here nosing around? This joint's got a reputation. I can't have every guy carryin' a badge scarin' my renters."

I jerked the door wide. Beyond it stood a slightly built man, barely over five feet tall—without the lifts in his new engineer-boots. He had a gaunt, bony face; a large nose; big ears, and bloodshot eyes. The latter were partially hidden behind gray tufts from a synthetic toupee. A white tank-top drooped from his bony shoulders down to a pair of baggy, gray workpants. These were neatly tucked within the boot-tops. I knew he was not wearing underpants because his zip was down.

"What's your name?" I demanded.

"Edgar Price." The reddish eyeballs blinked. The big nose sniffed. Then he complained, "I told the cops and your pal all I know. She lived here. She died someplace else. That's it. I got a business to run."

"Which pal?"

He gave me a suspicious look. "Special Agent Joel Kingsley."

"I know him," I said, moving past the superintendent. "This *was* his case. Now it's mine. That means I have to start from the git-go. Where's her apartment?"

"What for?" he complained. "There's nothing there. Didn't Kingsley tell you?"

I put my hands to my hips making sure the butt of the Beretta came into view. "I thought I'd made myself clear. Kingsley moved on. I'm assigned to this case. I want a look for myself."

The gnome-like little man looked stricken. "I ain't feelin' so good."

"I could make you feel a lot worse."

His head wagged, shaking the toupee like a dirty rag tied to the end of a long stick in a high wind. "The past two days, I've had the screamin' shits. I was on the can when you buzzed. I got a delicate constitution."

"I'll chance it."

Price gave the security door a closing shove. "You're not the one with knots in his guts."

I glanced around the hallway. The floor was black and white check linoleum. The walls were papered in a dirty floral pattern. Green wainscoting came up from the floor; covering the walls to waist-high. Instead of a ceiling fixture, a bare bulb dangled from the end of a tangled wire. Just to my right dark staircase went up.

"Ever since that bastard left Texas for the Whitehouse, you guys've been acting like fuckin' Nazis!" the superintendent whined. "Putting people out'a work. Harassing employers. Making life miserable. It ain't right—just because we don't like the asshole."

"I don't like the asshole, either. Who owns this dump? You?"

"Salvator Portello."

I was not entirely surprised to hear that. In an effort to legitimize his social image, Sal had invested heavily in real estate. "Would you prefer I had Mr. Portello picked up and dragged over here in shackles to give me a tour of her apartment? Naturally, I'd have to tell him your refusal to cooperate instigated his arrest."

Price's face contorted in terror. Then one of his bony hands went to his belly and squeezed. "Dear God, no."

Which way to her flat?"

"Up," he grunted, still clawing at his middle.

I started for the stairs.

"Mister, there's a complication," he called to my back.

I stopped and turned offering him my best do or die sneer.

Price whimpered, one hand leaving his belly to offer a beseeching gesture, "I already rented the dump."

"Who said you could do that?" I feigned fury.

"Nobody said I couldn't!" His hands clawed at his middle again. "Jesus, stop yelling! My diarrhea meds ain't kicked in yet."

"Who's in the apartment?"

Price chewed on his lower lip reflectively. "Nobody."

I took a menacing step toward him. "Are you jerking my chain?"

He gave his head a frantic wag. "No. Dear God, no! Not even if you had one."

"Why, if the dump is empty, is there a complication?"

His eyes wavered for an instant. Then they came back to me. "Mr. Portello's got a rule about not lettin' nobody in an apartment without the renter's permission. He gets pissed when somebody don't follow his rules."

Then it came to me. Typically, when someone is murdered in a house or apartment, no one wants to live there. It's as if any potential purchaser or renter fears there might be a repeat occurrence, because the place is cursed. In a neighborhood like this, where vacant apartments were the norm, the probability of Helen Martinis' apartment being immediately rented was beyond calculation.

"Who rented the apartment?" I demanded.

He drew a long, quivering breath. "Some broad." Price licked his lips, as if not quite decided as to whether he should expound or not. "She paid the first month's rent and the security deposit. Cash. But she ain't moved in. Not 'til a week, next Monday. Says she wants the apartment painted."

I took another step toward him. "Have you painted it?"

Another frightened wag. This time both his hands made a frantic lunge for his ass-cheeks, pressing them together. "Mr. Portello says she'll have to paint it, herself. Are you done yelling at me? Because, right now I got real problems in my guts."

I jabbed a thumb toward the steps. "Let's go."

Price hesitated, crossing his legs. "I don't think I can make it."

"What's wrong now?" I demanded.

The sudden sound of rapidly escaping gas accompanied by echoes of flowing semi-solids touched my ears. This was immediately followed by my nostrils being hit, like a swinging mall through a glass window, by the stench of freshly discharged feces.

"I just shit my pants," he groaned.

I fanned the air in front of my nose with one hand. "I'm trying not to notice. Let's go."

Price had to clear his throat before he could find his voice. "Couldn't I change clothes, first? I ain't got no shorts on. So the whole dump settled in my new boots."

"Only if you want me very unhappy. Whereupon I shall bust your soggy ass for cocaine distribution."

He gave me a bewildered look, his hands going out palm-wise. "I ain't got no cocaine."

"I do. Which means you will by the time I've handed you over to the locals. Now do we take a peek at Helen's apartment? Or do you and your dirty drawers make my arrest-quota for the month?"

Without another word he rushed up the stairs, soggy pants bagging, boots sloshing.

Two flights of darkened steps later, I followed Edgar Price and his now-familiar perfume down a dimly lit hallway. Several doors along, he stopped and fitted a key into a lock. I heard a click. He jiggled the handle for a few seconds, then he threw the door wide. After which, Price reached into the darkened room, felt around for a light switch and then gave it a flick.

When a fluorescent ceiling-fixture came to life, I brushed him aside and strode into the flat.

Only the desperate would rent that type of place. The kitchenette and living room shared space. A door led to a tiny bath. Another door gave access to an equally tiny bedroom. The walls were cracked. The ceiling drooped. The place was furnished with items manufactured several decades, earlier. It was, however, clean. Nevertheless, it was not what I would consider a residence in great demand—particularly for a Federal Agent.

"Is this Helen's furniture?" I asked.

He crept nearer, shaking his head. The place comes furnished. They all do. Mr. Portello thinks it's a great marketing scam."

"What do you think?"

"This floor's half empty so I'm not so sure."

"Is this the same furniture as when Helen Martinis lived here?"

Price circled his dry lips with the tip of his tongue. Then his eyes turned upward in that vacant stare people use to aid their memory. "I ain't sure."

I turned and faced him. "Why in hell not?"

He spoke hesitantly. "I don't 'member exactly. If she sold somethin' I might'a not known. People do that. They sell stuff that ain't theirs. Are we done?"

"How come you had such an easy time finding another renter?"

I could see him collecting himself. "Mr. Portello was surprised, too. He says to me, 'Why does the bitch want that flea-nest when there are twenty others in the dump, ready to rent?'"

"What did you say?"

"I didn't have an answer. I try real hard not to have too many answers when I talk to Mr. Portello. He gets pissed when somebody has too many answers."

"What's the name of this new renter?"

"Jessie Hampstead," said Price. "Said she'd come to town expectin' to split the rent with Helen. When she heard Helen died, she said she'd rent the place on her own."

The first name fit the blonde Mrs. Annie Chase had told me about. "Describe Jessie."

He wilted under my stare. "I don't recall her too good."

"Try."

"Bottled blonde. Nice accessories. Eyes you could die in." Price swallowed as if trying to get rid of his tongue. "Can we go now? Because I really out'a…"

I pressed him for more details about Jessie's physiognomy. But other than the blonde hair, what Price said did not match the description I had gotten from Annie.

"Where does Jessie work?" I asked.

"Said she was a Private Dick." He gave me a denture-grin. "Says she can put the fix in with the cops should I get in trouble."

I had never heard of a P.I. by her name. There are not many women in my business. So it followed Jessie was working under another's P.I.'s license. Regardless, she must not be the Jessie I was looking for.

"Did Jessie Hampstead mention her boss's name?" I asked.

He nodded. "Deacon Bishop. Mr. Portello talks about him, a lot. Every time he comes around, in fact. You know, to make sure I'm keepin' the dump clean. Sometimes that all Mr. Portello talks about. Bishop this. Bishop that. And how he's gonna' blow Bishop's balls off. Bishop must be a real asshole."

"You don't know the half of it." I wondered what game this Jessie Hampstead was playing.

Price followed me into the bedroom, taking a nervous, splay-legged position by the open door. The room was furnished with a double bed, a four-drawer bureau and a closet. Hangers dangled empty from a wooden dowel spanning the latter's width. I walked over to the dresser and pulled open drawers. They, also, were empty. Then I jerked up the mattress to look between it, and the springs. Edgar Price watched me with gaping concern, his face suddenly pale with guilt. He was obviously keeping something secret. Something, my searching had brought vividly to his memory. But I returned to the front room without saying anything.

"You done?" he asked. "I think the load in my boots is causin' my ankles to break out in a rash."

"All your tenants pay their rent in cash? Or, just the new ones?"

The hesitation was minimal. "All. Mr. Portello says it saves on chasin' hot-checks. This ain't the best part of town no more."

"Where did Helen work?"

"She didn't have no regular job. So I figure she had herself a Sugar-Daddy."

"Who?"

"I don't know. But if a broad can pay rent and don't never work, she's got to have somebody on a string."

"Did Helen have any visitors?"

"I guess."

"What do you mean, you guess?"

"Some women came by a couple of times."

"The same women?"

He nodded his head but replied, "Different."

I asked for descriptions. What I heard came as a small surprise. One of the women had been Rita Portello."

"Do you know Rita Portello?"

Again he tried to swallow his tongue. "Maybe. Yeah. I guess."

"Was she one of those women who visited Helen?"

"Maybe. Yeah. I guess."

"How many times was she here?"

"To see Helen?"

I went over to him as I suddenly envisioned my prospects of getting hold of a hundred-million going down the toilet. "How many times, damn you?"

"Three that I saw. Jesus! Is this any way to treat a taxpayer?"

"Any men visit Helen?"

He cleared his throat. "Which answer is going to make you the less mad?"

"The right one."

He gulped. "Only one I saw was Dominic Portello."

"How many times was he here?"

Price shrugged. "I only saw him the one time. But he coulda' come in the back way and I wouldn't see. He's got a passkey. You know, in case his brother's out of town and I need help or something."

"When was he here?"

"Two days, maybe three."

"The night Helen was killed?"

"I guess. Cruised in the front door. Went right up the steps."

If Price remembered correctly, that timeframe put Dominic Portello in contact with Helen Martinis. "How do you know he came here to see Helen?"

He shrugged. "The old lady living in the apartment next-door to Helen called and complained about people arguin'. But by the time I got up here, Helen was gone—that's what Dominic Portello said, anyway. He was comin' out of her apartment."

"You didn't go into Helen's apartment to verify what he told you?"

"Mister, when a Portello tells you something, you don't verify it—not when they're around, anyway"

"Where are Helen's personal things?"

Price avoided answering at first. "The cops took 'em." Then he looked at me pointedly. "I thought you'd know that."

I stared at him hard enough to drive his eyes toward the floor. He fumbled with his pockets, shifting his new boots like a man bearing a lot of guilt.

"What about the stuff in storage?" I asked.

More fumbling followed by furtive looks to the left and then to the right.

I grabbed him the throat and squeezed until I had him looking bug-eyed at me. "Where are the crates, damn you?"

"I don't know about no crates!"

I gave him a backward shove. "You'd better not be leading me down the garden path."

"Jesus!" he whined. "I shit my pants—again."

"Where's the renters' storage area?"

"Basement," he choked.

"Let's take a look."

He gulped, "There ain't nothin' of Helen's down there, no more."

I had all I could do to keep from dragging out the Beretta and shoving it down his throat. "She had the crates in the storage-area?"

"Just a small suitcase." His hands flew apart. "Look, I sold it."

"Suitcase?"

He nodded. "Helen kept a small suitcase there."

Who did you sell it to?"

"Rita Portello."

"What in hell did she buy it for?"

Price looked like he was seeing his own ghost. "I don't know, Mister. I swear to God I'd tell you if I did." His hands suddenly went to his backside and tears puddled in his eyes. "Jesus, Mister. How much more do you think these boots can hold?"

I shoved him backward. "Rita shows up and you offer her a suitcase?"

He stared at me like a mouse watching a hunting cat. "She came looking for it. Said Helen borrowed it. Said she wanted it back. If a Portello tells you they want something, you give it over."

"Did you see what was in the suitcase?"

He nodded, the toupee slipping and sliding atop his naked skull. "She made me open it. Inside there was a key with a tag on it."

"A name tag?"

He shrugged. "Just a tag—it had numbers and letters on it."

"A name?"

"There was a business name printed on one side. On the other was like a code of some kind."

"What was the business name?"

The little man's words ended in a hissing intake of breath. "I don't know."

"Is there anything else you haven't told me?"

He shook his head, giving the toupee another sliding. "Not a chance, Mister."

"Think back carefully," I told him. "Did you tell Joel Kingsley about Rita being here?"

He pondered my question for nearly a minute before shaking his head. "No. He come here the last time before she did."

"What about Dominic Portello? Did you tell Kingsley about Dom visiting Helen?"

He nodded. "Are we done?"

"Okay," I said. "That's it. Let's get out of here."

He led me up stairs into the main hallway. "You're done for sure, this time?"

"Yeah. Done and done—until I get my hands on that beautiful, brown-eyed…"

"Glad I could help." His tongue came out and wet his lips, like he was suddenly relieved about something that had him worried. "Sorry I couldn't have done more. But you know how it is."

I smiled, putting my voice into casual mode. "I'd like to speak with the new tenant—Jessie—in case she and Helen were close." I took out my notebook and pen. Then I handed them to Price. "Write down where Jessie said she was living."

He scrawled an address in the notebook and returned it and the pen. I left, heading back home. I was quickly regaining my strength. But my head was calling for sleep or a throat-slicing. I decided on the former. But my first stop, after breakfast, would be Jessie's Hampstead's last address.

CHAPTER EIGHT

The next morning I stopped for lunch at Garcia's Taco Run, just off the I-35 strip. It is best known for its egg-stuffed Jalapeños. But I was in the mood for breakfast tacos, so I took a chance on their sage-sausage special. While I braved a coconut-curry sauce and pork tasting a whole lot like dried rattlesnake, I kept my cell-phone busy trying to track down Rita Portello, and Hamilton Blake. According to Rita's friends, she had been extremely moody for the past several days. I had better luck with Hamilton.

"We need to talk, Ham," I told him, by way of greeting.

"Deke?"

"Is there anything more you want to tell me about your pal Benny?"

Another gulp. "It ain't my fault, Deke."

"Then you knew?"

"Not 'til I checked his pulse."

It took a few seconds for his reply to sink in. "What in hell are you babbling about, Ham?"

"Some guys plugged Benny. He's deader than a doornail."

"Killed? When?"

"About two minutes ago. I'm waitin' on the cops."

"Who shot him?"

"There was two of 'em. Didn't even knock. Just walked into my place, plugged Benny and put two rounds into me—well, into my bulletproof vest. I pretended to die. I figured I might as well, cause I was goin' to anyway. Then, them killers left. Damn! A thing like that ruins a man's prospective on humanity."

"Why do you wear a bullet-proof vest? Was it Benny's idea?"

"Thought it'd be the safest thing, Deke," replied Hamilton Blake. "You remember that transvestite I nearly married by accident. He threatened to kill me after I broke it off—our engagement, I mean. They say love is blind. But as God is my witness there are limits—especially if he's not really a she in the important areas like I was expectin'."

"Can you identify the shooters?"

"Not a chance, Deke. Benny was in my bedroom making a private call. No sooner does he come out and start telling me some wild shit about Elsa, some crates of money, Helen and some crazy blonde and a brunette from hell when these guys bust into my apartment. Bam! Bam! Benny's on the floor dead whimperin' like a kicked dog. Then bam, bam! And I'm thinking a mule kicked me in the chest. I hit the floor and closed my eyes figurin' they was gonna' blow my head off. Next thing I know, the door shuts. When I opened my eyes the killers were gone without so much as a by-your-leave."

"What can you give me?"

"One of 'em was in a plaid shirt and bib overalls. The other was in a t-shirt with 'Love Hurts' painted on it. They was both wearin' ski masks. One was little shorter than me. The other was real short. I'm thinkin' of giving up my marriage plans, Deke. If wives are gonna' start hiring other guys to kill their husbands, it ain't worth it. I don't care if Benny was a little weird around the edges."

"Trust me, Ham. Some women have no sense of humor. What makes you think Elsa was behind Benny's killing?"

"Because Benny was cursing a blue-streak just before he got shot about she and that redhead and some bitch named Rita and another named Jessie and how they stored some crates and moved 'em and did some other bullshit all because some other asshole was makin' trouble."

"Did Benny say where the crates were?"

"What for? I sure as hell didn't know what he was goin' on about! I'm not sure he did either. Dammit, Deke! I live in a security building. People with guns ain't supposed to come in unannounced."

"Think carefully, Ham. Did Benny say anything else?"

"Just how the frigid bitch is cold meat and how nobody knows where the shit is because she had the key. What in hell do I pay taxes for if I ain't gonna be safe in my own home?"

"Let's get back to the crates, Ham. Are you saying Elsa was the last one to have them?"

"No. The frigid bitch who's dead had 'em. At least as nearly as I could understand Benny's screamin'. He said Elsa went to move 'em but they all was empty. And how the shit was gonna' hit the fan and…"

"What makes you think Helen was frigid?"

I heard a telling gulp at the other end of the line. "I guess I forgot to tell you," he said. "'Member when I told you about seein' Helen piling money into them laundry bags? Actually, I made a pass at her. Nothing serious. You know. A little ass-grab and tit-pull. Helen kneed me in the balls and then slapped me silly. I could'a sat down and cried."

"Is there anything else you didn't tell me, Ham?"

"Just that Benny don't look too good. Neither does my carpet. I never figured a guy that small had so much blood. You think I should put in tile? Just in case a thing like this happens, again? 'Cause I'm here to tell you, Deke, that carpet ain't no-way gonna' get cleaned!"

"Get out a pen and paper, Ham. Write down everything you remember about the shooting. The investigating officer will want that."

"You gonna' keep on lookin' for Elsa, Deke?"

"I don't think there's much reason for that. Do you?"

"I expect not. Benny ain't gonna' care whether you find her, or not. And I sure as hell won't. That woman never quite took to me. You think it'd be all right if I put a sheet over Benny? I can't take them starin' eyes, Deke. He looks like a fish wantin' to ask a question of me, but not knowin' how."

"Leave things as they are."

After ringing off, I paid the tab for my meal—which included a roll of antacids for dessert. Then I headed for Dallas Street, the address Edgar Price had given me. With a little luck, by days-end I would be in my flop rolling around naked on top of a hundred million dollars.

Two hours later, I was at the door of a walkup over a leather-repair shop. The tag on the mailbox in the foyer had read, *Jessie Hampstead.* I knocked expecting to hear Rita's voice. Instead a soft, female voice I had never heard before made a vague reply.

"Jessie?" I asked, in disappointment.

"She's not here. Who are you?"

Immediately, I did a rethink. Possibilities abounded as to where my frolicsome lover had hidden Tandem's hundred million—including one of her brothers' warehouses. But what if Rita had taken a partner, in this hundred-million dollar gig? The real Jessie Hampstead, perhaps? What if that partner sold Rita out to the Chicago Mob or to Tandem after the pair got hold of the money? It wasn't like Rita to go off without touching base with her friends. Especially after a night with me—considering her feminine right to brag.

I identified myself to the voice. In an effort to intimidate the woman in the apartment into telling me anything she might know about Rita, I said I was making inquiries about stolen property—in particular, five large crates.

"The door is open," came her reply.

I grabbed the knob, twisted and followed it in.

The apartment was a four-room affair with high ceilings and two large windows. The windows had shades but no curtains and overlooked an approach-way onto the I-35 freeway. One wall was fitted with shelving lined with books in colorful jackets. But the reading material all looked too well-kept to have been enjoyed. It was as if she had joined every book-of-the-month club in the country, then stacked the books on shelves as they arrived. The other wall held a collection of clocks suspended as if they were pieces of art.

As for furnishings, the front room was full of severe modern stuff that looked backbreaking in its discomfort—or maybe it was the violent colors that gave that impression. The only decent place to sit in sight was an overstuffed, velveteen chair facing the doorway. But, like the rest of the furnishings, it was a patch-quilt of brash red, blinding yellows and mysterious purples. It was almost as if whoever had decorated the apartment had tried to copy a room seen in a magazine, and overdid it.

I let my eyes drift down a hallway and spotted two closed doors. But no hint of any crates. The imaginary bell in the middle of my head began a soft, warning din.

In the big chair facing me sat a petite, bottled blonde. Her soft, rich hair was tucked behind her ears. Her face was pale, lit up with dark, shiny eyes. She had a babyish brow, brown eyes and a narrow nose. Her crimson lips were firm and determined. There was just a hint of golden orange in the pink of her dimpled cheeks. She wore a red and blue plaid shirt under which she either had good breasts, or a smart bra. Further down were black jeans and red sandals. In her lap was a small, chrome-plated pistol. One of her hands rested casually on top of the weapon, a forefinger draped through the trigger-guard.

Instead of concerned by my presence, she actually seemed to be enjoying it. She calmly sat in the chair, watching me as if I were an intruding cat.

"Have you got a few minutes?" I asked.

She smiled like a kid who had cheated on a test to get a good report card. "I always take time to discuss stolen crates with rumpled old men." Her voice was a high, irritating squeak.

I pushed the door shut, took out a business card and carried it over. She looked vaguely familiar, but I could not tag her with a name.

Her eyes went greedy, and then suspicious. "Who hired you to find those crates?"

"Client. Do you live here with Jessie?"

"Not exactly." She took my card. "Did your client tell you what was in them?"

She was about thirty years of age, and not what I would consider pretty. She continued to stare, her eyes wandering over me like I was a hitherto unknown curiosity. It was more than possible Edgar Price had been mistaken about the two women being the same. This one fitted his bottled blonde description, perfectly. Her eyes were very large—not as beautiful as Rita's, but a man *could* get lost in them. Around her neck hung a thin, gold chain with a key dangling from it.

"What's your name?" I asked.

She sort of pulled herself together and leaned back in the chair. "Carla Dugan."

After putting on a pair of thick glasses, she read the print on my card. Then she took off the glasses and handed the card back. I tried not to gape in surprise as I realized who she was, but I did not succeed. I'd found Elsa Jacobson.

"Will Jessie be back soon?" I let my eyes drift down the hallway as I imagined Rita in one of those rooms, her pert ass perched upon one of the crates

She returned her gaze to me. "You mentioned stolen crates, Mr. Bishop." Her hand gently patted the pistol as is if it was a favorite pet. "Your client—you didn't mention a name."

"A little guy," I said, intending to bait her. "Called himself Benny Jacobson."

The pistol rose toward my chest as if alive. "What else did Benny tell you?"

"That there was a bonus if I could get the crates back quickly," I said. "I get the feeling you know Benny Jacobson. Friend of yours?"

She gave me a belly laugh, and then cut it off abruptly. "Go over by the door." Her mouth went hard and drew apart into a tight smile—a smile cold enough to shatter diamonds. "Don't try anything stupid."

"I'm not going to hurt you."

Her thumb cocked the pistol's hammer. "Damn right you're not. Now, move!"

I backed away, wishing I was anywhere else. "Have you seen Rita?"

73

Elsa stared at me, her thin lips moving as if she were verbally weighing options. Finally she quietly asked, "Benny gave you this address?"

She stood up and with her free hand dragged out a cell-phone. Her eyes had gone soft again as she said, "How'd he peg me so fast? Did Jessie tell him? Is Joel outside? Is he the one who hired you?"

"Joel?" I echoed, my mind racing back to Hamilton Blake's remark about the name he had overheard Elsa mention, when she was on the telephone. "Joel, who?"

She hesitated, not sure if I was kidding her. "Shuttup!"

I gave a good imitation of someone completely bewildered. "I don't know what you're talking about." Then I pointed at the weapon. "You're making me very nervous."

Elsa punched a number on the phone's dial-pad. Then she held it to her ear waiting for a connection.

I kept retreating until my back hit the door. Then I casually reached behind, gripped the knob and gave it a turn.

She spoke softly into the phone, listened and then spoke some more. After a few more seconds she screwed up her nose, cursed and put the phone away.

"Where's Benny?" she demanded.

Hamilton Blake's surmise that Elsa had been behind Benny's murder went down the toilet.

"He came by my office this morning," I lied. "He paid me advance for three days work. I asked how to reach him, but he said he'd be moving around and said he'd check back. He told me if I had the crates by the time he contacted me, I'd get the bonus. I can come back if this is an inconvenient time."

She waggled the gun. "Rita Portello has the crates doesn't she? The lying bitch!"

I gulped, wishing I had not asked about Rita. "According to the lead that brought me here, Jessie Hampstead has them."

"Then why did you ask about Rita?"

"A name mentioned by Benny. Look, if I didn't think Jessie Hampstead had the crates, why would I come here?"

Elsa smiled bitterly. "Somebody's trying an end-run. Get this detective: nobody makes a sucker out of me. Nobody!"

I pretended to remember her, hoping to redirect her intent. "You worked with Jessie at the Chicago Stork Club, didn't you?"

Her brows furrowed and her forefinger immediately coiled tighter around the pistol's trigger. "You're working for fucking Tandem!"

I twisted the knob and stumbled back as she fired. The round went wide splattering into the plaster to my left. A moment later, a hail of bullets erupted from her pistol.

I jerked out my weapon, pointed and pulled its trigger. But the hammer failed to fall.

She fired again.

Deadly Turn

I made a dive for cover and ended up tumbling down the steps. By the time I stopped rolling everything around me had gone black. On the plus side, I was having my favorite dream. Young, nubile women were dancing all around me— naked, of course. And I was getting stinking drunk.

When I came to, I struggled to my feet. My ribs were screaming complaints. My head was rolling out its own thunder. I checked my watch. Nearly two hours had passed since my confrontation with Elsa Jacobson. I had little doubt she was long-gone. I was equally doubtful she'd left the crates. I looked around for the Beretta, but it was nowhere in sight. I headed back up the steps, anyway.

To my surprise, Elsa was where I had left her. She wasn't very talkative, however. I chalked up her lack of animosity about my return to the gaping hole in her head. People rarely react negatively to uninvited visitors when their brains are spilling onto the floor. It was then I noticed my Beretta lying conveniently next to her chair. I went over, took out the pen I kept in my shirt pocket and stuffed it into the weapon's barrel. Then I raised the pistol to my nose. Someone had been more successful than I at firing it.

I toyed with the idea of reporting her murder but with my gun the likely murder-weapon, I decided to let someone else have that pleasure. My head and ribs did not need a four-hour interrogation at police headquarters. Instead, I carefully deposited the Beretta in my coat-pocket in hopes of maintaining the prints of the shooter, should I be accused of her killing. Then I headed down the hallway to the two closed doors. One led me into the bathroom. The other was a bedroom. Neither held five steamer crates full of cash. I closed the apartment door on my way out, after wiping my fingerprints from the knob. Then I limped down the steps and hobbled my way to the Buick.

An hour later I was home, enjoying the delights of two painkillers: Pinch, and the blissful vibrations emanating from my new recliner.

CHAPTER NINE

Rattling thunder acted as my alarm clock, the next morning. I got out of bed like man in a body-cast. Then, while emitting cries of anguish over my bruises and abrasions, I staggered into the bath. A shower, shave and the ritual clothes-donning had me in the kitchen eyeing my new microwave. I had decided it was fit to process ham, eggs, toast, hash-browns and coffee in one fell swoop, when the phone rang. I grabbed the handset and a voice on the other end of the line cooed low and soft—the tone a woman uses when she is hoping to get laid by the love of her life, or is trying to convince some old fool he has nothing to worry about. From years of experience with Rita Portello I assumed her call was intended as the latter.

"I've got a bone to pick you," I said.

"So I've heard. In fact, all over town I hear you're looking for me."

"Where's the money, Rita?"

There was a pause. "What money?"

"Rita, you know damn well what money. Tandem's hundred million."

There was another pause. Then in a shaky tone she said, "I need to see you."

Visions of naked blondes, brunettes and redheads rolling around with me on top of all that money flooded my head. "When and where?"

Rita's voice continued to quiver. "At your office. I'm there, now."

"My office? How in hell did you get in there?" Before the last words were out of my mouth I knew it was a stupid question. When Rita demanded entrance, no landlord owing money to her brothers would dare deny her.

"Is the money there?"

I heard a ragged breath. "Bishop, I'm scared."

A chill ran down my spine. Rita did not scare. She had steel for spine and cast-iron for guts. A nighttime visit by the trio of Frankenstein, Godzilla and King Kong would not even give her a mild shiver. Tandem must know she has his money, and was in hot-pursuit.

"What happened?" I asked.

"Somebody tried to kidnap me."

"Were you hurt?"

"No. I gave his eyes a good clawing, and got away."

"Did you recognize him?"

"I'd never seen him before. But he reminded me of a clothing-ad from a fruity men's magazine. Long blond hair and lots of sweet stink. He ran like he'd been kicked in the balls."

"He had. Call Sal. I'm on my way."

"I can't call Sal, Bishop," Rita sobbed. "I'm in too deep."

"Then call Dom."

I heard a sniffle. "I love you, Bishop."

"I love you too, Rita. In a hundred million different ways."

Deadly Turn

"I did it for you—for us—for family."

"Stay put. Don't let anybody in. I'll be there as quickly as I can."

Forty-five minutes later I stood behind my desk in my office. My empty stomach growled. My lungs screamed for another dose of nicotine. The crates of money were nowhere in site. So I managed a suitable glare in Rita Portello's direction.

"I'm here. You're safe. I don't want any stalls. I don't want any bullshit. Where in hell are those goddamn crates of cash, Rita?"

She crossed her arms and offered me a defiant glare as one of her shoes gave the floor an impatient tap-tapping. "I tell you some asshole tried to kidnap me, and your only concern is that damn money?"

"Stop playing me, Rita! You got it. I want it. Where is it?"

Her arms fell. Her words went soft. She looked like a little girl caught doing something she should not.

"Dom and I have it. You were too late from the git-go. So forget about becoming a dirty-old-man-version of a millionaire."

My greedy heart sank at the mention of Dominic Portello. If Rita had acted alone, I might have been able to con her out of several million. There was no way in Hell Dom would let me see dime-one. Like it or not, I was out of the running.

With a frustrated curse, I told Rita to take a seat in one of the customer chairs. Then I opened the windows to bring in what little fresh air Austin mornings offered, between rains. After which, I sat down in the swivel-chair behind my desk trying not to look disappointed about my future lack of luxuries.

"Day late and a dollar short," I grumbled. "Dom has it at his warehouse, I take it?"

"That joint's a cracker-box. So, I picked the spot." A flash of anger appeared for a moment in her beautiful dark eyes. "But if you expect to cut in on our action, it's not going to happen. Not, unless you marry me."

With three failed marriages under my belt, a fourth was not likely to succeed under the best of circumstances. Considering who was offering marriage, I could not help but consider prospects for post-marital bliss as the worse-case scenario. As soon as her brothers learned I'd made Rita into an honest woman, they would cement our vows by casting my ankles in it and dropping me several hundred miles out at sea.

On the plus side, they would make certain their sister enjoyed widowhood.

"Does Sal know about the money?" I asked.

Rita colored and her look took on an odd intensity. Her face showed emotions quickly and completely. So much so, that conversing with her often gave the impression of talking to several women at the same time. Her dark eyes were like those of a child who was almost certain the big person—me—was lying to her.

"No—and you'd better not tell him."

I offered up my greediest leer. "Are you offering to buy my silence?"

Her face turned dead-white and her voice went flat. "If you tell Sal and I'll kill you."

Rita meant it. I felt a slight tinge of remorse, but I shrugged it off. Love never lasts forever—at least in my experience.

"Okay," I said. "Let's start again. Has Tandem contacted Dom about his hundred million?"

She shrugged. "Why should he? Tandem doesn't know we've got his money."

I lit a cigarette and leaned back in my chair. I tried to blow a smoke ring. But my unsated greed kept my heart out of the nonsensical endeavor. After several tries I finally managed it.

"Of course Tandem knows. Why do you think he sent a man to abduct you?"

"What makes you think he was Tandem's man?" Rita shook her head with the impatience of one who longed to be understood and accepted without qualification, without need of explanations.

"I had a run-in with the guy and gave him his current running problem. The creep's name is Joey Fortuna."

She jumped up, cursing Tandem's lineage and my less than encouraging observations.

"Think about it, Rita," I persisted. "Grabbing you is how Tandem figures he can force Dom to return the money. Unfortunately for you, Tandem does not realize the depth and breadth of your favorite brother's greed." I pointed to the telephone on the desk. "Get Dom on the horn. We'll settle this right away. Tandem gets his money in return for leaving you alone. If Dom balks, tell him I'll get Sal involved."

"I meant what I said about Sal, Bishop. You leave him out of this or…"

I jerked out the Beretta and rattled it across the desk toward her. "You want to kill me? There's the means. Go ahead! Because if Dom doesn't move on this immediately, I'll see that Sal does."

She grabbed up the pistol and took aim at my head, her forefinger coiling expertly around the trigger.

For a moment I was certain she'd kill me. Then the gun wavered. Rita's hand shook causing the gun to dance up and down in the air. Her mouth trembled. Finally her arm fell.

"I can't do it." Her hand opened and the gun thudded back onto the desk. "Damn you Bishop!" Rita offered me her back amidst a tirade of vile Sicilian. "No way in hell am I giving back that damn money. Not after all the effort I invested to get it!"

"Do you really think Tandem will keep quiet after he grabs you? Do you really think Salvator won't find out about the money, then? You and Dom have put this entire city at risk. Hanging onto Tandem's money would instigate a gang-war. Your father would never have touched another Mob's money. Old Frank knew what would happen. If you won't give back the money for your own safety, then do it for Momma's. Because if Tandem doesn't get the results he wants from grabbing you, she'll be his next target."

Rita grabbed up the phone receiver, her fingers whitening with pressure. A second later she dropped it back into its cradle and pulled her hand back.

"Dom's not at his store, today. I don't know where he is."

"Stop playing me, Rita. Tandem isn't some small-timer who breaks into a worried sweat when your family's name is mentioned." I indicated the chair she had vacated with a finger-jab. "He's got the juice to bring in enough hired guns to wipe out your entire family."

"You're blowing smoke, Bishop." She sent one of the customer chairs spinning with a vicious kick. "You want me to tell you where the money is so you can grab it!"

I shook my head. "All I want is your safety."

A tear tumbled down one of her cheeks. "Dom would've told me if Tandem was onto us."

"Who are you kidding, Rita? For a hundred million, your favorite brother would feed you to the dogs. Get him on the phone. If Dom won't budge, we'll get Sal to handle it. Either way, you've got to give back Tandem's money."

"Fuck you, Bishop, and the goddamn horse you rode in on. You don't own me. You don't tell me what to do."

"Have I ever lied to you, Rita? How many times has Dom lied to you, conned you?"

She cursed me up one side and down the other before settling into the upright customer chair. "A hundred million, Bishop. Do you know what we could to with a hundred million?"

"I know what *I* could do with it. I get palpitations thinking about what I could do with it. But it's no longer an option. Call Dom or call Sal. We're going to resolve this, today."

She leaned back in the chair, crossed her arms over her chest and looked away from my stare. "Dom wouldn't leave me hanging. There has to be another reason that creep tried to grab me."

I lit a smoke, wishing I could tell her my concerns about her welfare were unfounded. But a lifetime of knowing Dom's evil mind proved otherwise. A hundred million would put him above Sal in both wealth and power. If little sister had to be sacrificed to hang onto it, so be it.

Dom could not take out Tandem on his own: he did not have the manpower. But if the Chicago mobster kidnapped Rita, Dom wouldn't have to. Regardless of Tandem's justification, Salvator would wade in with all the men and guns he could beg and buy. The end would be a massacre on both sides.

If bullying wouldn't do the job, I would have to ease her in the right direction with a little flattering nestled between bouts of schmoozing. But that would not be easy. There was an animal inside her: one that was fierce, frantic and extremely dangerous.

"All right," I said in my best conciliatory tone. "I admit I'm more than a little jealous about your success. I admit if I had the chance, I'd grab that money and I'd run with it. Since I that won't happen, at least tell me how you figured it out?"

Rita wet her lips with the tip of her pink tongue. Her eyes had lost their usual luster and were now a dull, angry purple. After a moment, she tapped one side of her head.

"I used my brains, Bishop."

"I knew Dom hadn't done the mystery-solving. How about a little inside information? Such as where, when and who?"

"Jacob Tandem paid Dom a late-night call shortly after arriving in Austin." She smiled, then. It was the teasing, bad-girl smile Rita used after winning the day. "Tandem admitted the embezzlement. He had to. He wanted Dom to help get the money back from the people who had stolen it. He said the Chicago Mob was going to have him hit unless he moved quickly. So Tandem offered Dom five million out of what he recovered in exchange for helping."

"Christmas in July for Dom," I quipped.

"Dom agreed, of course." Rita's coloring had returned to its normal, sexy glow. "Who wouldn't? Tandem told Dom what he knew about the people involved. After Tandem left, Dom came to see me. He knew a job like that required smarts. He also knew that Sal would refuse to get involved no matter what Tandem offered. So Dom offered to cut me in for an even split."

"Whereupon you convinced your brother that the two of you would secrete all the money somewhere and tell Tandem a tale of woe over failing in your quest."

Her brows puckered prettily. "Why settle for five million when we could have a hundred million in untraceable cash? Tandem embezzled it. He deserves whatever the Chicago Mob figures is his due."

"Tandem talked about Helen Martinis?"

Rita nodded. "Helen was what he called her—no last name. Tandem said that she, Benny and Elsa Jacobson, Harold Maybe and two others Tandem had not identified stole the money. Tandem had been hiding it behind a false, concrete wall in the basement of his house."

"It had to have been someone very close to him who tipped off the others."

"It was Harold Maybe." Her head tilted to one side, her dark eyes on mine for an instant. "Harold was Tandem's nephew. Tandem trusted him and made the mistake of bragging about how he had fooled the mob into believing Gino Picot stole it."

"What happened to Harold Maybe?"

"Family ties are not as tight as in Texas."

"A city this size and you pulled off a miracle in locating that money-pile by knowing only a few names?" I asked, in genuine awe.

She studied me as if wondering if I was taunting her. "I had a bit of luck in the form of Jessie Hampstead."

"I've heard the name."

"Jessie is Tandem's bit of fluff. He brought her here from Chicago. I hooked up with her when she and Tandem first visited Dom." Rita paused a moment, her brows furrowing as she gave consideration to something. "I know I've seen Jessie before. But I'm not sure where."

"Have you been to Chicago?"

She nodded. "Sal took me a few years back. It was after he completed a business deal with Frankie Gravano."

"Frankie 'The Wop'?"

"Yeah. You know him?"

"He and I had a brief run-in during my last visit to Chicago. That was years back, when he was still a torpedo for the Profaci Mob."

"Frankie invited Sal to Chicago to show appreciation. Since Sal isn't married or involved, he brought me. We went to the Stork Club. Pretty snazzy place." She snapped her fingers. "That's it. That's where I saw Jessie."

"Jessie worked there?"

"No. I saw her on the arm of one of the Chicago Mob. Gino Picot. He was second in command, then. Sharp dresser. Handsome guy." Rita scowled uncertainly. Then her face brightened. "Yeah. That's why I remember Jessie."

"If Tandem brought her down here, Jessie must be more than fluff."

Rita shrugged, smiling slightly. "Maybe. Guys his age don't often form long-term attachments—as you and I both know."

"I'm completely devoted to you."

"Liar." She smiled faintly. "Jessie's mother lives at any bar where she can get credit—Maria, I think Jessie said was her mother's name. Could be Jessie asked to come so she could visit family."

"What about the money?"

"I figured that if Helen, Elsa and Benny were hiding in Austin it meant the money had not yet been divided."

"I don't understand your reasoning."

"Think about it, Bishop." She spread her arms. "If you had tens of millions in cash, would you hang around Austin? There are more tantalizing places far beyond Tandem's reach."

I snuffed out my cigarette in the ashtray on my desk. "Point taken."

"I thought there was a good chance at least one of those unidentified two still works for Tandem. When you steal from the devil and you're unable to run away with his loot, it is a wise thief who sleeps with him to keep tabs on his efforts at recovery."

I could hardly keep from smiling at her jaded, folksy philosophy. "Which pinpointed one of the unidentified thieves as Jessie?"

Rita nodded. "Pillow-talk is always full of secrets. I could write a book on what you've told me." She glanced about the room. "Jessie's one shrewd lady. She makes a point of knowing all that's going on in Tandem's life. Her interests come across as that of a devoted lover. But her body language says otherwise. She hates Tandem. She's terrified of him. She oozes affection to keep him telling her everything she wants to know. If he finds the others, she knows that Tandem will get them to identify her."

"Did Jessie admit as much to you?"

"Of course not. But because of my suspicions, I made a point of cultivating Jessie. A short time later, she and I were out at one of the malls, shopping. We ran into two women who she claimed were old friends—Elsa Jacobson and Helen Martinis. Coincidentally I had met Elsa three months earlier, over a business deal. At that time Jacob Tandem was still in Chicago and I had no idea a hundred million in cash was missing. With the names Tandem gave Dom also being pals with Jessie, I not only confirmed my suspicions about Jessie but penciled-in Helen Martinis as the third player in the hundred million dollar game."

"I'm surprised Elsa and Helen openly approached Jessie."

"They were hot under the collar." Rita scratched the side of her delicately chiseled nose. "Funny thing about the three of them. They all wore the same necklace—a simple gold chain with a key dangling from it. Almost like they were in a club."

"Dom's club? Helen said he had her key."

Rita gave me a dirty look. "Dom isn't in the joy-house business."

"What deal did you make with Elsa?"

Rita hesitated. "Girl stuff. Anyway, they excused themselves and went off to a quiet spot for a private chat. I didn't dare try to listen, but I watched them carefully. Something had the three of them worried."

"You told Dom about Helen and Elsa?"

"Yes, but not at that time. I wanted to find the money first. Dom is like a bull trapped amongst a collection of crystal, particularly with women. His threats would've sent those three running—with the money."

"And to think I had images of you seducing the three women into telling you…"

Her full lips went thin, and taut. "What do you take me for, Bishop?"

I laughed in a dirty way. "A greedy liberal?"

Rita gave me a disgusted look. "When Jessie and her friends finished chatting, I think they were concerned about what I might think if they simply parted ways. So they came back to me and we went for lunch." She smiled loosely. "During our meal I learned where Helen lived. I pretended to be looking for an inexpensive apartment for a friend. The next day, I staked-out Helen's apartment building. When she left, I searched the basement storage area, and her flat. Sal owns the building, so it was no trouble getting Edgar Price, the building manager, to cooperate. Much to my disappointment, the stolen crates of money were not there. That, to my mind, meant Elsa had the stuff. So, I drove out to her house and did the same routine. Again, I came up empty."

"How is it you knew where Elsa lived?"

She narrowed her eyes defensively. "I conduct business ventures in an orderly fashion, Bishop."

"Jessie didn't try to justify being friends with Helen and Elsa?"

"Why would she? Jessie's mother lived in Austin." Rita's feet shuffled. "Why shouldn't Jessie have friends, here?"

I lit another cigarette. "I think I'd feel the need to explain why I was hanging out with a couple of gay men."

Rita tapped a forefinger against her chest as she spoke. "Unlike men, we women don't panic over homosexual inclinations. We accept it as another way of life and we move on." Jabbing at me through the air, she continued, "The cash had to be somewhere in town. The problem I had was time. If Tandem suspected Jessie, there was a good chance he was having her followed. Austin is a small city. If his people were watching her, they may already have spotted Helen or Elsa or Benny. To beat them to the cash, I had to work faster and smarter. So, I went back to Helen's apartment building with the Sicilian Brothers. When Helen went out, I had them bug the joint using small, high-tech stuff that uses encryption in transmissions. They're expensive, but I couldn't afford an eavesdropper. Then I rented an apartment a few blocks away."

"Somehow I don't see you hunched over speakers listening to what Helen Martinis was doing."

"I didn't." Rita sniggered, "I had Ramón set up a computer to monitor the transmissions from Helen's apartment. It filtered out dead space and consolidated time by storing only what was said."

I tilted toward Rita curiously at the sound of a name I had not heard her mention before. "Ramón?"

"Ramón DaVita. He's Sal's computer hacker—an import from Sicily. A real wiz."

"Why would Sal need a hacker?"

Her shoulders hunched up and down impatiently. "That's where the big money is, these days – hacking into banking systems. Get with the times, Bishop."

"I'm not as out of date as you might think. I'm just surprised Sal is involved in that type of operation. It poses a number of risks in terms of the bank's ability to track those electronic transactions."

"Trust me when I say Ramón can cover tracks. Anyway, I did the same thing at Elsa's house, renting a place within transmission distance to record what went on, there."

"Didn't the Sicilian Brothers ask what you were up to?"

"Of course not. They know from past experience it is better to do what I ask and not wonder why. If they ask, they might hear something that Sal would want to know about—something they would have to tell no matter how upsetting. You know, like who I'm bedding—you, for example."

"What about this Ramón guy? Wasn't he a little curious?"

"Ramón thinks I'm the new wing in the family's secret operations. He also has the hots for me."

"You made at least one visit to Elsa's house when she was there. Was that before or after you located the money?"

"How did you know that?" Her brows furrowed.

I blew smoke at the ceiling and grinned. "I'm a trained detective."

Rita offered up a tired smile. "The first meeting at Elsa's house was a girls' night thingy. I was invited. Even though I had the bugs working, I was not about to turn down the invitation. Nothing makes a woman more talkative than a pile of money and a good buzz from wine. I thought if I played it cool and cagey, I might direct the conversation around to what I would do with millions. I hoped by doing that I could find out where they'd hidden Tandem's. But it didn't happen." She gave me a searching look as if trying to guess what was going on in my head. "The other visits were me playing the good friend. You know, to keep in touch in case she should decide to leave town with the cash. Shifting five crates of cash would require muscle. I thought that my family history was such that she would ask me to help. I did the same act with Helen."

"So your bugging operation gave you the location of the money?"

"No such luck. I heard a great deal of complaining about not being able to divide the money. And I heard how the theft came about—bits and pieces in terms of them rehashing what they should've done instead of what was done. That's how I learned that the money was in five wooden crates."

"How long did it take to get you that far?"

"Nine days. Then on the tenth something happened that changed things."

"Benny and another guy came looking for their end of the heist."

She stamped one foot in surprise. "Damn but you're good!"

"Who is the other guy?" I asked. "Did you see him? He was described to me as tall and blond."

Her head shook sharply. "I never saw either of the men and the women never mentioned your blond's name. My recordings caught Benny over at Elsa's several times ragging on her for money. But that day, he threatened to take the bundle if they didn't cooperate. Later on, the other guy showed up at Elsa's house and threatened to kill her if she didn't tell him where the money was. She must've been armed because he left without making good on his threat."

"Did Benny know where the money was stored? What's your take?"

"As near as I can tell, they gave the money to Helen and Elsa to bring to Texas. Benny and the others stayed behind for whatever reason. By the time Benny and the other guy got here, the money was already stored. I got the impression that Elsa and Helen did not trust either man. If you don't trust somebody you don't tell them everything."

"Why not split it up? Each could go his or her way and it's all the tougher for Tandem to track them down."

"From what I heard in the recordings, the original plan called for them to hang onto the cash until the Chicago mob took out Tandem. Jessie refused to budge on that issue. Originally Elsa and Helen agreed. But during the last few days of my bugging efforts, Jessie was more and more at odds with Elsa and Helen over that part of the plan."

"So Jessie was running the operation?"

"That how it looks to me."

"Which one of them let Tandem's ex-playmates know he had embezzled the hundred million and not Gino Picot?"

"Jessie, as near as I can tell," she said. "To make sure the Chicago Mob believed her claims, she told them where Tandem had been hiding the money. It must've been enough. I know for a fact that a contract was put out on Tandem—Sal told me a few days ago. Sal also told Dom to sever relations with Tandem because of that."

"Elsa, Helen and Jessie must've thought Chicago would take out Tandem immediately."

"They did. But the Chicago Mob wants its money. So the hit is on hold while they see if Tandem recovers it. That way they take him out and collect what is rightfully theirs, at the same time. It makes good business sense. You can only kill the guy once. Why not profit from his search?"

"I think it's likely Jessie's agenda does not include sharing the money," I said. "Which leaves, in the interim, multimillionaires without ready-funds."

"As near as I could tell, the women are bearing up financially. What I heard on the recordings suggests that Benny and the other guy are beyond the point of being patient. That's why, after the last bout of threats, the women decided to have five crates built. They planned to put the empty crates into the storage area and haul the cash-full ones someplace else—which they did. Then if Benny or the other guy showed up with force being the plan, the women would simply tell them where the empty crates were and hand over the key. Then, the women would hook up and make tracks with the loot."

"But if you knew where the money was, why did Dom go after Helen?"

She blinked in surprise. "How did you know he went after her?"

"A little boot-wearer with loose bowels told me."

"The crates with the money were to be stored at Elsa's house, temporarily," said Rita. "Since the men had already been there, it was not likely they would think to search the house again. That's when I made my mistake and told Dom what I had learned." Her beautiful face took on an expression of disappointment. "We piled into his furniture-delivery truck and went out there. Only when we got there, the place had already been cleared out. Dom went ballistic. I tried to point out that all we had to do was keep an eye on Helen. By following her we would find the money. But he was tired of waiting. Dom wanted the hundred million, and he was going to get it from her."

"How did Helen get away from Dom?"

"As usual, Dom made the mistake of using scare-tactics," Rita explained. "Helen snuck out her bathroom window. He came home fuming. I figured the hundred million was history. But, Dom, ever the brutal optimist, sent his people looking. A few hours later, a couple of Dom's men found Helen. They dumped her in their car and told Dom they were on their way to him. Lucky for her or not, those clowns hit a truck on I-35. Dom's men were killed. Helen got out, apparently without a scratch, and took off before the cops arrived. She must've gotten a ride with someone."

"A guy with roving hands who dumped her out on the highway when she wouldn't come across," I reflected.

Rita made an impatient gesture. "In any event, Dom figured if he didn't get her that night she'd get to the money and leave the state. He had his people running all over the place. They were stopping cars, searching the rest-areas—the whole nine yards. It was crazy."

"So it was his men who pulled me over?"

She nodded. "When they saw Helen in the car, those two guys thought it was bonus-time. It wasn't until they radioed the good news to Dom and he told them all about you that they understood how much trouble they were really in. Their plan was to take you out. But Dom figured a shootout would get everybody killed—including Helen. So he told his men to send you on your way. Dom then sent another crew out to keep a tail on you. Once you dropped Helen off, the plan was to make another attempt on her. Somehow between the original guys letting you go, and the next group of Dom's people picking up your trail, you and Helen got run off the road."

"Why didn't you tell me it was Dom's men when I first told you about it?"

"Because I was afraid you'd go after him. He didn't kill Helen, Bishop. His people didn't run you off the road."

"Who did?"

She made a despairing gesture. "I honestly don't know. But it has to be someone who thought they had the money. Elsa's brother or the other guy, I suppose."

"But they didn't know where the crates were stored—the empty ones or the full."

"How do you know?"

"Because of a key on a chain. The dangler to be handed over if the men got rough. No. Elsa must've been behind it."

"I don't see her pulling that off on her own. She sure as hell wouldn't have hooked-up with the men from the theft to take out Helen."

"You don't know her as well as you think," I said. "But I agree she did not do it alone. She must've mended bridges with either her brother or the other guy—maybe both."

Rita shook her head. "I don't buy it."

I started justify my assumption when another thought came to mind. "I'm wrong. It was Jessie. She probably used some of the local talent Tandem had hired."

"But Tandem would know about it."

"What better way to prove her devotion to him than to turn on her counterparts? See what I mean? She knew where the money really was. She had access to it."

"But how would she know where Helen was? And why didn't she take the money afterward? That theory has too many holes, Bishop."

"Not if Elsa and Helen did a second switch of the money to cut her out."

"Why would they do that? She was their information source on what Tandem was up to?"

I shrugged. "Probably because of Jessie's insistence they wait on the split. Let's talk about the suitcase."

She pretended innocence, again. "What suitcase?"

"The one you conned Edgar Price out of."

Rita laughed. "So you know about that, too," she said. "Well, I figured Helen would not dare keep anything that might disclose the money's actual location with her. She also would not hide it in her apartment where it could be easily found. Most people have a suitcase. I just guessed about it being in storage."

"Helen told me Dom had the key."

"He did. She had been wearing it on a necklace – the same as the other two wore. When Dom grabbed her by the throat, the necklace broke. But he didn't know what lock the key was for. It was just some key."

"That must've warped his mind."

"It did! As it turned out, it was not the same key as I found in the suitcase. The one she and the others wore was a red herring to the original location."

"The key inside the suitcase was tagged?"

Rita nodded. "The key was to the padlock on the storage door from a self-storage place. The tag had the pass-code to get into the storage facility's secured area. I went and opened it on my own. Inside were five crates that weighed about a ton. So, I rented a spot at the same place. Then I called the Sicilian Brothers, told them to bring over a forklift and they shifted the crates from where Helen and Elsa had hidden them to my spot."

"How did Tandem trace Helen to Texas?"

"Elsa and Benny have family here," Rita replied. "Tandem guessed they'd run to where they might get protection. It followed the money went south. Tandem came to Austin because it was his only lead."

"Did you know that Elsa and Benny are dead?"

Her Adam's apple bobbed several times. "Elsa and Benny are dead, too?"

"Like I said, Tandem is not some amateur you can bluff."

Rita crossed her legs, giving me a good look at her thighs. "I don't believe you. You're trying an end-run on me for the money!"

Before I could say anything further, two men appeared in my office doorway with guns drawn. One was Thomaso. The other was Pietro. Both worked for Salvator Portello. Both were known among their mob connections as the Sicilian Brothers. Both smiled out of one side of their mouths like matching manikins. Rita shot a look at the door, then she stood and retrieved her purse.

"Mr. Portello sent us to fetch you, Miss," said Thomaso. "When he got your call, he got very concerned."

"Not Mr. Portello, Thomaso," chided Pietro. "Mr. Dominic. We must be precise."

Thomaso nodded his head in agreement. "Yeah, we must be precise. It was Mr. Dominic, Miss. He sent us to fetch you."

"Thanks for keeping me safe, Bishop," she said, with heavy sarcasm. Rita thumbed her nose at me before moving toward the door.

"Nice to see you again, Mr. Bishop," said Pietro, as he holstered his pistol. "You done real good keepin' an eye on her."

"Yeah, Mr. Bishop," chimed Thomaso. "You done real good keepin' an eye on her."

At the door Rita turned and looked back at me. For a moment it seemed some sort of expression—guilt, maybe—came into her big brown eyes. But it did not remain long. Then, without a word, she turned and left.

I watched the Sicilian Brothers follow her out, taking with her my dreams of a hundred million and leaving me in a haunting, empty silence.

After they left, I did some thinking. As Tandem knew Dominic had the money Rita would never be safe—until the cash was returned. But with Rita refusing to cooperate and Dom willing to trade her life for that money, there was only one thing I could do. I had to get Salvator Portello involved. It would be unpleasant. It would be dangerous. But I had no choice.

I telephoned Sal and requested a meeting. In response, I heard the usual threats, promises and vows concerning my future suffering. But in the end Sal agreed to see me—in two hours. I rang off thinking two hours was just long enough for him to get the dip-tank ready.

I was hungry. Since my next meal might be my last, I decided to head for Romero's BBQ Café, just off SH 183. I now knew Joel Kingsley's had lied to me about Helen. I also suspected he was the big blonde described to me by Annie Chase. Since Kingsley had been Henrico Romero's handler after Henrico entered the Federal Witness Protection Program, there was a chance that Henrico had the inside scoop on Kingsley. It wouldn't get me the hundred million. But Henrico might provide me with enough information to link Kingsley to Helen's death. Her dying was a still a very personal issue for me.

CHAPTER TEN

When I arrived, Romero's Barbeque was doing a brisk business. I could not help but salivate as my nose detected the smells of grilled beef and pork mixed with the pungency of Henrico's spicy sauce. He had a special way of combining roasted serranos, tomato paste, honey, cloves, chili powder and a secret ingredient Henrico vowed to take with him to his grave. Having missed breakfast, I was ready to devour anything he wanted to let crawl onto a plate.

As I made my way past to an empty booth near the fire exit, I gave a nod to the eighty-something, pink-haired number sitting on the stool behind the cash register. I got a winking leer in reply, plus several blown kisses. Every time I visited Henrico's restaurant, she gave me the same greeting. I couldn't tell if the old girl appreciated my business or was hoping I'd ask for her as my dessert.

At the far end of the near-full serving-counter, a shabby old drunk sipped coffee while having an animated conversation. No one was near him or paid him heed, but the old fellow talked up a storm, turning his head to the wall and then to the vacant stool on the other side before nodding at the empty space on the other side of the counter. It was as if he was hearing voices from all three sides and sharing his views with each. Not unlike some of my Monday mornings after a long weekend with Rita Portello.

I spotted Henrico Romero through the serving passage cut in the wall beyond the counter. He stood barking orders and swilling at the grill as several young men in cooks' uniforms shoved plate after plate filled with steaming-hot food through the passage, to the waiting servers.

Henrico was quite short—barely over five feet. His obesity—he was nearly as wide as he was tall—made him appear even shorter. Henrico was about my age. I did not know if his eyebrows had always been white or if their color was the result of long-term worries coupled by terrifying dreams. But the hairs were so pale against his alabaster skin that they were nearly invisible. He was bald except for an untrimmed circle of shoulder length hair growing at ear-level and of a deep yellow hue. There was no sign of a beard growing within his dead-white skin. Henrico's eyes were unusually large and the irises an odd yellow hue. Each eyeball bulged from its socket like a hardboiled egg, giving him a permanently shocked appearance.

The counter-help scrambled to keep customers served with food, and beverages. When a waitress finally had time to visit my table, I told her I needed to speak with Romero.

She made an apologetic face and told me it might not be for a while because they were so busy.

I handed her my business card and told her to let Henrico know I was waiting and to bring me a glass of ice tea and the biggest plate of ribs on the menu.

She gave a quick nod and then hurried off.

Thirty minutes later, I was sucking the last bit of sauce from my fingertips and pondering the prospect apple pie a la mode, when someone from my past strolled in—a stoolie of low repute by the name of Sherman 'The German' Tate. The last time I had laid eyes on Sherman was nearly a year ago, just before I stumbled into a private party where one of the participants took great pride in sending three nine millimeter rounds into my belly. I would not normally have attended such a gathering in that flatfooted fashion, but Sherman had assured me the man I was looking for would be there. He was. The man was also dead.

Sherman caught my stare and shot a quick look at the door. He probably would have been made a run for it had I not been reaching inside my coat. Instead of fleeing, the six-foot-six snitch and came over, slinking in the fashion of a long dog toward its abusive master. I grinned and pulled out a smoke.

"Take a load off, Sherman." I pointed across the table.

He hesitated a moment, his pale blue eyes dipping to the patch of floor between his scuffed brown shoes. The frightened man's gray brows furrowed and worry lines formed around his mouth.

"How's it hangin', Deke?' Sherman choked, still staring at his shoes.

His long face had the sooty-tan of someone who spends a lot of time on the street. The green suit covering him looked new. The brown shirt and orange tie complementing it were old, and stained. He stank of stale gin and unwashed sweat.

I purposely waited several seconds on my reply, enjoying the sight of nervous sweat rolling from his gray temples. "Thanks to you, I'm lucky things still are."

Sherman slid into the booth across the table from me, still averting my gaze. "I didn't know what them Russians had in mind, Deke," He tried to make the quivering corners of his mouth rise. "You know how unpredictable that mob is."

"I want to believe you, Sherman. Truly I do."

Tears streamed down his hollow cheeks. "I didn't figure it for a setup. Honest. On my life, Deke." He clasped his palms together in prayer-fashion, pressing his thumbs to his forehead while resting his elbows on the tabletop; his eyes still down-turned. "On my fucking life, I didn't know!"

I pulled out my pack of cigarettes and tossed it onto the table in front of him. "Maybe I got it all wrong. Maybe your phone-call wasn't a ruse to get me into the hands of the Russians who were doping him. Maybe it was just the result of bad information being passed around."

His watery green eyes finally came up. "You got it in one, Deke! You can't trust those fuckin' Russians. No way can you trust 'em!"

"That's what I kept telling myself those three weeks in the hospital. But the more I told myself the less I believed it, Sherman. Do you know why?"

His quivering fingers grabbed up the pack of smokes and rattled several out onto the table. I grabbed one, turned it filter-toward-his-mouth, and shoved it between his whimpering lips. Then I brought out the Zippo and gave his cigarette some flame and then mine, before dropping the lighter back into its keep.

"You see, I kept wondering why you never came to visit me," I continued, "during that painful and lengthy recuperation. I tried to make myself believe it was because you were too busy. But..."

"I was! I was!"

"A man isn't busy all the time, Sherman. See what I mean?"

He dragged one sleeve across his running nose leaving a dingy stain on the cuff. Then he took a deep drag on the cigarette before coughing out, "I can't tell you how many times I started for your flop. But I got caught up in action I couldn't put off."

"For nearly a year, Sherman? You see, for nearly a year I've been asking around about you. And for nearly a year, I've been hearing how you're purposely avoiding me. A thing like you and me playing hide and seek could ruin our friendship. Know what I mean?"

His boyish hands fanned the air between us. "You ever need information," he quivered, "just come to old Sherm. It'll be on the house, Deke. Don't worry about that. You and me go too far back to let a little misunderstanding come between us."

I eased back in the booth pretending to smile. "That's what I like to hear. An old friend offering to help. Let's talk about a red sedan, Sherman. Lots of horsepower. Phony tags. Rumpled right front fender. Plate number XYC 519. I want to know who was behind the wheel, when my old Buick sprouted wings."

He gulped. "Heard about that. Right away I knew you'd want the lowdown, so I went digging"

"And?"

"Them plates are hot."

"I knew that much, Sherman. Where's the goddamn car?"

"That little number got sent to the crusher."

"Which one?"

"Algoid Auto Parts."

I sat up straight in surprise, resting my forearms on the tabletop. "That's Salvator's operation, isn't it?"

He gave the crowd in the restaurant a nervous glance. "You and Sal ain't never been what might be considered close. Makes a guy think."

It did. Had I been wrong right from the beginning? Had Sal's people run me off the road? It didn't make sense if they wanted Helen Martinis alive. But maybe the plan had been to kill me and she was just a side issue.

"Jacob Tandem," I said, blowing smoke into Sherman's face. "Ring any bells?"

His lips went tight. "Chicago," he whispered, as if God might be listening.

"Tandem walked off with a hundred-mill in mob money. More recently, six people relieved him of those ill-gotten gains. Harold Maybe, Helen Martinis, Elsa and Benny Jacobson were involved. Who were the others?"

Sherman Tate shifted about like a man with a pack of fire ants stinging his backside. "A guy who talks about Tandem is liable to end up with broken bones —or worse."

"Alternatively, Sherman, I could pop you on some dark rainy night during a bout of depression over our failed friendship."

"You're right about somebody grabbing the dough," he confided. Sherman shook like a man waiting his turn at the urinal behind three million beer guzzlers. "But those six didn't lift it here." He gave another glance around the café. "Chicago. Four of the six are dead. Tandem's got a line on the other two —maybe."

"Who are they?"

I could barely hear Sherman's voice. "Joel Kingsley is one."

I smiled. "You're certain?"

He nodded. "As certain as Tandem is."

"And the other?"

"I don't know. I don't think Tandem knows, either. But he ain't about to give up. He's got no choice. The Chicago boys put out a contract on him. His only hope of stayin' alive is to give back that cash and he knows it."

"Where can I find Joel?"

His eyes did a quick tour of the place before coming back to me. "He's dug himself a deep hole and crawled in. Tandem tried to whack him last night. Kingsley dropped two of Tandem's men before making like the invisible man. Tandem's offered a hundred-thousand dollar reward for Kingsley's whereabouts —Tandem's not shy with the bucks when he wants revenge."

"Who did Chicago send to do the job on Tandem?"

He took a long draw in the cigarette before saying, "Alls I know is the shooter's been in place since Tandem was in Chicago, waitin' for orders. Close enough to Tandem to do the number on him on a moment's notice."

"I need a name, Sherman."

"I don't got one, Deke." He paused to fill his lungs with smoke. "But I'll keep digging." His eyes gave me a pleading look, then. "Does that square us?"

I nodded. "I understand Dom's got a new business."

Sherman's brows went into a telling arch. "Claim's he's gone legit."

"You don't believe it?"

"Not a chance. Somebody's supplying him with hot merchandise from out of state." Then he leaned closer. "For a c-note I can give you something that'll wet your dreams."

"It had better be worth it." I took out my money-clip, peeled off two fifties and set the bills on the table.

"Dom's gonna' have Sal hit," said Sherman, snatching up the cash.

"I don't believe it."

"I heard it from the horse's mouth," he insisted.

"Dom? How?"

Sherman leaned back grinning slyly. "I hired on as night-watchman at Dom's store. Been there since it opened. It's a big place full of nice, soft beds.

So why pay rent? I just sorta' moved in. During the day I stay out of sight up above the false ceiling over Dom's office. I got a little mattress between the trusses, all nice and cozy. That's how I heard the plan. Tandem's backing his play."

"When did you hear this?"

"Not more than two hours ago."

"You're certain it was Tandem and Dom?"

He raised one hand and crossed index over middle finger. "They're like that. Tandem's been coachin' Dom. Tellin' him how Sal's gotten too old to run the family business. Tellin' Dom how Sal should retire and put Dom in charge."

Perhaps I had it all wrong about why Tandem went after Rita. Maybe the attempt on her had nothing to do with his missing money? Maybe it was intended as the first step to getting rid of the Portello clan? Whether Tandem reclaimed the hundred million or not, the Chicago Mob would not cease their efforts to kill him. Tandem's only hope of continued breathing was to offer his former associates something worth more to them than revenge. Something like the rackets now run by Salvator Portello. Tandem would use Rita as bait. Then he would wait for Sal and Dom to come for her. Dom, thinking he was going to move into the top spot after Sal was hit, would lead his brother to the slaughter. Tandem would kill Sal and while Dom was still relishing the prospect of finally coming into power, Tandem would take him out. Rita would be hit as an afterthought. Then 'The Wop' would move his troops into place here.

"When is Dom to make his move?" I asked.

He let his eyes drift down his chest and then dart back up to mine. "If either of them find out I talked, I'll be sent to hell—along with Sal."

I parted my lips to give him a good look at my front teeth. "You know you can trust me, Sherman."

Sherman Tate's face suddenly turned the color of boiled pork and he abruptly convulsed.

"What's the matter, Sherman? You don't look so good."

"I got a bad ticker," he whimpered. "Just thinkin' about Tandem finding out I talked to you, makes it jump around in my chest."

"You know you can count on me to look out for you."

"I don't have a date. But it ain't gonna' be long." He tilted forward in agony, one hand clutching his chest. "Are we done? 'Cause I think I'm overdue for my funeral."

I nodded.

Knowing Joey Fortuna and matching Rita's description of her attacker to him had been a fluke. Tandem probably thought his plans for the Portellos was still a safe move. All he had to do was get his hands on Rita—no mistakes this time. Then it was just a matter of waiting for Dom to get his courage up.

Sherman slid out of the booth. Then he stood up slowly; his teeth chattering; his blue lips quivering, his breathing ragged. "See ya, Deke."

I watched him stagger out, not noticing Romero heading my way.

"How's tricks, Deke?" Henrico Romero grinned, as he settled across the table from me.

"That depends on what's going on between you and Joel Kingsley, Henrico."

He gave me a plastic grin. In a confidential voice, he said, "I ain't talked to Kingsley in months. He ain't my handler no more—you know that."

By the way his lower plate bounced against his tongue, I could tell that Henrico was lying. I let it pass—for the moment. "Tell me about Helen Martinis?"

I watched his Adam's apple bob like he was trying to swallow his tongue. "I think I read something about her in the paper."

"Stop playing me, Henrico. I'm one of the few friends you've got. Do you know who ran me off the road?"

The bugged, yellow eyes grew larger. "I never had nothin' to do with it, Deke."

"Who did?"

His shiny head with its yellow mane wagged. "Honest to God, Deke. If I knew I'd tell you."

I reached out and lightly tapped his forearm with a forefinger. "I've always played it straight with you. I've always been there when you needed help. You know something, Henrico. What is it?"

After glancing around to make sure he would not be overheard, Henrico tilted toward me. "Two or three days back, Joel Kingsley comes in. He shows me a picture. Redhead. Not beautiful. But nice."

"Helen Martinis?"

Henrico nodded. "I'd seen her in here a couple of times. Come in with my daughter."

"Daughter?"

He grinned. "I got two kids, Deke. Boy and girl. Grown up, now. They took their mother's name after I went into hiding—Jacobson. Benny calls once in a while. He's in Chicago. Bookkeeper for some hot nightspot. I'm not sure what Elsa does. I ain't seen her in years. I guess Benny told her where I lived. Anyway, she shows up out of the blue with this redhead."

My stomach fell in sympathy, but I did not say anything.

Henrico made a vague gesture. "I used to owe a bundle on this place. I wasn't making enough to meet the mortgage, keep the equipment working and still earn a living. Elsa asked what I owed. I told her. The next day I was free and clear." He jabbed a thumb over one shoulder. "I even bought a new grill. That thing's big enough to fry half a cow at a time. I don't know what Elsa's doin' for a livin', but whatever it is she's got the bucks."

"What did Joel say about Helen?"

"He was looking for her. Wouldn't say why. I didn't press the point—none of my business. But I could tell Joel was steamed about somethin'." Romero paused a moment. "I'm not sayin' he was the one who did the number on you and her but…"

"But what?"

"Joel Kingsley's got the temperament for it. That's why they kicked his ass off the job."

"Joel Kingsley's no longer with the F.B.I.?" I asked in surprise.

He glanced around before giving his chin a slight dip. "Not unless they took him back—which them guys ain't known for."

"Why was Joel dumped?"

"Kingsley wasn't taking care of business. Always on the prod about some Chicago hood."

"Jacob Tandem?"

"That's the ticket."

"Anything else you can tell me?"

Henrico shrugged, looking much relieved for telling me the truth. "Nothin' about the redhead. But Kingsley wanted to rent my house on Lake Travis. Said he needed someplace quiet to get his head together. I'd already rented it to Rita Portello. He didn't like hearin' that."

"I didn't know you had a house on Lake Travis?"

He nodded. "You remember. I got it when my aunt died. I rent it out during the summer. Brings in a few grand each year—enough to cover the taxes and keep me in beer-money. I'm thinkin' of moving there after I retire."

I recalled the place, then. "Your aunt picked my pocket when I attended her ninety-first birthday party. Took me for over a grand."

He gave a sympathetic groan, and leaned back. "Bad habits are the hardest to shake—especially among senior-citizens."

"When did Rita move to your house?"

"Can't say. She come to me a few days ago—paid in advance a full three months. Said she might want to stay longer. I don't cotton to them Portellos. But she's okay."

I stood up suddenly feeling greedily ecstatic. Perhaps those crates weren't locked away where only she and Dom could get to them. Perhaps they were sitting in the living room of Henrico's lake home? A truck and forklift rental. A few sturdy day-laborers. And I would be in heaven—financially speaking. Of course I had to determine Tandem's motives for grabbing Rita. If Tandem planned to take out Sal and Dom, I could offer to help in order to keep Rita clear of it. Alternatively, I could just hand Tandem his cash and tell him to leave town—less a small carrying charge. Nothing excessive. Just enough to keep a dirty old man in blondes for the rest of his days.

"I think I'll take a swing past, there," I said, making like it was a casual consideration. "I'm heading out that way, anyway. What's the address?"

"16127 Fillmore."

"We'll have to get together for a brew, Henrico."

"Sure," he said, getting to his feet. "I'd like that. I'll bring my kid along. You'll like her, Deke." He tilted toward me and whispered, "Do you want me to call you if Joel comes in?"

I nodded. "But keep what we talked about between us."

"Sure, Deke. Sure."

We shook hands. He told me my meal was on him. After thanking Henrico I went out to the Buick where I checked my watch. There wasn't time to drive to Lake Travis before my appointment with Salvator Portello. But I was still optimistic. If what I hoped was there, this would be my last interaction with the angry Mafia-Don.

CHAPTER ELEVEN

At the agreed upon time, I was sitting in Salvator's office at his home in an exclusive part of West Austin. Sal was propped behind his desk, an eighteenth century mahogany item embossed with carved cupids and gold filigree. The Sicilian Brothers, Thomaso and Pietro, were parked in chairs behind me. Sal was in his usual foul mood, his fulminating voice rattling from the walnut-paneled walls.

"You've got thirty seconds, Bishop," he growled. "Then I'm going to pack you in cement and drop your stinking carcass into Lake Travis."

"For what?" His words took me by surprise. "Usually I get death threats after I've explained the reason for my visit, not before."

Salvator Portello glared at me, his gray eyes cold, humorless and flinty, the kind of eyes you expected to see behind a hoodlum's gun or in a rogues' gallery. "You've been hustling Rita."

I shrugged and smiled bleakly. "Since when?" Then I muttered a silent prayer that he had not bugged my flop.

Sal skewered the air between us with a jabbing index-finger. "I heard Rita on the phone, talking to some broad. She was making marriage-plans; talking about babies. Rita mentioned you. So help me God, if I thought my sister was crazy enough to hook up with a son-of-bitch like you..."

I tried being friendly in hopes of placating what surely must be his worst nightmare. "Do you think I'd risk ruining my best suit by coming here after enticing your sister into marriage, knowing Rita's off limits?"

He made a disgusted face while his eyes assessed my wrinkled and slightly rank ensemble. "A lye coating would improve the looks of that rag," he growled. "And you, too."

"Let's agree Rita is not on my hit list, Sal—never has been, never will be." I suddenly had a guilty conscience, like a kid talking to his girlfriend's father after a very eventful prom-night. "Obviously, she was talking about someone else— probably thanking God that her husband-to-be is nothing like me."

The mercurial Portello, like a manic-depressive on the downswing, twisted his face into an ugly snarl. "That has to be it. No woman in my family would be crazy enough to give you a second glance."

Then I got to look at another shaking finger. "What's this about you and that Martinis woman? Was she a Fed? Did you kill her?"

"First, explain why you went through my flop with a bulldozer."

"What in hell are you babbling about, Bishop? I wouldn't be caught dead in your flea-trap."

"I didn't mean you personally, Sal," I said. "But somebody went to a lot of trouble turning my little piece of Texas paradise into a sewer."

He gave the Sicilians an angry, questioning glare. In reply came the rapid rustling of shaking heads on thick necks within tight shirt-collars.

"Nobody's been near your dump, Bishop," Sal scowled. "Now, what's with you and that Fed?"

"She was one of six who put the grab on your newest pal's finances—Jacob Tandem—embezzler of a hundred million. He had it. She got it. Now she's dead."

The tip of Salvator's tongue suddenly showed pink between his thin, bluish lips. "I don't have any idea where that money is." Then his voice became ominously soft. "Has Dom done something stupid—again?"

"Dominic's name has been mentioned."

"Jesus Christ!" Salvator strode through his office, his voice throbbing with fury. "Dom knows the rules. You don't fuck with another mob's money."

"My gossip's an irrefutable source, Sal." I stayed purposely vague so as not to link Rita to the problem. "Dom has the money stashed. Tandem wants it back. When was the last time you chatted with your brain-dead brother?"

Salvator Portello returned to his desk and reached for the phone. A second later he caught himself. Then he gave me another dirty glare. "Who fed you this?"

"What difference does it make? I'm telling you that Rita's at risk and it's not going to end until Dom comes clean."

"You're lying, Bishop! You have to be." Salvator Portello pointed at me and yelled at the Sicilian Brothers, "Take this piece of shit out and shoot it."

"Killing me won't change the truth, Sal."

"My brother wouldn't dare! Not that. He wouldn't dare try that!"

"You're lying to yourself and you know it. Everything Dom's ever touched has turned to shit. Think about it, Sal. A hundred million. For the first time in his life Dom would be a success—a bigger success than you. He'd have all the money he'd ever need. No more running to big brother for handouts."

"Damn my brother's eyes!" Having let go his curse, his stare bored into me almost hypnotically. "Do you know where the money is?"

"No." I made a supplicating gesture. "But Dom has a warehouse, doesn't he?"

The gray-haired gangster thumped his chest. "What the fuck does my brother have against me? Answer me that, Bishop. I've cleaned up every mistake he's made, his whole life!"

"There's more, Sal. One of Tandem's men tried to abduct Rita."

He rushed over to me as if his feet were on fire. "Is she okay? Did you ask if she was okay?"

I heard the Sicilian Brothers shuffle feet and clear throats. They did not want to admit they had done a job for Dom on the sly. But they knew they were obligated to admit it, having taken Rita from my office.

"Don't worry," I said, jabbing a thumb over my shoulder. "Your men took her in hand."

The gangster almost smiled with relief. Then he looked past me with a questioning stare.

"We done just like Mr. Bishop said, Mr. Portello," said Thomaso. "We took Miss Rita in hand."

"Yeah, Mr. Portello," chimed Pietro. "We done just like Mr. Bishop said. We took her in hand and brung her here where she'd be safe."

Salvator Portello let go a sigh of relief. "Thank God for that." Then his face choked with blood. "Tandem, that fucking piece of shit! I knew he was up to something, coming here, playing up to me. I should've had the bastard hit right out of the fucking gate." He tilted toward me. "Which one of his men did it? Did she recognize him? I'll make an example of that bastard if it's the last thing I do!"

"From Rita's description it was Joey Fortuna."

Salvator jerked erect glaring past me at the Sicilian Brothers, again.

"Leave him to us, Mr. Portello," said Thomaso, his voice low and unemotional.

"Yeah," chimed Pietro. "Leave him to us."

"Taking out Fortuna won't cure the problem," I interjected. "You'll still have the source to deal with. Why not let Fortuna stew for awhile?"

A second later I felt the crack of Salvator's hand as it slapped my face. "You telling me my business, Bishop?"

"I'm telling you the truth," I said through gritted teeth. "Tandem is the problem and until he's put away, you and your family will continue to be at risk."

"I'll take care of Tandem." He jabbed a finger at the Sicilian Brothers. "You get it worked out. You set it up. You let me know when you're ready to move. Don't do shit unless I say so!"

"You know us, Mr. Portello," said Pietro.

"Yeah, Mr. Portello," chimed Thomaso. "You know you can count on us."

Sal looked over at me as if seeking my approval. I gave him a halfhearted shrug.

"But you got even bigger problems," I said.

The Mafia-Don's eyes rolled back in his head and shouted at the heavens, "What the fuck is going on?"

"Did you know Dom tried to put the snatch on Helen Martinis the night she was killed in my car?" I asked. "Did you know after she got away from him, his men abducted her? Your brother's the reason she was at that rest area where I stopped. Did you know the car used to run me off the road was run through your auto-parts crusher?"

For a moment Salvator Portello gave me a blank, stunned look. Then he pointed at the door to his office and ordered the Sicilian Brothers to find Dominic. A split second later, I heard heavy men scrambling out of chairs behind me.

"What about Mr. Bishop?" asked Thomaso. "I don't think it's safe us leaving you alone wit' him—considerin'."

"Yeah, Mr. Portello," chimed Pietro. "Mr. Bishop can be unreasonable when he's miffed. And when he's got a red neck, he's miffed—like now. Probably because you whapped him, a little."

"I'll give you two, miffed!" Salvator screamed. "Now get out there and find my goddamn brother."

As the Sicilian Brothers tore out of there, Salvator returned his attention to me. "You're sure Rita was okay?"

I nodded. "She said she clawed Fortuna's face and got clear of him."

He dragged one hand through his thinning, gray mop. "Christ almighty. What in hell is that idiot Tandem playing at?" Then he strode behind his desk and grabbed up the phone. After thumping a number, he waited a few seconds before speaking, "*La madre, Rita è con lei?*" There was a pause and then he rang off. "The crazy bitch went out shopping! For paint, no less."

"Did Rita take anybody with her?"

He nodded. "Deuce. She'll be okay." He made a beseeching gesture. "Who the fuck goes shopping for paint after nearly being kidnapped?" Then he came around the desk waggling a finger at me. "You know what else? Rita wants to convert the room next to hers into a damn sewing room. That's what the paint is for. Blue or pink. She can't make up her goddamn mind. Rita even wants to cut a door in the wall of her bedroom so she doesn't have to go out into the hall to get to her the sewing room. She's gone crazy! And you know what else? She wants bars on the goddamn windows so nobody can break in. See what I mean about crazy? Who puts bars on the windows of a goddamn sewing room?"

"Sounds like Rita's finally found a hobby that'll keep her around home, Sal. Don't knock it. For years you've complained about her nightlife. With that sewing room to keep her occupied, Rita will be the little house-mother you and your father always hoped she'd be."

He gave me a dirty look. "You know something, don't you? What aren't you telling me?"

I splayed my hands. "Know what?"

"About the knitting. Pink and blue wool. She says she's making a scarf. Well, let me tell you something, Bishop, that damn scarf looks a whole lot like a pair of baby-booties!" Then he stormed behind his desk and dropped into the swivel chair. "Is she pregnant? You son-of-a-bitch, you'd better not be holding out on me."

"I'm not her goddamn keeper, Sal. What Rita does and who she does it with is none of my business, and that's the way it's going to stay."

"Get the fuck out of my sight."

I stood and stated for the door.

The phone rang and Salvator answered it. As I gripped the knob, his voice hit the walls like a clap of thunder, "Deuce is dead! Rita's missing!"

The blood drained from Sal's face. He slammed down the receiver and his next words boiled out. "That goddamn fucking Tandem! I'm gonna' take a month dipping him!"

"If you touch him before we get her back, Rita's as good as dead," I warned.

"You're going to bring her to me, Bishop. If something happens to her in the meantime, I'm holding you responsible. Understand?"

"I didn't kidnap her. You got grief talk to your brother and his pal."

Salvator pointed at his office door. "What are you standing here, for?" There was a trace of rue in his voice, a quirk of regret I would not likely ever notice again. "Find her, damn you!"

I lit a cigarette. "Does Rita keep an apartment or a house?"

His hands went to his face and rubbed. "16127 Fillmore. That's it." Then he grabbed up the phone and dialed. After a few seconds he hung up. "She rented some dump on Lake Travis. No answer there."

"Try her cell-phone."

He dialed again. Again, no response.

"Something's happened to her," he moaned. "Dear God…"

"I'll start at the Lake Travis address and then contact her friends," I said. "In the meantime, I don't want you to let on to Tandem about any of this."

He bolted around his desk over to where I stood. "You think I'm gonna' take this lying down?"

"If Tandem has her, he's not going to do anything stupid. He just wants his money. You get Dom to cough it up while I have a chat with Tandem to give him assurances you've got things in hand. Rita will be okay, Sal."

"I can't ignore this, Bishop," he growled. "If I do, every punk in town will start making moves on my action. I have to react and react fast and hard!"

"If you want Rita back alive, you'd better listen to me and not your gut."

He turned away cursing a blue streak. Then he turned to face me. "Okay, hot shot. Do it your way. But if anything happens to her, don't think I won't come for you."

"If Rita dies because of me do you honestly think I would care?"

Salvator Portello clawed at the back of his neck as if I had stabbed him. "My father must be rolling in his grave." Then he fell silent, his eyes clenched, his hands coiling into white-knuckled fists. "My father always liked you—why I cannot figure. He used to talk about you with a mix of chuckling and curses. He always claimed he could count on you to take care of Rita and Momma—maybe that's the reason. No threats this time, Bishop. You talk to Tandem. You tell him if Dom has his money, I'll see Tandem gets it back."

"What if Dom doesn't know where it is?"

"You said he did!"

"For argument's sake, what if he doesn't?"

"Agree to anything Tandem wants to cut Rita loose. Whatever it will takes, you agree to. Then you call me. By the time I'm done with him, they'll hear his screams all the way back to Chicago!"

CHAPTER TWELVE

I drove to Lake Travis and the address Henrico provided—the same Salvator tried to telephone. It was a pleasant little place of white stone and blue tile roof standing two stories high and about as wide as the average Austin mansion. A veranda painted off-white held sway along the roadside where I parked. Half a dozen Adirondack chairs rested there, all of them carrying thick coats of dust on their forest-green surfaces. The windows on that side were so thick with grime they looked gray. Through the filthy glass I could see a collection of colored curtains hanging as if too frightened to pull aside. If Rita was staying there, it was not out of choice. This house was too unkempt for her to tolerate. It was likely she had rented it with another purpose in mind—possibly to store a hundred million in cash.

With my palms sweating over the prospect of a hundred million dollars, I got out of the Buick and strolled up to the front door. After glancing around to make sure I was not being observed, I used a credit card to slip the lock and get inside. The kitchen was small but functional with appliances and walls reminiscent of the yellow-craze during the seventies. A short, narrow hallway papered in roses and ferns brought me to the front room. It was fairly large, with ceiling and walls covered in swirled plaster, its concrete foundation topped by cream-colored tile.

The room's main element was a large window that looked out onto Lake Travis. The water, glinting beneath the sun, looked like a bowl of diamonds as it made its river-like flow toward parts elsewhere. Resting in front of the window was a grand piano, all black and shiny. Beyond it was a presentable secretary-desk with some brainy-looking books stored behind glass doors. The top row was given over to a set of encyclopedias, plus a little bit of Freud, Jung, Homey and Menninger for visitors who might take an interest in psychiatry. But if one looked carefully on the lower shelf, there was a nice collection of adult reading —the type I prefer. Most of these paperbacks had naughty pictures on their covers.

On a small table set near one wall was a personal computer, some stacked ledgers and several racing forms. Adjacent to the table was an ancient slot machine. Its display showed three lemons, as if a reminder to the risks inherent in gambling. Set slantwise near the one-armed bandit was a roll-top desk of age-darkened oak. At a respectable distance was an oak filing cabinet. The latter's corners were reinforced by tarnished brass plates screwed top and side. On another wall several neatly framed photographs showed racehorses from the thirties, forties and fifties: Native Dancer, Polynesian, Case Ace, Nasrullah, On-And-On and others. On another wall were silk-screen prints that looked like museum pieces. But up-close I could see they were merely good copies. In the center of the room was a big round, oak table covered by a spread of white linen. In one corner of the room was a massive bronze statue of Buddha. It was as tall as me. The rest of the furniture was ebony and teakwood; the lamps, vases and ashtrays were rose quartz and jade. All looked expensive.

I went over to the Buddha and patted its fat belly without having to bend down. As I turned back, I caught a glimpse of the dining room through an open doorway. I walked over and peeked inside. The dining table was an intricately carved piece of mahogany inlaid with ivory. Surrounding it were eight matching chairs. A matching sideboard went from floor to ceiling and displayed chinaware that must have cost a fortune.

From the general covering of dust, no one had been in the house for some time. Nevertheless, I set about searching it floor by floor from top to bottom.

Thirty minutes later I was back inside the Buick. I did not find anything indicating Rita's presence, or evidence she'd ever used this place to secure all that illicit cash.

If Tandem had kidnapped Rita, he would have made his demands to Salvator Portello. Since he had not done so, there was a good chance Rita had slipped through his fingers. With that thought giving me reassurance, I lit a cigarette and nosed the Buick toward my office.

I knew I would not be received warmly at Tandem's home. In fact, it was likely Tandem would view of my uninvited presence as a transgression of the lowest order. This would result in fisticuffs at best, or gunplay at the worst. I decided to put it off until I could load up on aspirin and check with Rita's friends in hopes of finding her hiding out with them. If not, I would take on Tandem and his goons. I tried to convince myself it would be a cakewalk. Deep down, I knew it would likely be my last effort on earth.

After reaching my office and giving the phone a workout in an effort to locate Rita, I contacted Salvator for an update. He had heard from neither Tandem nor Rita. The Sicilian Brothers had not, so far, located Dominic. They were still looking—if they valued their hides. I rang off, promising to visit Tandem before the day was out. Sal actually thanked me. Then I leaned back in my desk-chairs and stared glumly out the window.

My thoughts were a blur, like the kaleidoscope of rolling cars, hurrying people and darkening clouds outside. I clapped my hands over my face and massaged my tired eyes. Still, there was no shutting out the rest of the world. It continued to flog my brain through a cacophony of sounds: human cries, blaring horns, roaring engines, squealing tires. Finally, I dropped my mitts and looked out the window once more.

Most people would have accepted the view from my office window as the intro to a movie about life in all its many colorful patterns. I wondered how many of those passing below would be dead by tonight. How many would be crippled? How many would be shedding tears of grief over missing loved-ones? How many would go to bed sick with remorse over violence committed?

The phone rang.

I picked it up with little enthusiasm—until I heard Rita's voice at the other end.

"Where in hell are you?" I demanded.

"I went back to the car and Deuce was dead—shot!" Her voice quaked.

"Are you home?"

"I'm at a place I own."

"What's the address?"

"I'm okay. I just want to be alone. I have to work this through—that damn money!"

"Rita, you have to call Sal. He's worried sick about you. He thinks Tandem is behind Deuce's killing and your disappearance."

"I just talked to him. Why did you tell Sal that Dom had the money?"

"I had no choice, Rita."

"Dammit, Bishop! He's got his people out looking for Dom and I don't know what's going to happen when they find him."

"Nothing that hasn't happened before. Sal will give Dom hell. Dom will promise to be a good boy and tell Sal where the money is. And that will be the end of it."

"Dom doesn't know where I hid the money. He can't tell what he doesn't know. What if Sal doesn't believe him? What if Sal kills Dom?"

"Frankly, the world would be a better place. But if you want to help Dom, call Sal back and tell him where the money is."

On the other end of the connection I heard knocking sounds, like knuckles rapping on a door.

"Don't answer it," I told her. "Call the police. If there's a cruiser in the area they'll be there in two minutes. Regardless, don't answer the door."

There was a pause. Then she said, "I'll talk to you later, Bishop."

"No! Rita! Wait! Tell me where you are!"

There was a click at the other end of the line, as she rang off.

"Just once," I grumbled, "I wish that little bitch would listen me."

I jumped up, not knowing what I could do but needing to do something. Then a brainwave inspired me. Davey Kenyan and Rita had a long time relationship before he was gunned down. Considering Salvator and Dominic's racist views, she would have purchased a little hideaway for her trysts with Davey. If anybody besides Rita, knew the location of that place it was Blind Ray. I grabbed my keys and headed down to the Buick.

Except for the help, *Adam's Rib* was empty when I arrived. Two brown-skinned waitresses shared a cigarette as they rested their plump backsides on the serving counter. The heavenly smell of rib sauce and grilled meat filled the place. I was not hungry, but my tongue still salivated at the aromas floating out of Ray's kitchen. Who would have thought that a big man with such an evil heart had a culinary soul?

"Where's Ray?" I asked the chatting waitresses.

One of them pointed to the kitchen.

I followed her guidance and ten paces later I saw him. All six-foot six inches and four hundred pounds of black gangster. He stood in front of a massive gas stove, his big mitts using a gigantic steel spoon to stir a three foot high pot of delectably-smelling BBQ sauce. Ray wore a white shirt and gray slacks with a bright red apron wrapped about his big middle. A bottled blonde barely over twenty with headlights big enough for a Peterbilt, stood next to him encased in a something pink and skin-tight. While the big man worked the spoon, she rubbed her breasts against one of his huge arms.

A couple of young black men stood a few steps away, by the grill. They grinned with envy while watching her teasing. When the smiling pair spotted me, both of them did a quickstep out the back door; shoving hands into pockets to dig for anything a Narc might find interesting.

I watched them leave wishing I was still in Austin's Narcotics Division, where accepting bribes was encouraged. Perks like that would go a long way to satisfying my need for funds. In particular, I had in mind paying for surprisingly expensive and newly-arrived apartment-furnishings.

"Got a minute, Ray?" I called to the big man's, broad back.

He jerked upright. Then Ray turned toward the blonde, white cane in one hand, gigantic, stirring-spoon in the other, red sauce dripping from the latter's gleaming tip. "Who's that?" he demanded; his blind eyes darted back and forth while his brain chugged through decades of memories, comparing my voice to those he had heard over a lifetime.

"Old white man," the blonde replied, giving me a scathing look.

"Arnold! Budgie!" Ray shouted. "Throw that honky out'a my kitchen!"

"They ran out the back when the white dude come in, Ray," confided the blonde.

"Damn it to hell and beyond, it can't be him!" groaned Ray. "How white is that honky?"

She shrugged, still looking at me. "As white as old coots get, Ray."

"Damn again and damn again and damn yet again!" Ray cursed. "Is he mean-lookin' and ugly?"

"Mean-lookin' enough, Ray."

"Damn and double-damn! Lord Almighty, has he got on a wrinkled suit and socks what don't match?"

"I can't see his socks, Ray. But that suit ain't been pressed in a dog's age."

Ray whirled to face me, the stirring spoon waving through the air like club, spewing B-B-Q sauce in all directions. "Bishop, you lowlife son-of-a-bitch! You get the hell out'a my place. God dammit! Every time you show up I get trouble comin' down the pike."

"I just want a few words about Davey Kenyan, Ray," I said.

Ray moved toward my voice like a bulldozer approaching a building to be demolished, the big spoon still swinging, the white cane banging from side to side on the green linoleum floor. "What in hell for? Davey's dead! Now get the hell out before I bust your goddamn head."

"Five minutes of your time, Ray," I pleaded.

"Ask him about that Fed, Ray," chimed the blonde.

"That's right," Ray bellowed with renewed gusto. "I'm gonna' bust your head for pointin' that Fed to me over that dead-bitch." He made a wild swing with the spoon. "Stay put, Bishop, so's I can bash-in your brains. Am I getting' close, honey?"

"Keep goin', Ray!" the blonde encouraged.

"I didn't tell anybody you were involved in the Helen Martinis business," I protested, beginning a retreat.

"Then how come I got a visit from Joel Kingsley?" Ray demanded. "How come he's sayin' he's gonna' bust my chops for doin' somthin' I didn't do and how you put him onto my case claimin' what was done was done by my men, which it was not? Explain that, you miserable old bastard!"

"I don't know what Joel Kingsley's trying to shake out of you, Ray. But he's not a Fed, anymore. You don't have to answer to him."

"You're lying!" Ray shouted, still swinging. "Quit movin'! Am I getting' close, baby?"

"That's it, Ray," the blonde called. "Keep goin' like you're goin', honey. You'll nail that crazy white man real soon."

I sidestepped on my tiptoes.

"He's gone to the left, Ray," she coached.

Ray grinned and made a wild swing in the opposite direction from where I stood.

"My left, not your left, Ray."

He stopped his attack and looked back in the direction of her voice. "I don't know how many lefts you got, bitch, but I only got the one. And since we both facin' that same damn honky, my left is at least one of your lefts. Now, which left is it, dammit?"

"Ray, all I need to know is if Rita Portello bought a house for her and Davey," I said.

The big, blind man jerked toward my voice and lowered the spoon. "What's your interest?"

"I'm looking for Rita," I explained. "She's had some trouble. I need to find her. Did Rita buy a place for her and Davey?"

"Don't trust him, Ray," chimed the blonde. "That old man looks so crooked a fair wind would screw him in the ground."

"Maybe Rita did, maybe she ain't." Ray tilted his massive form toward my voice. "I've said my piece. And as far as I'm concerned, you said yours. Now best face the alley, Bishop, and get the hell out'a my place before my boys get back. 'Cause when they do, I'm orderin' them to blow you're honky head off."

"Tell me where the place is, Ray. In return, I'll see this dump gets a four-star review in the Food Section of the *Austin Chronicle*."

He wrenched erect in surprise; his head twisting as he tried to locate me with his ears. "How you gonna' do that?"

"Sheila Parrot," I suggested. "You remember Sheila, don't you?"

Ray grinned. "Shady Sheila. She still writes that food column?"

"As good as ever," I assured him.

"She's still one of your personal, closest friends of the female persistence?"

"Me and Sheila are like two sets of lips in synch, Ray," I replied.

Sheila did write the restaurant review column. However, at the moment she and I were not on speaking-terms due to a not-so-minor misunderstanding over a loan extended to yours truly, during a string of track-losses. But I kept that little tidbit to myself.

The huge man giggled like a schoolboy. "Hells bells! Why didn't you say so in the first place, Deacon? A review in the *Chronicle*. That'd almost make up for all the grief you've given me over the years." His face turned grim as he added, "*Almost.*"

"You believe' that devil-lookin' old man, Ray?" scoffed the blonde. "He's lyin' through teeth he probably stole from somebody else!"

"Sheila's a big rib-fan, Ray," I coaxed. "Once she gets a whiff of your sauce, and wraps her lips around one of your cutlets, you'll be beating off customers with a stick."

"Beatin' 'em off with a stick! Damn, I like that." He held out the spoon and gave it a waggle. "Shut your lip, Baby, and get your big butt over here."

The blonde hurried to where Ray stood, and took his hand. "I'm here, Ray."

"Me and this gentleman has business to discuss," he solemnly declared.

She made a disgusted face. "He don't look like no gentleman to me, Ray. I swear on all that's holy, he's the devil himself."

"Mr. Bishop may be lackin' a certain savoyee-farey in the clothes department," Ray confided to her, "but he and I go way back. He ain't gonna' try nothin' stupid—not with me, anyway."

"Elgin and Julian will be back soon," she pleaded. "Why not wait 'til they're here—just in case?"

He waggled the spoon. "Never mind that, Baby. You keep stirring that sauce whilst I and Mr. Bishop retire to my office."

"You're right about his socks, Ray," she whined, taking the spoon. "They don't match."

"Elgin and Julian?" I asked him.

"My bodyguards," Ray replied, proudly. "Nephews on my mother's side. Good boys, the both of 'em."

"If you like men who crotchet," jibed the blonde as she headed back to the stove.

"Crotchet?" I echoed.

"A great stress-reliever—or so they tell me," confided Ray. "I'd take it up myself. But the directions don't come in Braille."

With cane banging, Ray led me to a small room at the back of the café. There he slumped down behind a small desk. I took a seat on a blue velveteen davenport against the opposite wall.

"Rita did buy a place." Ray gave his head a sad shake. "Davey told me. She's as mean as a snake as far as I'm concerned. But, lord, how Davey loved her."

"Where is this place?" I asked.

Ray grinned. "You been gettin' it on with Rita, I hear."

"I've got a kinky streak only she can satisfy. Where, Ray? It's important."

His smiled faded. "You gonna' marry her?"

"Not if I don't want to become another statistic. Is Rita's place in Austin?"

He gave his big head a wag. "Leander."

"Address?"

Ray leaned back and propped is big feet on the desktop. "Does she know you're goin' there?"

"Hopefully not. Address?"

The huge man made a vague gesture. "That's expectin' my memory to perform miracles, 'cause Davey never told me no address. He did say the place was red brick and just outside of town. Sits in a grove of pecan trees, or so he said. I'm real partial to pecan pie. Like it warm with a bucket of ice cream on top."

There were any number of houses on the outskirts of Leander. Of those, several were probably brick. And of those, one or two might be red. However the odds Rita's hideaway was not the house Elsa Jacobson lived in, was beyond calculation. As Rita said, she and Elsa had completed a business arrangement several months earlier. If my luck was running good for a change, that business arrangement was a lease on Rita's property. I stood up feeling much relieved.

"I think I know the place."

"Glad I could help, Deacon." He tapped the manicured nail of his right forefinger on the desktop. "What makes you think Joel Kingsley ain't no longer a Fed?"

"Sherman told me."

"Sherman the German?" Ray nodded. "I never liked him, much. He'd sell his own mother." The big man paused a beat before saying, "Joel Kingsley's come by not too many weeks ago. He was lookin' for somebody. Offerin' ten grand for her location."

"Her, who?"

"Redheaded number, according to him. Big eyes. Milky skin. A hooker. Said her name was Helen. Said she owed him a pile of dough." He tilted toward me asking, "Is she the one you were with the other night?"

"Helen Martinis."

"You think maybe she's the reason Joel Kingsley got kicked off his job? Maybe Kingsley's runnin' his own stable and she talked?"

"Thanks for your time, Ray."

His big feet hit the floor with a resounding clunk. "You won't be forgettin' our deal about Shady Sheila?"

"I'll have Sheila put you on her to-do list. I'm thinking she should title the article, *God Gave Austin Adam's Rib*. What do you think?"

He rose up grinning from ear to ear. "Damn! That's as good as it gets!"

There was a chance Sheila would forgive and forget. But first she'd cut off my personal equipment with a jagged chunk of dirty glass, and then force-feed me the bloody lump. Nevertheless, I would have to risk the encounter. Ray was not the type to be played for a fool. The trouble was getting my hands on fifteen grand to repay Sheila's loan.

I went out to the Buick and headed for Leander.

An hour later I parked in front of the red brick affair I had searched in my efforts to locate Elsa Jacobson. I got out of the Buick and went up to the front door. This time, the key was not under the mat. I knocked, hoping that Rita was inside. When I got no answer, I tried the knob. The door was unlocked. I went inside calling her name.

When I still did not get an answer, I did a quick sweep of the place.

Rita had been there. In the master bedroom her purse had toppled onto the floor. A small smear of blood was on the doorjamb inside the bedroom—the kind the injured leave when trying to keep from being dragged away. My stomach knotted in grief and anger. There was no guarantee Jacob Tandem had Rita. But considering his earlier attempt, I felt it likely.

With her purse tucked under my arm, I went outside and hurried to Annie's house next door.

I rang the doorbell. Blue haired Annie Chase responded holding a cup of coffee in one hand and a sweet-roll in the other.

"You're back, huh?" she said by way of greeting.

I tilted my head in the direction of the red brick house. "Did you see a man and woman leave there, today?"

She nodded. "It was Rita. But she didn't leave. She was carried out by a lean guy with long hair wearing an expensive suit. He wasn't moving very good under her load—walked with his legs splayed like he had a bad case of crotch-rot. It looked to me like she'd been hurt. I told him I was calling the police but he waved me off, dumped her in his car and drove away. Leander P.D. came out and took my statement. But since then nobody's reported anything back. They treated me like an old woman who was turning the outcome of a drunken party into something sinister. I kept insisting she was abducted. But the two cops kept snickering that it was just some poor slob trying to get his drunken wife home. I doubt very much they're going to do anything. She a friend of yours?"

I nodded my head. "What time did you see them?"

"Hour and a half ago."

I fished a business card out of my pocket and handed it to her. "If you see either of them, again, please notify the police and then call me."

"I couldn't give the police her full name. It might help them locate her."

"Rita Portello."

Annie's eyes widened in surprise. "Sounds like what's to come will be far from boring."

"Did you get the plate-number?"

"Didn't have any. It was a gold Cadillac convertible; new, white top, brown interior."

I thanked Annie for her time and then headed for Sgt. Leon Martin's office. I wanted details on what had happened to Deuce, and to get him involved in the search for Rita. En route, I telephoned Salvator and gave him the bad news.

Surprisingly, he actually said 'please' when asking me to continue searching for Rita. He was talking to Dominic when I rang. From Dom's pleading voice in the background, they were not having the brotherly interaction one might expect from a closely-knit family.

I told Sal that Dom was telling the truth about not knowing where the money was. But I did not tell him I suspected Joey Fortuna was behind Rita's abduction. The one thing Rita did not need is to have her eldest brother loose his temper and go gunning for Tandem. I told Sal to claim I now had the money if Tandem contacted him. It was a weak stall, but I wanted to protect Rita from interrogation over the money. I also expected that little ruse to make my reception at Tandem's home slightly upbeat and filled with homespun humor—before he had his goons start working on me.

CHAPTER THIRTEEN

Lt. Leon Martin greeted me with hands juggling file folders while muttering curses about police commissioners with paper-fetishes. It was the noon-hour so we were alone in the squad room.

"I empathize with your complaint, Leon," I said, as I followed over to his desk.

"I don't need understanding, I need a suggestion. At this point, I'm open to anything."

"Besides killing the bunch of them?"

He gave me an over-the-shoulder glance. "That's my backup plan."

"Success in any paper-related matter is done by passing the job onto a junior."

Martin groaned. "Bishop, I don't have a junior."

"That's because you're too honest. An honest man, according to our Mayor, doesn't warrant a watchdog—which is the role of each and every junior. They aren't assigned to learn the job of their superior. They're assigned to catch you with your hands in somebody else's pockets. To keep that from happening, you shift all paperwork in your junior's direction. It's a tried and true technique."

Leon Martin dropped the files on top of his desk and turned to face me. "You're not suggesting I rob a bank?"

"You don't have the stomach for a corrupt lifestyle. Just start an unfounded rumor about having been bribed. The day it reaches the Mayor's ears, you'll get a junior. That's how I got Herby Mann as my partner."

"You started a rumor to get a junior?"

"No, I took a bribe."

"Just for my own information, Deke," he said, sitting down behind his desk, "were any of the tales about your corruption unfounded?"

"Of course not. But I was a class act. You've got too much conscience to follow in my shoes, Leon. The guilt would kill you—if your wife didn't."

His eyebrows arched in bewilderment. "Your wives knew what you were pulling?"

"Why do you think they all asked for so much alimony?"

He gave his head a dismal shake. "How can you sit there telling me this without an ounce of shame?"

I crossed my legs in the chair fronting his desk. "The way I look at it, Leon, too much honesty is a bad thing. Herby Mann is a prime example. That's why he'll never make captain. I, on the other hand, would've easily made captain—except for a single moment of honest impulsivity."

"You call shooting down the Mayor's son an honest impulse?"

"Considering how he was beating that old woman to get her purse, I'd say it was my finest moment."

"Well, my finest moment will be when I fill out my pension papers."

"I keep hearing the same thing from Herby Mann. But neither of you will be happy sitting around doing nothing."

"Me, no. But Herby? I beg to differ with you on that, Bishop. Can you believe his wife? The most beautiful thing on two legs! The woman has jugs the size of Hawaii and an ass as round as a bowling ball. After he retires Herby will be able to have her anytime he wants." He tilted toward me and whispered, "She used to be a stripper. Can you believe it? The man has his own private strip-show whenever he wants." Leon let go a dissatisfied groan as he slumped back in his chair. "God, what I wouldn't give to be married to somebody like her. What in hell does she see in Herby, Bishop? He's got no money. He's overweight. He eats like a slob."

"I ask myself that each time I see her. But he's got something. I see love in her eyes whenever she's with him."

"I'd cut off my left nut for a night with her."

"Nonsense! Your wife would kill you."

"But I'd die a happy man."

"Happiness is overrated, Leon. Do you know how many happy men commit suicide each year?"

"Meaning the personal misery I married is someone I should cherish for the rest of my days—no matter how drearily long my life might be?"

I grinned. "Because you keeping her happy means you're keeping her off the singles-market so suckers like me won't get trapped by her barbed claws."

Leon offered me a Gaulic gesture. "I'm tired of doing my bit for the benefit of you free-wheeling singles." Then he gave his head a dismal wag. "My wife moved her mother into our house despite my objections. I swear to God, I'm going to kill both of them. And no jury would convict me."

Martin leaned back and crossed his arms over his chest. "Now that I've vented my frustrations, what's up with you?"

"Three things. First, I have reason to believe Rita Portello has been abducted by Joey Fortuna—one of Tandem's men."

"No one in their right mind would try that. Rita's more dangerous than a rattler shedding its skin. Then there are her brothers to consider…"

"The woman next door, Mrs. Annie Chase, says she saw Fortuna dumping an unconscious Rita into his car. Annie notified Leander police." I gave him her address and a description of Fortuna's vehicle. "The problem is the car has no plates."

He grabbed pen and pad from one of the desk-drawers. "Lay it out for me."

I told him what Annie had told me and what Rita had said about nearly being abducted. When I finished, Martin gave me a confused look.

"Why in hell would Jacob Tandem order a snatch-job on Rita Portello? That's begging for a gang-war. And considering the Chicago Mob is already after him, Tandem needs any friends he can make."

"Jacob Tandem thinks Dominic has the hundred million you and I were hoping to find."

"That dirty bastard!"

"My sentiments, exactly. But not for the same reason. Dom actually doesn't have it. But Rita does."

Leon made a sour face. "I'll put out a pickup order on Joey Fortuna. But with her having all that money my heart won't be in it."

I said, "There's more. You had a homicide reported earlier? Paul 'The Deuce' Abbandando."

He nodded. "What about it?"

"Deuce was playing bodyguard for Rita when he was killed. Somehow they got separated. When she returned to the car Deuce was dead. I talked to Rita shortly before Fortuna got to her."

His eyes widened in surprise. "You mean Joey Fortuna capped Deuce to get to Rita?"

"Likely. But he was unable to get to Rita before Rita realized what had happened, and made tracks. Rita owns the house where she was abducted. It's next door to Annie's."

I went on to tell him, of my chat with Blind Ray and his help in locating the house. Then I said, "My second point, if you're ready."

"Is it going to upset the mayor?"

"That depends on whether the gang-war rumor I wanted you to start becomes real."

"Dear God…"

"Joel Kingsley is no longer a Fed," I said. "He's been booted out of the F. B. I. for reasons I haven't been able to verify. But speculation is it has to do with the heist of Jacob Tandem's embezzled millions. My information source says Joel Kingsley was in on that job."

Leon let go a low whistle. "How in hell did Rita get the money from Kingsley? She's as nasty as Gila Monster. But Kingsley's nobody to mess with."

"As you said, she does have Gila Monster leanings." I took out a cigarette, lit it, then took a drag and sent a curling stream of smoke over his head. "My third point: Helen Martinis was not a Fed. She was one of Kingsley's partners in the theft."

"But why would he kill Helen if he didn't have the money? It'd be like shooting himself in the foot."

"I don't think he did it. In any event, Joel was conned into believing he had the money. The hundred million was crated up and put in a storage area. What Joel didn't know was that the crates with the money were moved and empty ones where left behind. By the time he figured out the switch, Helen was dead.

"One last thing before you get too far ahead of the evidence in your assumptions about Joel. The car used to run me off the road was run through the crusher at Salvator Portello's auto parts yard. That could mean Sal was involved or Dom was involved, But I don't think so."

Leon Martin picked up the telephone and pushed buttons. A few seconds later he was giving someone on the other end of the line instructions to take Joel Kingsley and Joey Fortuna into custody for questioning in the murder of

Helen Martinis, Elsa Jacobson and the disappearance of Rita Portello. When Leon rang off he said, "I assume you've told Rita's brothers about her?"

I nodded. "I told Sal. But I did not tell him who I suspected. I've never heard him more worried in my whole life."

"Any idea where Tandem might be holding Rita?"

"Not a clue."

"What about Kingsley's location?"

"Also nothing. But I was told that Kingsley dusted a couple of Tandem's men, last night. I was told they came gunning for Joel and he was the better man."

"We did bring a couple of corpses to the morgue early this morning. They haven't been identified yet. Both shot by the same weapon." He scratched his head. "I'll send someone out to chat with Jacob Tandem. It won't do much good. He'll have dozens of witnesses proving his men were never near Rita Portello, but we'll make the effort anyway. Maybe, considering his Mob problems, he'll cut her loose to keep us off his back while he looks for his money."

"Can you hold off questioning Tandem until tomorrow? I'd like first crack at him."

Leon shrugged. "It'll take me that long before I can get someone over to his place. But that's not official."

"Do you have Tandem's address?"

He nodded. "2876 Crestview. Don't let the casual view fool you when you arrive. The place is dotted with cameras. And for God's sake, don't try anything heroic. You'll just get Rita and yourself killed." He reached into his desk, dragged out the Mauser and slid it across to me. "You'd better take this. The clip's full and in place. Herby says the shooting review board gave you another passing mark. He also says the Mayor is, again, trying to get your P.I. license lifted."

I nodded. "One day I'll get the goods on our mayor. Then it will be my turn to squeeze his balls. How did the hit on Deuce go down?"

He tilted toward me across the desk to whisper, "One round to the temple, contact range, twenty-five caliber round, silencer. Professional all the way. The way Tandem would've done it." He gave his fingers a nervous snap. "I almost forgot. That woman you were looking for… Elsa Jacobson. She's in a drawer at the morgue. Somebody popped her, too."

"She was another of Joel Kingsley's playmates. So was her brother, Benny. He's also dead—in Dallas. Benny was gunned down in Hamilton Blake's apartment."

He shifted in his chair. "I got a message on that, but I didn't realize there was any connection between the two Jacobson's." He paused a moment to thumb his lower lip. "Dallas forensics claims Benny Jacobson was killed with a .455 Webley. Who in hell carries around a canon like that, anymore? Why would you want to? And where would you buy ammunition?"

"Hamilton Blake told me there were two shooters. They didn't verify their kills so they were amateurs."

"Not any more they're not," he growled.

"One more bit and then I'll get out of your hair," I said. "I have information which links Dominic Portello to Helen Martinis. He visited her the night she died. Further, Dom's people abducted Helen sometime later. She got loose during a fatality-accident on I-35 that same night. One way or another she ended up at the rest area where I agreed to help her."

"Two of Dom's goons were killed in a crash, that same night. Considering what you told me about that car being run through the crusher, Dominic jumps to the head of the suspect list."

"Any news on who's in town with Tandem?"

"According to my snitch, Tandem brought half a dozen shooters from Chicago. All experienced. All dedicated to his protection. If the Chicago Mob does try to take Tandem out, they'd better be ready for a war."

"Jessie Hampstead? Does the name ring any bells?"

He shook his head. "Which camp? Portello or Tandem?"

"Tandem. She's supposed to be his current love-interest. She's also supposed to have a mother in Austin—Maria. I assume the same last name."

"I'll see what I can find on them."

"What about local talent? Did Tandem take on any?"

Martin nodded. "Tandem took on several, mostly small-timers—including Angel Rico."

"You interrogated Rico?"

Leon nodded. "He admitted working for Tandem. He claimed they were supposed to keep a watch on Kingsley. You weren't on their list of concerns. Have you told Herby any of this?"

I shook my head. "I didn't feel like ruining his day."

Martin sighed. "With a wife like his, nothing could."

I pointed at the Styrofoam cup on his desk. "That's what's souring your outlook. Herby may have nights you and I envy. But you've got an adoring family and I—well, you've got an adoring family."

"I've also got a vicious mother-in-law who'll never move out." Martin's fingers made a nervous rat-a-tap-tap on the desktop. "Bishop, the Chicago Mob isn't going to wait forever on Tandem's hit. At some point they'll make their move. If Tandem has Rita Portello, you can bet she'll become a bartering tool for him to get Salvator involved on his side. If the Portellos take on the Chicago Mob it'll mean a bloodbath."

I nodded. "Next stop, Jacob Tandem. I'll let you know how I make out."

"Assuming you live to tell about it."

CHAPTER FOURTEEN

I drove out to the house Jacob Tandem rented on Lake Travis. At first glance, the place seemed modest—for a medieval Spanish castle. The austere whiteness of its four sprawling stories of gleaming white stone was relieved by vivid splashes of red in the form of paint-coated shutters. This cozy monolith rose from the midst of a velvety, green lawn and was shaded by magnificent pecan trees. In well-ordered flowerbeds surrounding the foundation were profusions of color from roses, carnations, sweet peas, snapdragons, petunias, pansies and tulips. At the east and south corners of the house patches of tiger lilies and alstroemeria were coming into radiant bloom. The concrete driveway was lined with fig trees. At its terminus, a wide screen of star-jasmine cut off all view of the lake, from the street.

The house offered the usual amenities such as a garage big enough to play soccer in and a pool the size of Lake Michigan. A decorative sandstone wall separated the property from neighbors.

After giving the place a thorough visual going over, I decided a guy with a hundred million in the kitty could afford a place like this. The shame was my kitty sorely lacked in content.

I parked the Buick in the turnaround, then got out and headed up two flights of flagstones to the front door. From somewhere beyond the house came the sounds of women laughing. This was quickly followed by the blast of a man's deep guffaw. I was about to ring the bell when a pink Mercedes convertible squealed to a stop beside the Buick. The car was beautiful. The slinky, thirty-something, blonde in its driver's seat was even more so.

When she climbed from the Mercedes I noticed tight tan slacks and a see-through cream blouse; neither had anything, underneath—much to my delight. The blonde was only a few inches more than five feet. But the grin she offered was broad enough to have been spawned by a giant. I smiled back, wishing I was twenty years younger and rich enough to be bone-idle—except in bed.

Bouncing strides brought the beauty and her jiggling, pink nipple-points up the steps. The pixie in me hoped a raft of buttons would suddenly let go to send everything sloshing and sliding beneath her blouse, nakedly into view. Unfortunately, that did not happen.

I got the usual greeting when she reached me. In reply, I offered lust everlasting. Her blue eyes twinkled, lighting up the type of face often found on magazine-covers. It was probably the gloss decorating her full lips in pastel-pink, which made the blonde irresistible. But the dirty-old-man in me wanted to believe my desires stemmed from her unspoken need for masculine attention from a very experienced P.I. type.

"Party crashing?" she asked.

"I'm the impulsive type." I shifted slightly to one side to get a clearer look at her dark, blue eyes. In so doing, my shadow briefly crossed her expressive face. "Who are you and how does Jacob Tandem fit into your life?"

Her teeth peeked from beneath the soft curve of upper lip like a row of white pearls. Then her head tilted back and a laugh filled her throat. For a moment I thought she had noticed the ring around my slightly seedy shirt-collar. But then her eyes locked upon mine, her brow wrinkled with curiosity and she gave me an honest smile.

"I'm Jessie Hampstead, Jacob's bed-warmer," she declared without embarrassment. "So he fits into mine." Then her right hand came out; palm open. "If I were to guess, I'd say your name is Deacon Bishop."

Up to this moment Jessie Hampstead had only been a name. Now she would play frolicsome parts in my favorite dreams—the very naughty ones. I gave my eyes another treat at her expense, not unlike a jockey sizing up a new horse. Jessie, I thought, is the way all women should be. Friendly. Uncomplicated. Straight-talking. She let opinions be said and to hell with what others thought. I covered her fingers with my paw feeling deep envy for Jacob Tandem.

"You were expecting me?" I asked, trying not to drool.

Her hand squeezed mine. Then her middle finger curled within my grasp and tickled my palm; sending a jolt of delight up my arm and down my thighs. I dropped her hand with a start, my cheeks warming and my loins taking note of my excited palm.

"I've heard *all* about you."

"Nothing good, I presume?"

"Depends on who is speaking. There's a brunette I met recently who carols your virtues. Her brothers, on the other hand, make a different assessment. I'm curious as to where the truth lays."

"Somewhere between my being much worse than Rita claims, and slightly better than Dominic and Salvator describe. How goes the fitting with Tandem? Anything in short supply? I'm noted for my lack of commitment and lengthy probing."

For my slightly off-colored remarks, I got a light tap to my cheek from her hand. "If only you were younger…"

"I say the same thing to the mirror every morning. Sadly, I keep getting older—but better."

Jessie looked at me thoughtfully. "Has Jacob bought your allegiance? Or did someone sinister send you?"

"I'm running on my own nickel. When was the last time you saw Rita Portello?"

"Not for a few days," she replied with casual honesty. "You sound like a man hooked on Sicilian cooking."

"I prefer a female smorgasbord. What about Joey Fortuna? Is he around?"

Her smile collapsed. "He might be. I've been out shopping. Friend of his, are you?"

I gave my head a shake. "I'm here to give his next manners lesson."

The smile returned and her arms crossed. "Ah, so you were the one. The way Joey told it, an army descended upon him."

"Fortuna's not what I would describe as an apt student. I kept my left hand in my pocket, during the first lesson, but this time I intend to go all-out. He won't feel like talking about anything after that."

"What's Joey done since you left him by the curb?"

It was my turn for a smile to fade. "He abducted Rita. There's a witness, so it's no mistake. Salvator's trying to accept Joey's actions as a foolish prank. I, on the other hand, view it as an intrusion worth killing over. Where does Fortuna live?"

She gave another shrug. "I was expecting a boring afternoon. Now it sounds like I have a lot to look forward to."

"I'll try not to disappoint you." I nodded toward the door. "Shall we join the others?"

Jessie pointed at my wrinkled togs. "In that suit, you'll never get past Harvey."

"Harvey?"

"Jacob's butler."

I glanced down at my less than fashionable apparel. "I'm between trips to the cleaners. I take it Harvey's a prissy guy?"

"Who comes with a Makarov hitched under one arm." Her face became serious, again. "Harvey's got years on you. But he still knows his stuff—even if he wears a trick-suit."

"The same thing is often said about me—usually during breakfast and as a result of after-glow. How tight is Fortuna with Tandem?"

"Nobody's close to Tandem but me. Are you absolutely certain Joey grabbed your Sicilian play-toy? Witnesses often make mistakes."

"Not this one."

She gave my scuffed wingtips a nudge with one of her shiny Papagallos. "Harvey wears crepe souls and likes to creep around in shadows. You prefer big clunky things."

"You know what they say about a man's feet."

"Harvey's the kind who makes others worry about their backs." The words were spoken slowly as if she had chosen them carefully. "Joey Fortuna's the same way."

"I just make people worry."

She paused a moment. "If Joey grabbed Rita, it wasn't on Jacob's orders. Jacob's got too much riding on keeping the Portellos cooperative."

"Good thing I came, then. I can help Tandem mend fences with Salvator—after I give Joey his last lesson in the all-to-brief art of living."

She reached out and patted the Mauser's silhouette beneath my suit. "Harvey will take away your toy."

"That would take a better than man than me. So far I've never met one. Where would Joey stash Rita?"

"I'll ask around. I can probably do you some good. Where will you be after you're tossed out of here?"

I took out a business card and handed it to her. "I can do you some good, too, with the Portellos. Just so you know, if Rita isn't safe and sound at home by nightfall, you and everyone here will not likely see sunrise. There'll be no bodies. There'll be no blood. Neighbors won't hear a sound. It will be the biggest disappearing act in Austin's history. No threat. Just forewarning on how Salvator operates. So if I were you I'd put a rush on getting that information."

"I get the message." Her head tilted toward the flagstones wrapping the patio, just beyond the front doors. "If we skip the front door I might be able to get you to the drink cart before you're spotted."

"And if we don't?"

Jessie tilted toward me and kissed my chin. "I'm almost tempted to find out."

Like a schoolboy trying to impress the new girl in class, I reached over and pushed the doorbell. From within the huge house came a soft clanging.

"I think you and I could get along, Bishop."

"Only because you don't know me. But I'm willing to spend the next twenty years helping you figure out my quirks. What are your thoughts concerning ceiling mirrors—and being handcuffed to headboards?"

She grinned. "Now, I know we can get along."

With a slight nudge, she steered me along the flagstones past the door. As we walked, I took out a pack of cigarettes and sloughed one up for her. She took it and I grabbed another. Then I put the pack away and brought out the Zippo. We stopped and I lit both smokes.

"You, Elsa, Benny, Joel Kingsley, Harold Maybe and Helen," I said, as we moved on. "A hundred million reasons to remain friends, I take it?"

Abruptly, Jessie's steps faltered.

"Elsa, Helen and Benny are dead," I continued. "As is Harold Maybe. Rita had you pegged from the git-go, Jessie. She didn't have to, but Rita kept your secret from Tandem and her brothers. Keep that in mind as you make inquiries into her health and welfare. If not for her discretion, I shudder to think what Tandem would do to you when he finds out the truth."

Jessie glanced around as if expecting demons to strike. Then her eyes met mine squarely. "I knew nothing about Rita's trouble with Joey until you told me," she whispered. "If Jacob wanted her picked up, I would've heard about it before it happened. I didn't. I don't know what Joey's got in mind. But he did whatever he did on his own. You've got to believe me."

If I had doubts about her previous claim, I no longer did. Jessie was scared. Too scared not to do whatever I wanted to keep me happy. "Has Dominic Portello been around?"

She nodded. "He was here earlier—before I went out."

"Angry or calm?"

"He and Jacob are buddies. So I don't think Dominic would've approved had Jacob ordered Joey's actions."

"You don't know Dominic Portello."

Her chin dipped and she studied the tip of one shiny shoe. "If you know about me and the others, you must know Helen and Carla did a runner with the hundred million."

"Must've been frustrating to you. All that money gone and the only two people in the world who knew where it was being dead. If only they had confided in someone else."

Her eyes rose up to mine. Jessie stared into my face, searchingly. "Did Helen tell you where the money is?"

"All five crates of it. That's why I'm here. To offer it to Tandem in exchange for Rita."

She gave me a doubting smile. "You wouldn't be leading me down the garden path?"

"I'm saving that for when I get you naked."

"Before you make an offer to Tandem, let me make a call."

There was a tense undertone in her voice that suggested Jessie was not playing me. "Why?"

"Because Jacob doesn't have what you want."

"Who does? You?"

"Joel Kingsley—maybe."

A sickness formed in my belly as I pictured Kingsley knocking Rita around to get her to talk. "He has Rita? You're certain?"

Jessie moistened her lips. Twice she started to say something and changed her mind. And then quite simply she said, "I don't know. But what I do know is Joey disappeared several times last week. When Tandem asked about it, Joey claimed he was just getting a feel for the area. I don't think Jacob believed him. I know I didn't. Maybe Joel's involved. Maybe Joey did the grab on spec, trying to impress Joel. Maybe."

"You know where Kingsley is hiding?"

Her head wagged slightly. "I have his cell-phone number."

"Why would Fortuna risk his setup with Tandem to get involved with Joel Kingsley?"

"Joey's the type who craves recognition. The trouble is he doesn't have the talent or brains to warrant it. Tandem keeps him around for easy jobs. Joey has big plans, but he won't see them working for Jacob Tandem."

"I don't have time to assess possibilities, Jessie."

She stopped to face me. "If Joel knows where Rita is, you'll have her back by tonight—provided you're willing to deal on the money. Not my rules—if he's behind Rita's abduction, it's the money Joel's after. I want Rita safe just as much as you do."

"Tell him Joel can have the bundle. All I want is Rita."

She took another drag on the cigarette; tossing me a greedy grin. "Did you count the money?"

"I'm a spending kind of guy. I only count when it's running low."

"It's all there?"

"The crates are locked and loaded."

She moved off dragging me along. "I'll be waiting for you by your car."

As we turned the corner a group of people came into view. Jessie's mood changed to one of serious concern. "Don't trust anybody."

With a slight tilt of her head Jessie indicated the elderly man in the black tuxedo chatting with half a dozen young women around a circular umbrella table. Standing in the shadows behind him were four big men in dark suits. These, I assumed were bodyguards.

"Jacob Tandem," she said. "Trust me, if he finds out you have the money you won't leave here alive."

"I'm tougher than I look."

"So is Jacob."

The ex-Mafia-Don looked more like somebody's grandfather than a cold, calculating killer. His white hair was neatly coiffed. His face was average: neither handsome nor ugly. Despite Jessie's assurances, I intended to deal with Tandem and Fortuna over Rita: Tandem for edification purposes, Fortuna, as part of my package-deal covering pre-burial services.

"Remember what I said about watching your back," Jessie whispered. With that, she moved toward the women to distance us, casually calling out to Tandem.

I let my eyes follow her, enjoying the sight of swaying hips and flexing buttocks. Jessie made no sound as she crossed the neatly trimmed lawn. She did not need to, to be noticed. No matter the outcome of this afternoon's visit, the sight of Jessie's movements made the trip worthwhile. And if I should survive the day—the sight of her in motion locked down my plans for tonight's dreams and those in the foreseeable future.

By the time Jessie reached Tandem, he was staring at me with hooded eyes.

Her fingers brushed his cheek in quick caress. Then she moved off in the direction of the bar.

A snap of his fingers sent two linebackers in my direction. I was about to pat myself on the shoulder for getting somebody's attention when I heard soft footpads approaching from behind. I glanced back to see a burly man in a swallowtail suit limping my way.

Considering he and the other two were not the type for casual discussion, I felt I had only two options: wait and see what would happen when the four of us started swinging, or follow through with my usual tactics in violence. The pixie in me chose the latter.

With a grin on my puss, I quickened my strides.

The linebackers made the mistake of trying to grab my arms. When they reached out, I dropped the one on my left with a kick to the groin.

The other dug inside his coat looking for something deadly.

I countered that effort with a well-practiced spin and caught the side of this head with my heel.

He grunted out a desire to sleep before dropping to the grass. After which, I casually took out the Mauser, turned and took aim at the butler.

To my surprise, the burly man in the trick-suit did not even break stride. Instead he reached inside his coat and jerked out something big, steel-blue and menacing.

"Let it go, Harvey!" a male voice called out. "Mr. Bishop was expected."

The butler stopped. Without giving consideration to the possibility I might shoot him anyway, he reholstered his weapon, made an abrupt turn and went back to wherever butlers go until needed. I twisted toward Tandem; still holding the Mauser and feeling rather foolish for having drawn it.

"I don't like violence, Mr. Bishop," Tandem called out. His face was now sour, his eyes fulminating.

The women he had been entertaining stared at me, their eyes wide, their mouths gaping, their cheeks pinking with fear-tainted delight.

Jessie gave me an encouraging grin from the liquor cart.

I pointed down at the two fallen men. "Silly me." I reholstering the Mauser. "You sent these guys over with bouquets, and congratulations. My deepest apologies, Mr. Tandem."

Tandem forced a lip-curling smile. "You're upsetting the ladies, Mr. Bishop."

I glanced at the women as I continued my approach to Tandem. They were smiling; their ears crimson with anticipation, their chests heaving with pleasure.

"And doing a damn good job of it," I said. "Do we talk here or in private?"

His eyes narrowed unpleasantly. "Drink, Mr. Bishop?"

As I drew close, I gave Jacob Tandem another assessment. He might have been eighty, but in actuality he was sixty-eight. He was slightly taller than me and weighed about 300 pounds. His cheeks were pallid. His nose was large and hooked. His mouth was a thin red slash across an icy map. But it was the eyes that captured my attention. They looked straight through me, saw everything, and betrayed nothing. As they moved over my body their color changed. One moment they were agate. The next they were glinting steel. Tandem had dangerous eyes: cold and inhuman.

I gave the staring women a wink. "No thanks," I told him. "It might weaken my aim."

Tandem got red in the face. He made a casual wave toward the house, trying to appear at ease. But he was not. "We'll do business, inside." Then he strode off after excusing himself to his guests.

I blew Jessie a kiss and followed him. To my surprise, the remaining pair of bodyguards remained where they were. Either Tandem knew why I was there and did not fear me, or he had other people inside to give me cause for worry.

As houses go, his rented bit of heaven was more than just nice. But, then, several million in stone, furnishings and decorations should look a bit upscale. Otherwise you are not getting your money's worth. I particularly like the paintings on the white walls. Very colorful. Very confusing. But abstracts always hang well in lush surroundings.

Tandem led me down a long hall to a big room containing a snazzy billiard table—ten by six feet of rosewood, brass and green felt. I stopped in the doorway and let my eyes drift, looking for other eyes. Other than the game-table and the black phone hanging upon one wall, all I saw were high, wooden chairs with cigarette ashtrays and bottle holders in the arms.

"Do you play eight-ball, Mr. Bishop?" Tandem's voice crackled across the room.

I nodded and moved toward him. "Frank Portello taught me when I was a kid. Each lesson cost me ten cents a ball."

Jacob racked the balls. Then he selected two cues, tossing me one. Surprisingly it was straight and well-balanced. I found a cube of chalk on the arm of one chair and scuffed the cue's leather tip. Tandem watched genuinely interested in what I would do next.

"Where's Joey Fortuna?" I asked.

"What's your interest in Joey?"

I gave out a good impression of a casual shrug and lit a cigarette. "He put the snatch on Rita Portello today. I want him dead. I want her back—not necessarily in that order. I thought you might want to help on both counts."

His eyes narrowed a moment. "Who told you Joey abducted Rita Portello?"

"A little bird. But if you don't want to believe me, let's ask him. Fortuna tried to grab Rita earlier and got a face full of scratches from Rita's claws. If I'm lying, he's got a puss as smooth as a baby's butt. If I'm not, he's dead—that's a promise."

I watched his jaw-muscles work. Tandem was fighting a sudden fury, but not toward me.

"You've seen him since," I said. "Otherwise your face wouldn't be taking on that nice plum color."

The telephone rang. Tandem leaned his cue against the billiard table, went over to the phone, and grabbed the receiver. There was nearly a minute of silence while he listened to somebody talking at the other end of the line, his head nodding and his eyes darting from side to side. After a few muffled words, he rang off and retrieved his cue.

"I gave Joey no such order," declared Tandem. "I have a great respect for the Portello family. I would never stoop to such a vile act against friends."

"That's what I tried to tell Sal. But he refused to believe it. I told him that as big a louse as you were for embezzling a hundred million from your employers, you wouldn't risk ruining new friendships by doing anything so stupid as kidnapping Rita. Unfortunately, Sal made a good counterpoint. He kept asking why Fortuna would pull such a bonehead play on his own? I didn't have an answer."

His words chewed angrily off his tongue. "Why would *I* put the grab on Rita? Tell me that."

"To get back the hundred million. The hundred million Dominic has or should I say *had* been holding out on you."

Jacob Tandem glanced at me sharply. "Dominic?" His voice sounded like a betrayed wail.

"The money was in Dom's warehouse. Fortunately for you, I arranged a little party. I personally delivered five crates of cash to a nice out of the way spot where they could not be mislaid again."

"When did Dominic find my money?" His words came out aching with disappointment.

"A moot point, Tandem. I came here ready to drop that hundred million back into your lap in exchange for Rita."

One of his hands went into his pocket to grip something small and transmitter-like. "The problem, Mr. Bishop, is I don't have Rita."

"How disappointing. However my offers still stands. If you don't know where Rita is, Fortuna does. I'm sure he'd be willing to tell me where he's hidden her—once I get his undivided attention. I hope you don't mind. The pixie in me promises not to break anything other than his bones."

Tandem jerked his head around to look at me. "That won't be necessary, Mr. Bishop. I'm sure Joey will tell us what we want to know." His eyes were cold and venomous. "You're certain my money is safe?"

Three men rushed into the room with guns drawn. One of them was Joey Fortuna. From the quadrate of scratches along both of his cheeks, Rita had done herself proud. The other two looked to be Irish. Both had rust-colored hair and freckled faces. Both wore dark green suits. One was about thirty years of age, tall, and angular with a long puss. He had a sinister scar over the left eye. A moth-eaten mustache sat beneath his hawk-like nose. His eyes were deeply set, looking like pools of hot tar. The other was short and stout with a round face and pouting lips. The three men approached. I spun the cue-stick around until I had it in my hand like a club. A glint of amusement showed in Tandem's eyes.

"Mr. Bishop and I were having a friendly chat about my missing money and Rita Portello," Tandem announced. "Apparently Rita Portello is missing. Mr. Bishop has offered to hand over my money in exchange for her freedom. I find that a very tempting offer. Unfortunately, I do not know where Rita is. Do you three have any ideas?"

Joe Fortuna went wide-eyed and his face went gray, like moldy oatmeal. The other two goons relaxed and holstered their weapons as if the question completely bypassed them.

"Put the gun away, Joey," Tandem cooed. But the Mafia-Don's knuckles had gone dead-white around the cue-stick, his eyes had narrowed, his jaw muscles had started flexing, again. "We're all friends, here."

Fortuna's glance flicked nervously across the faces of his companions, and then to mine; hoping someone would tell him the answer to the question he dared not ask. Then, with obvious reluctance, Joey Fortuna did as instructed.

I lowered the cue-stick hoping my chance to get my hands on Fortuna was about to take place.

"Perhaps you can help us out, Joey." Tandem leaned over the edge of the table and took aim at the cue-ball.

Deadly Turn

"Me, Mr. Tandem?" Fortuna quaked. "I don't know nothin' about Rita Portello."

The room became silent except for Fortuna's wheezing breath.

Tandem glanced past Fortuna at the other two men. Although no words were spoken and I saw no visible communication, they suddenly moved forward—each flanking their terrified companion.

I could tell from their faces they did not know what had prompted Joey Fortuna's actions with Rita. But they recognized, from past experience, that Fortuna had proof Joey was dirty and was about to part ways with the rest of the world. Whatever friendship had developed between Fortuna and the men watching him was now as dead as Joey soon would be.

There was a sharp click as Tandem thrust his cue against the white ball. It darted toward the multicolor triangle of balls at the other end of the table; sending the stripes and solids in all directions. We waited—all of us—for the balls to stop. Then Jacob Tandem turned to Joe Fortuna. A quizzical smile twisted Tandem's mouth into an angry sneer.

"Mr. Bishop thinks I ordered Rita picked up, Joey," Tandem said. His voice was very pleasant, like a bartender recommending a Manhattan. "Salvator Portello is of the same mind. I told Mr. Bishop I had not done so. I hope—for all our sakes—that Mr. Portello believes it."

Fortuna looked for a place to run. The other two men closed ranks, blocking his path. Their eyes were on Fortuna. Their fists were locked. Their jaws were set. Their shoulders were bunched. Whether Joey Fortuna realized it or not I could only guess. But, he was breathing his last breaths.

"I...I... don't know what you mean, Mr. Tandem," Fortuna stammered.

Tandem called his shot on the fifteen-ball. Then he leaned down and lined up with the cue-ball. But he thumped the cue too hard. The cue-ball struck the fifteen, bouncing it into the pocket and then back out, nearly leaving the table.

As if furious with the shot, Tandem let out a roar and swung the stick at Fortuna. The cue splintered alongside the young man's head.

Fortuna's knees sagged and he dropped to the floor in a praying position. The other two goons rushed over and grabbed him by the arms, jerking the dazed Fortuna upright.

Tandem went over, pulled the Makarov from Joey's shoulder holster, and stuffed it into his own coat pocket. Then he gently patted Fortuna's face to bring the young man back to consciousness.

"Your touch is a true gift, Tandem," I remarked, as Fortuna's eyes flickered open.

"Where'd you get those scratches, Joey?" Tandem asked. He spoke as if a father talking to a naughty child.

Fortuna tried to struggle free but the two men holding him were experts at their craft. I had to hand it to Tandem: at least *some* of his men were well-trained professionals.

Fortuna panicked, his eyes bugging and his mouth gaping. He finally realized he was on borrowed time.

"Don't make it hard on yourself, Joey," cooed Tandem. "Where's Rita Portello?"

The young man chewed the air, his entire body trembling. "I don't know, Mr. Tandem."

Tandem's head moved from side to side in dismay. Then he turned to look at me.

It must have been a signal because the two holding Fortuna went into action. One smashed a hard right fist into Fortuna's face.

Joey's nose crushed noisily. Blood spattered and smeared against his cheeks and chin.

The other goon then took his turn. He hit Fortuna in the face several more times. Then the pair went to work in concert.

After each blow Fortuna tried to scream, but before he could get it out, one of the goons would hit him again. They did not try to knock him out. They wanted him conscious: they wanted him to feel pain again and again.

Fortuna tried to crouch, his hands covering his face. But that merely signaled the pair working on him to combine forces, each sending a simultaneous, crushing blow to each of Fortuna's mitts. There was a crackling sound as the metacarpals in Fortuna's hands splintered apart.

This time, Fortuna screamed.

His cries fell upon deaf ears.

Jacob Tandem softly cleared his throat.

Instantly, the two goons backed away from Fortuna.

Joey collapsed to the floor, cuddling his broken hands against his chest and whimpering like a kicked dog. His soft mutterings were interspersing with short, sharp yelps in response to any attempt at finger-movement; his swollen face looked like a pile of raw beef on a white plate.

"Let's try it again, Joey." Tandem turned back to look at the dazed and battered young man. Once more he was a father coaxing a slightly uncooperative child. "One last time for your sake."

"If I knew, I'd tell you," whimpered Fortuna.

"Somebody told you to grab Rita, Joey." An understanding smile formed upon Tandem's lined face. "You wouldn't have done such a thing on your own. Who was it, Joey?"

"Kingsley," Fortuna mumbled through swollen, bloody lips. "Joel Kingsley. He has Rita Portello. I don't know where he took her."

"That might be the truth," I told Tandem.

The aging mobster looked back at me. A slow smile creased Tandem's lips. Then he turned back to the fallen man.

"You brought her somewhere, Joey," pressed Tandem. "You must know that much. Where, Joey?"

"I don't know, Mr. Tandem," said Fortuna. "I delivered her to Kingsley. We met out of town on a dirt road. He drove her away. I'm sorry, Mr. Tandem."

Jacob Tandem looked over at me. A deadly shadow appeared briefly in his eyes. Then the Mafia-Don gave the two men rubbing their knuckles a nod. They reached down and pulled Fortuna to his feet.

"Deliver him to Salvator Portello with my apologies," Tandem said in a grieving voice. "Inform Mr. Portello that I will make every effort to locate Rita, and return her safely to him."

As I watched, the two Irishmen dragged Joey Fortuna out.

I was angry at Fortuna for what he had done to Rita. Nevertheless, I shivered over what would happen when Joey Fortuna was delivered to Salvator. Fortuna was dead as far as Tandem was concerned. He was dead as far as the rest of the Tandem's goons were concerned. Fortuna, himself, realized there was no avoiding it. But what Joey Fortuna did not know was there would be a long, painful time in the dip-tank while Salvator got that killing done.

"Kill him," I urged Tandem. "If you have any feeling for the man at all, kill him."

"I want to be certain Salvator realizes I have held nothing back. If Joey knows any else, I'm certain Mr. Portello will hear it in short order."

Jacob Tandem was correct. Sal would hear everything and anything until Joey's screams were muffled by the dip-tank's acid.

Tandem looked over at me. His stare was now mean and sharp; his eyes were dark shards of glass beneath cliffs of gray brows. "Why not make a gesture of good faith and hand over my money now, Bishop?"

"You deliver Rita, you'll get your money. Not before."

He jabbed a thumb in the direction Fortuna had been taken. "Hard or easy," he said. "Either way you'll tell me."

"You obviously don't know me, Tandem." I went over to the nearest chair and snuffed out my cigarette in the ashtray. Then I returned to the table and sent the fifteen-ball into a pocket with a three cushion bank-shot. I cued twice more, sinking the seven, twelve and eleven balls. Then I purposely missed on the fourteen.

"Talk," he growled. "Before I have my boys give you the business Fortuna got." His voice had become harsh and hostile.

Joey Fortuna had confirmed Jessie's assumption that Joel Kingsley was holding Rita. So, I was wasting time with Tandem I should be spending with Jessie. I dropped the cue, jerked out the Mauser, cocked it, and took aim at his head.

"Go ahead," I told him. "Call your boys. Since you don't have Rita, you're no good to me. Kingsley's who I should be dealing with."

He chuckled grimly, "I don't like you, Mr. Bishop."

"Not many people do." I backed over to the door. "Sometimes, I find that distressing. In your case, it doesn't bother me a bit. If you should find Rita before I do, my offer stands. You know where to find me, Tandem."

He put his cue back into the rack. "I do indeed, Mr. Bishop. And don't think I won't be long in coming."

When I got back to the Buick, Jessie Hampstead was there as promised, leaning against the trunk. "You're not the brightest bulb on the Christmas tree," she remarked. "No offense meant. But I saw what happened to Joey Fortuna."

"Not my workmanship. Did you talk to Kingsley? According to Fortuna, Kingsley has Rita."

"I told him what you'd made an offer—Rita for the hundred million. Joel's willing to trade."

I gave her a look at my canines. "When and where?"

"Soon. I'll be in touch. He said he'd deliver her any place you say."

"You pick the spot. When I'm satisfied Rita's okay, I'll take him to the money."

"You're my kind of man, Bishop."

Jessie Hampstead tilted toward me, her mouth pressing against mine.

I tangled my fingers in her hair. Her lips felt like burning velvet. I leaned into the caress. But she touched my face with the tips of her fingers and drew back.

I watched her walk away as I climbed into the Buick, wishing Rita was not part of what was to come.

Jessie's kiss had been a throwaway teaser. But for an old man like me, it was a nice one. All the way back to Austin I tasted her lips, the warmth, the wetness and the tantalizing flavor of her lipstick. It was like I was sixteen again, driving home after my first date.

"Get a grip, old man," I chided myself. "She'd cut your balls off to get that money." But I did not want to believe it. It was too much fun fantasizing about how she could improve my lonely nights.

CHAPTER FIFTEEN

The next morning, I tried to fry an egg in the Microwave. Two minutes later, I tossed egg and oven into the trash and went out to the Buck. I had endured enough quick-cooking for one lifetime. From now on it would be fried foods with all the grease and resulting cholesterol I could tolerate. But before I could unlock the door, I heard footsteps behind me.

"Put 'em up, Bishop!"

I turned toward the voice, flat-footed and emptied handed, the threat going unregistered to my food-preoccupied brain.

It had come from a tall, lanky sort wearing bib-overalls, biker boots and a plaid flannel shirt. He held an old .45 automatic. It was the kind of pistol WWII GI's threw away as soon as they got their hands on a Mauser.

The ancient relic's barrel pointed ominously at my belly. The man's forefinger was tightly curled on the trigger. Its hammer was cocked.

Slightly behind him and off to the right side I spotted another guy. This one wore pink chinos, green sandals without socks and a T-Shirt bearing the slogan, 'Love Hurts'. He brandished an ancient Webley-Forsby .455 revolver. Both men were in their early twenties.

The automatic did not worry me. Even at twenty feet there was a good chance a fired round would miss a target my size. But the Webley was a more sinister problem. At fifty yards, it could send a round barely an inch off target-center.

"Trick or treat?" I quipped, as my memory darted back to Hamilton Blake's description of Benny's killers.

"You heard him!" T-Shirt shouted. "Up, or we'll plug ya."

I raised my hands forming two fists in hopes I would get an opportunity to use my favorite tools of the trade. Lanky must have read my thoughts. He gripped the automatic in both hands, came within six feet of me and took aim at my chest. T-Shirt sidled over trying to give an impression of John Dillinger. While I patiently waited, he gave me a sloppy frisk. Like the bad-guys do in the movies he made a production of confiscating the Mauser before sticking it behind his belt.

"Let's take a ride, Bishop," T-Shirt grunted; backing away like he was on the F.B.I.'s Most-Wanted list and I should be worried to death.

That was their first mistake. They did not kill me on the spot.

"Tandem sent you clowns?" I asked, still not believing the pair were for-real.

T-Shirt nodded. "You got somethin' of his. He wants it back. He sent us so there'd be no mistake in gettin' it."

As kidnappers, they were pitifully unprepared amateurs. Either Tandem wanted to avoid making their next paychecks, or he had grossly underestimated my experience and determination. Or he was shorter on qualified professionals than I had thought. I assumed it must be the last.

"Sounds like you guys are Tandem's first-line team," I remarked, doing my best not to laugh at them. "How was Big-D?"

T-Shirt grinned, giving me a peak at his green teeth. "Just how in hell did you know we was in Dallas?"

"I'm a professionally trained detective."

I had no doubt I was looking at the pair who killed Benny Jacobson. But I was not worried. As far as Tandem was concerned, I was his only hope of reclaiming a hundred-million dollars. That knowledge all but guaranteed they would fail in their quest. It also gave me enthusiastic hopes justice would soon prevail on Benny's behalf—with my help, of course.

"Get movin'." Lanky ordered.

I considered trying to convince them of the foolishness in their actions. Words came to mind, of course. But because my utterances would be accompanied by chest-wincing laughter over the pair's ineptitude, I felt it best to remain silent. Why cheat myself out of an opportunity to demonstrate the error of their ways in a graphically painful manner?

"Anyplace in particular, fellas?" I asked.

Lanky motioned me to follow as he backed toward a weary-looking, bald-tired sedan. I lowered my fists and complied.

His partner trailed several paces behind me, still trying to get the Dillinger impersonation right.

As I moved, I glanced behind every step hoping he would grow impatient and rush forward to prod me. But T-shirt kept his distance. He also kept the Webley trained on my back.

At the car, Lanky opened the driver's door and sidled off a few paces. Then he gave me a John Garfield sneer. The one from *Dust Be My Destiny*. I was almost impressed.

"You drive, Bishop," he ordered.

That was mistake number two. Putting me and my impulsive pixie in control of rolling steel was begging for an impromptu funeral. Once they were in the vehicle with me, I would soon have them both by the short hairs—so to speak.

I let my mind dart to the delights of bridge-rail jumps and median-rollovers. Almost instantly, an amiable smile spread across my face. With a wink of appreciation in his direction, I crawled into the aging car and settled behind the steering wheel.

Lanky strolled back over, his ugly face beaming with confidence, and slammed the door shut.

"I hope you guys aren't anti-cigarette fanatics," I remarked, through the open side-window. I buckled myself in, tightly. Then I took out a smoke and lit it. "I always like a little weed while driving. Helps calm my nerves."

T-Shirt got in the front seat from the rider's side. It took him three slams to shut the door. Then he quickly twisted towards me, grinning proudly and giving me another look at the Webley.

I winked back. Lanky crawled into the back seat. After another concert of car-door beating against tired latching-mechanism, this time from him, he settled back; directly behind his partner.

They had now make mistake number three. That position kept both men within my peripheral vision.

"Uptown or down?" I asked, brightly. "On a day like this, I don't really have a preference."

A set of keys from the back seat landed in my lap. "Head for the Freeway," ordered Lanky. "After that, we'll tell you where."

That was mistake number four. Soon, I would have speed on my side. The only concern from my standpoint was how fast this wreck could go. Less than seventy meant I was limited to side-by-side rollovers. Past that, and I had options on bridge-rail jumps followed by the ever-exciting nose-to-tail flip-over.

T-Shirt cackled confidently, "Yeah, Bishop. We'll tell you where."

I laughed, too—but not for the same reason. My joy came in knowing this was going to be the last trip of their young lives.

"You're playing with the big boys, now," Lanky declared.

"Sounds like it," I snickered, starting the heap. "You guys got me covered from all angles." I dropped the gear-lever into drive, and tapped the accelerator. The old car belched blue smoke and rolled out of the parking lot.

The one beside tilted over. "Tandem says he wants you alive so's you can talk. But don't think I won't plug ya if I have to."

I pretended to shiver with fear. "You've got no worries there, buddy. An old man like me wants to enjoy as much time as he can get."

Mistake number five came in the form of not fastening their seatbelts. In the throws of a high-speed rollover, unrestrained bodies go into painful motion. I, too, would be at risk because of their neglect. But tricks I learned on many previous outings of this sort would be enough to shield me from any terminal damage.

I said, "I've already had lunch. But nothing says we can't enjoy a scenic drive to a place of your preference."

"What the fuck do you take us for?" demanded Lanky, from the rear seat. "Idiots?"

I tossed him an over-the-shoulder grin. "Not you guys. You're professional all the way."

Three blocks of holding in laughter later, I swung the ailing sedan onto I-35.

Once settled in the far left lane, I pushed the accelerator to the floor.

The engine coughed in complaint. But after a moment it sputtered into a crazy-sounding whine that grew louder and louder as the vehicle picked up speed.

"What's your itinerary?" I quipped. "I'd like to pick up my laundry before the place closes, at five. We could stop off for a beer after that. My treat."

"Just drive," shouted Lanky impatiently, from the backseat.

The car struggled to get past sixty. But that was fast enough. The traffic was normal for this time of day. And fortunately, for my plans, the State Cruisers were absent. I glanced at the speedometer, again. We were almost going seventy.

"Take it easy," the guy beside me ordered.

I kept my foot to the floor. "I don't want to keep Tandem waiting."

Sweat ran down my back as the speedometer touched eighty. It was not so much the speed that made me nervous or the animosity my passengers felt towards me. It was the thought of those skin-thin tires rolling across hot asphalt that really jangled my nerves. Blowouts at high-speed make keeping control of a vehicle extremely difficult. A planned rollover was one thing. A surprise, due to failing rubber, was quite another animal. I tightened my hands on the wheel, trying to make my thudding heart believe that if the worst happened, this was not going to be a bad way to die.

For some reason my erratically pumping organ was not completely convinced.

T-Shirt jabbed the Webley against my ribs. "Slow down or I plug you right now!"

"Go ahead," I countered, no longer shamming. "You'll be just as dead two seconds later when this heap crashes."

T-Shirt twisted in the seat to look back at his companion, completely bewildered as to what he should do. A moment later I felt something cold against one ear. It was the old automatic.

"Slow down or I'll blow your fucking brains out," Lanky roared.

"Same answer," I chuckled. "What a pair of dip-shits. You clowns couldn't play with the big boys if you paid Tandem's millions."

The speedometer slipped past eighty.

The car was shimmying so bad, I was not certain how much longer I could keep it between the lane-lines.

They glanced at each other, neither one knowing what to do.

"When I get this pile of shit up to top-speed I'm going to fly it off a bridge," I warned. "Don't worry. It will be a short flight with a quick landing."

"He's gonna' kill us!" croaked Lanky.

"Alternatively," I said, "you can hand me the Mauser. After that, I'll pull over and let you two out. We'll go our separate ways—no harm done."

The engine sputtered again. Even if I had another yard of accelerator play, the rattling car would do no better than ninety-five.

"The tires on this thing won't hold up much longer," I continued. "Better make a decision quick. I've got my heart set on taking flight off that bridge coming up. See it? In twenty seconds we're going to see how far this heap can soar. Bishop to radio-tower. Bishop to radio-tower. Permission to take off, please?"

"He's crazy!" Lanky shouted, the barrel of his gun leaving my ear.

"So I've been told and told and told," I taunted. "Ever been in a roll-over? I mean a high-speed one. It's quite an experience. The whole process seems to go in slow-motion—except for the pain. That comes on real fast—again, and again and again. If course, that all stops along with living when your internal organs rupture. The heart breaks loose first—the aorta can't take too much rough jiggling before it tears. A few seconds after that... Well, say your prayers."

"What'll we do?" screamed Lanky.

"At this speed, the pixie in me prefers an end-over-end flip," I said. "That really gives a rush. But I'm willing to settle for the sideways-flop. Suggestions? Requests? We're at top speed, passengers. Permission to leave the ground has been provided. Flaps are going down. Take off point is just ahead. Counting down – 10 – 9..."

The one beside me licked his lips; his eyes growing wide. The transmission began vibrating like it was trying to give birth. The differential sounded like it was in a howling competition. The tires whined like they were going orgasmic.

"What'll we do, Hal?" the Lanky one whimpered.

"Five seconds and counting," I interjected. "Four – three..."

"He don't scare me!" shouted T-Shirt. "He's bluffin'!"

"Give him his goddamn gun!" Lanky shouted.

"Let's all sing *In The Sweet Bye and Bye*," I shouted, and set myself.

Lanky reached over the seat, grabbed the Mauser from his pal's belt and dropped it into my lap.

I thanked him, grabbed up the weapon, cocked the hammer and sent a round into his throat. The second round hit T-Shirt in the ribs as he fired, at me. His bullet burned a wedge in my suit-sleeve. I sent another round into him to make sure he did not repeat his ventilation tactics , then I holstered the Mauser and took my foot off the accelerator.

Almost simultaneously, one of the car's front tires blew, throwing the vehicle into a wild, snaking skid. I spun the wheel back and forth trying to regain control. However, every other change in inertia caused T-Shirt's corpse to flop into me.

I did my best to keeping it elbowed away while I played dodge-car with the bridge abutments, but I finally lost the battle and the car careened across the Freeway where it did a side-kiss against the concrete, center-barrier.

The jolt gave my head a bang, temporarily stunning me into dropping my hands from the steering wheel. Before I could grab the wheel again, the car bounced back and made a frantic trip into the ditch adjacent to a gravel frontage-road. There the vehicle left the ground in a spiraling flight.

While airborne it toppled twice, nose to tail, before flying over a section of barbed wire bearing a no-trespassing sign. That's when the slow motion, side-to-side roll started.

I was giving odds on a wheels-of-the-car slam-down when the vehicle made an abrupt change in course pointing its wheels toward the clouds.

"Shit." I set myself against the door, twisted my feet onto the seat and bringing my knees up to form a barrier against the tumbling corpses.

Ten seconds later, both corpses had banged their way between roof and floorboards into what was left of the backseat. I was still gripping the steering wheel, even though the car was resting on its top. All about me I could smell gasoline fumes.

A few seconds of super-human efforts later, I braced one hand against the roof of the overturned wreck and unhooked the seatbelt. Then I managed to crawl out through the open door-window. After that, I did my best imitation of a stagger in an effort to cross a field of knee-high weeds before what I had been driving exploded.

I thought I had made it far enough away and stopped to catch my breath when the car exploded. The blast knocked me flat on my face.

I twisted toward the vehicle expecting to see a fire-slide coming my way. But the flames had merely engulfed its interior.

I got to my feet grinning. It was good to be alive—painful, but good. It would be better to be found a discrete distance away, in case the police should arrive sooner than expected. Some cops have no sense of humor in situations like this.

I got up and hobbled onward. With a little overdue luck I would merely appear to be a stunned onlooker who was emotionally scarred by all I had seen.

When I got to the frontage road, a redheaded kid on a motorcycle skidded to a stop, near me. He looked from me to the plumes of rising smoke in the field behind the fence.

"What happened?" he asked.

"I'm not sure," I replied, feigning confusion. "I was sitting in that field enjoying a brew and a burger when this old car flew in. I had absolutely no idea it could do that."

"It's on fire," he exclaimed, as if having a revelation.

I casually glanced back at the smoke. "Naw. That's my barbeque. The driver got pissed when I wouldn't give him a hotdog, and shot it full of holes. Can you give me a lift to a phone? I'd like to let the cops in on this. No telling what that lunatic will start shooting at next. Are you wearing a bulletproof vest?"

He gave a frantic head-wag.

Without invitation, I climbed onto the motorcycle's buddy-seat. "Then we'd better hurry," I warned. "How fast can this thing go? That guy's probably on his way over here, right now."

"Holy shit!"

A split second later the kid had the rear tire smoking, the front wheel chin-high and the gears jamming like pebbles being processed through a meat-grinder.

I hung on for all I was worth while offering encouragement in the form of, "I think he's seen us! Crouch low. Was that a shot?"

After changing cabs several times, I made it back to my flop. I did not report the incident to the police. I thought it best, under the circumstances, to let them root around for their own brand of answers. In time, they might determine the burned corpses of the men in the car had been shot. But since both rounds I fired passed through the men and out of the car, there would be little to link me to the event. Even if the kid came forward, I would merely be a fleeting memory from a frantic time. The kind that gives bald men hair and women beards in witness-statements.

After showering, I checked my body for damage. There were a few fresh scrapes and bruises, but those were not any more serious than what was already healing.

I slipped on another pinstriped number and went into the kitchen.

After turning on the radio, I poured a tumbler of Pinch and lit a cigarette. Then, I telephoned Salvator Portello. I wanted to give him a report on my search efforts, and to find out what he may have discovered.

Dom answered the phone. Between a flurry of Sicilian cursing and English vows of revenge for my costing him a hundred million, I learned that Sal and the dip-tank were busy with Joey Fortuna.

I rang off feeling slightly sick with pity for the suffering Chicago gangster.

I took my drink back into the front room and turned on my new television. A number of channel-switches later, I paused in my remote-controlling to watch a news broadcast. The announcer was talking about a fatality car-crash just off I-35. The occupants had not been identified as yet, but the vehicle had been reported stolen hours earlier. The police assumed the corpses in the wreck belonged to the thieves, however both had been burned to a crisp so identification would be difficult.

I turned off the TV, snuffed out my cigarette and toasted the report's accuracy. Then I set down my empty glass and drifted off to sleep smiling about the promise of confusion to come during the wreck's ongoing investigation.

The telephone rang me into wakefulness. I opened my eyes and checked my watch. It was nearly six o'clock in the evening.

I got up and limped into the kitchen. There, I grabbed the receiver from its wall-mount. For many seconds all I heard was a vague silence, on the line. Then a woman's voice said, "Jessie Hampstead, Deke. Busy?"

"I had a couple of silly things to take care of before getting home. But I'm free at the moment. What's up? Or, should that be your question?"

There was more silence. Then she said, "Joel Kingsley says he wants to make the trade tonight at the Double-Tree Hotel in Austin—seven o'clock."

"How's Tandem doing? A little miffed about the two losers he sent to pick me up this morning?"

More silence. Then she said, "I'll be there, waiting in the bar."

Before I could respond I heard the knob on my apartment door creak, as it turned. My hand became white-knuckled on the phone. Tandem was not easily dissuaded.

I cradled the telephone with my shoulder, jerked out the Mauser and waited as the knob rotated.

"I'll be there," I whispered. Hopefully without wings on."

Then, whoever was toying with the knob released it. On tiptoes I crept from the kitchen, through the front room and into the bath. There I raised the window and peeked out. Nobody was in sight.

With muffled whimpers of agony, I hoisted myself past the sill, slid out, and dangled for a moment before dropping uncomfortably to the grass.

Out on the street I saw a dark sedan parked at the curb. It looked empty.

I took out my keys and pressed the remote door-lock release to unlock my Buick. The sound of its clicking echoed softly to my ears. Then, I dropped to a crouched-posture before duck-walking over to the Buick—using the other vehicles in the parking lot as a blind.

Five seconds after climbing inside, I burned rubber on my way down the street. In the rear view mirror I caught sight of the two goons who had worked-over Joey Fortuna in a dead run, heading for the parked sedan.

I glanced at my watch. Six-twenty. It would take me forty minutes to get to the hotel. When I got there, Jessie would lead. I would follow. And Joel would probably wait for her to tease me into a spot where shadows prevailed and witnesses were invisible. If I actually had Tandem's millions, the problem would be minimized to a simple trade—Rita, for the cash. But with empty pockets, I was playing a bluff that left me only one chance for Rita and I getting away in one piece—to get Joel in the Mauser's sights when Rita was with him.

Of course there were Tandem's men to consider. Admittedly they were a bungling complication. But more than one bungler had gummed my actions in the past. Then there was the Chicago Mob and its shooter to consider. If he had told them I was holding the hundred million, I would have a third set of forces planning my doom. Still, there were other concerns. First and foremost, should I stop at my lawyer's to make out a will?

After reflection, I decided it would be a futile effort. Assuming I did not get my mitts on Tandem's money, there would be nothing to bequeath. I had an outstanding balance with my bookie. Then there was the fifteen grand I owed Sheila. Not to mention past due taxes, car payments and the leases on my office and apartment. On the plus side, my funeral would not be one of those dry-eyed affairs. Everybody I owed money to would be there, weeping.

I caught the freeway and merged into traffic with the Buick pushing ninety. I checked my watch again. Just enough time for another cigarette and a little soul-searching—assuming that black sedan tailing in the distance was not Tandem's men. I put the accelerator to the floor. The Buick's V-8 let go a confident growl, quickly burying the speedometer-needle. Slowly the black sedan in the mirror disappeared amidst slower-moving traffic.

CHAPTER SIXTEEN

Seven-eleven. At least that's what the digital clock on the wall behind the bar at the Double-Tree Lounge displayed. I had just settled on a stool in front of a slack-faced barman, who was using one hand to idly picking his teeth with the corner of a matchbook, while the other mashed a white bar-cloth. He was eying me with little interest.

I chalked it up to the suit. Pinstripes with repaired bullet-holes do not reflect the high-tipper image so often preferred by those in his profession.

"What'll it be?" he asked.

"Sidecar," I told him.

The matchbook found his pocket as he moved off.

I glanced around looking for Jessie. I did not see her.

I dragged out my money-clip and set it on the bar.

The bartender returned with my drink. I slipped him a five spot and told him to keep the change. He said there wouldn't be any and I was a buck short.

I handed him a dollar bill—after silently wishing upon him all the pain I had been suffering since Helen Martinis died.

After feeding the cash register, he moved away a few paces. There he worked the cloth on the bartop, making small tight circles.

A second later I felt movement at my elbow. I looked over to see a floozy blonde lugging a red plastic purse the size of a watermelon. Her lips were thick and painted red. She had sullen, heavy-lidded eyes. A loose plain blue smock covered her from neck to knee. She was plump, lots of veins in her fat legs, and her moon-shaped flabby face was topped with dirty hair braided in a circle around her head. Her eyes were red and the skin around them looked raw. She had a heavy way of breathing, almost like a sleeper's snore. I leaned in the opposite direction to give her room as she struggled to climb onto the stool next to mine.

Once perched, she fumbled her purse onto the bar top. That is when I noticed she wore two flashy rings – the kind sold in dime stores—and a thin marriage band. I could not help but wonder what kind of guy had married her – and if that guy had a smile on his puss after he killed himself.

She glared over at the bartender with the impatience of an unsated sow waiting on a boar.

The bartender pretended she was not there, moving one lip slowly over the other, his rag still making small circles.

After a frustrated snort, the blonde tilted toward me. I felt the heat of her nearness and looked over. The angle of her pudgy chin, near my shoulder, smoothed the wrinkles around her jowls. It was an improvement. But her sudden nearness brought with it the smell of something sweet, and dead.

"Bishop, ain't it?" she asked, her voice low and confidential.

"Maybe," I said.

The blonde paused, her gaze intent upon my face. "You're Bishop." She squirmed her ample backside as if trying to scratch an indelicate itch. "We ain't never been introduced. But I seen you before, plenty when you was a cop."

"Nothing bad between us, I hope."

There was a slight drawing up of her flabby bosom. Then her head waggled sloppily.

"What's your name?" I asked.

"Maria." She scratched the back of her neck, shook her head and then glanced at me obliquely, as if wondering if I thought she was beautiful.

"What brings you my way, Maria?"

"You did me a good turn, once," she replied. Her fat jaw moved as she flexed her lips. "I figure I owe you a good turn, back. That's why I said I'd come."

I waved the bartender over and told him to give her a drink. She ordered Bushmills neat with a beer chaser.

He moved off to satisfy her craving.

I returned my attention to Maria and asked if the 'good turn' she mentioned included cash.

She leaned toward me again, her breath sour upon my face. "They're settin' you up."

I picked my drink and gave it a taste. "Anyone special? Or just the run-of-the-mill types hired by local politicians to hassle me for being insightful about the Governor's secret incomings and outgoings?"

The bartender returned with her drinks. I handed over my money-clip and told him to peel. He left me with a limp ten-spot and a wink.

"They're putting the snatch on you," she confided. Then the blonde grabbed up the Irish whiskey and threw it back with an expertise acquired only from decades of practice. "Torture," she added with a shiver, like she was sitting naked on a block of ice.

Then she set down the empty shot-glass and picked up the mug of beer. "Didn't catch no names. But you're good as had—as they say."

"Is this fun going to happen anytime soon?"

Maria shot me a meaningful glance, permitting her eyes to lick over me. "Tonight. Here. Or outside, to be on the straight." She took a long draw on the beer before wiping her mouth with the back of one hand. "They're out there now. Waitin' for it to get dark. You won't make it to your car."

"How many?"

The floozy grunted softly, a bitter sound. "Two."

"Who's behind it? Jacob Tandem?"

"Does it matter?" Maria cocked her head like a curious bird, letting her eyes drift over me, again.

"Call it a dying need to know."

"Never said." She took another slurp of beer. "Those two you dusted earlier were low-talent locals. Tandem turned 'em out thinkin' you were a pansy. That gig you pulled gave him a much better appreciation for your talents."

"Somebody just laid it all out for you, huh?"

The blonde's eyes darted away as though startled by my question. "Jessie told me."

I set down my glass, and took out a pack of cigarettes. I gave her one and stuffed another between my lips. Then I lit both and gave her a questioning look. In return I got a sloppy leer.

"Talkative woman, Jessie," I remarked. "What makes her want to confide in you?"

"Jessie's my kid," Maria explained, without any pride. "She's ridin' high, now. But it'll soon come to an end. You wouldn't know it to look at me. But I did the same when I was her age. New York was my town." She took a deep drag on the cigarette and blew smoke across the bar. "Trouble is, it don't last. I turned thirty and had to come back here, to live with my mother. It was either that or turn tricks. I got my pride."

"What makes you my friend, Maria?"

She eyed me dazedly. "My mother was the one the mayor's kid beat up when he was trying to get her purse; the old lady who died, later on. You killed the little shit. He'd have gotten off if you hadn't done him." She waved her cigarette as if it was a baton. "That put me in your books. I've been waitin' a long time to settle-up. This puts us even."

"Where's Jessie?"

"Not here like she told you." Maria fell silent, slouching in her chair as if trying to recall something important.

"I assumed that. Where?"

The blonde gave a nervous glance around the room. Then she leaned over and whispered, "At a place on Anderson. Number 5612."

"Is Kingsley with her?"

Maria shrugged. "That deal with him was supposed to be done—what she set up between you, and him. But Tandem got the idea she could get you someplace where his lowlifes could collar you." The blonde waved one hand disgustedly. "Jessie didn't dare cross him. So she handed Tandem this arrangement because it was close to where I live. She wanted me to come and warn you."

"Dangerous business, playing both ends against the middle."

"They'll kill her one day," Maria agreed with a dismal head-wag. "They got that boy she was going to marry: got him good, the poor wop." There was a pause as she sniffed. "Jessie gave me money for her funeral, just in case. I'm hopin' I won't have to use it." Maria offered a suggestive wink. "I got other expenses—not having a man of my own."

"There's nothing like a mother's love," I remarked.

Maria nodded, not catching my dig. "Jessie said to tell you the deal with Kingsley's still good for tonight. She also said you might want to tell me about some crates—in case things go bad, here."

"Where do I meet with Kingsley?"

"That place on Anderson," she said, behind teeth that tried to close hard. "Jessie'll call him when you get there." A harried look took over her dull eyes. "About them crates…"

"Where does Jessie live?"

Her mascaraed brows furrowed suspiciously. "What've you got in mind?"

"Talk—in case I miss her party."

Maria's his eyes flicker around the room. "You think you'll be able to talk at all if you miss that party?"

"I'm always optimistic."

Maria cleared her throat. "Jessie lives over on Barrington." She gave another look around. "The Saw Mill View Apartments—number 517." Then she grimaced impatiently. "What about them crates? They sounded real important—what with Rita Portello's name being mentioned and all."

"They are important—in a hundred million different ways. Tell Jessie they're buried deep. So deep nobody will ever find them unless I'm around to dig them up. Tell her I'll be at her party and to get Joel Kingsley wound up to deliver."

Maria's face twisted in greedy disappointment.

I took the remaining ten from my money clip and dropped it on the bar next to her empty glass. "Thanks for tipping me off, Maria."

Her facial muscles were writhing and twisting, her mouth contorting into a bestial snarl. "But them damn crates…"

I crawled off the stool without responding.

Maria exhaled noisily with exasperation.

I gave her a wink and then headed out the way I came in.

When the night air hit my face, I headed for the Buick, keeping my chin tilted down and my eyes roving.

Three steps later, I spotted a suit moving parallel to me on my right. Crouched beside a red Mercedes just beyond it was another suit. They had me marked well enough. But for reasons I did not understand, neither was ready to make a move. It made no sense. It was dark. In my current physical state, I was a slow moving target with few options on escape.

I glanced behind considering my chances of ducking beside a car, and sneaking way. That's when I noticed a police-cruiser. The uniform assigned to it was chatting up a skinny brunette. That explained the two suits's hesitation to act. But the brunette looked edgy. Which meant the lovelorn cop would soon be driving off. I kept moving, hoping for a little luck.

A delivery van cruised down the roadway separating the parking sections. As it drew near, I darted in front of it. Then, as the van shielded me from their view I ducked down beside an old four-wheel drive pickup. The springs had been jacked up giving it clearance enough to drive over tombstones without scraping bottom. I crawled beneath and waited.

The two suits ran into the roadway, both rubbernecking to catch sight of me. They met up to work out a strategy. After a brief confab they split, one coming directly for where I was hiding.

Deadly Turn

As he hurried between cars looking left and right, he did not notice my big foot slide out.

My toe caught his ankle. He dropped with a curse and before he could rise I was out and on him. My fist caught the back of his head: one, twice, thrice. His skull gave way with the last blow. He went still, his breathing stopped.

Going through his pockets, I claimed another Makarov for my collection, as well as a set of car keys and a ball of cash held tight by a rubber band. Then I dragged him over to the truck. There, I quietly lowered its tailgate, and hoisted his body onto the bed, pushing the tailgate back into place, and wiping off my fingerprints with my coat-sleeve.

That taken care of, I looked around, but the other suit was nowhere in sight.

My eyes darted to the police cruiser. It was just pulling away from the brunette.

I dropped to my haunches. Then I crept from car to car making a circuitous return to the Buick.

By the time I reached it, my leg muscles where cramped and I was nearly out of breath. I was still in a crouched position when I grabbed the handle.

I might have crawled inside except for the touch of cold steel at the nape of my neck.

I did not look to see who was holding the gun. I spun on my heels and caught the weapon with my forearm. There was a pop from a silencer and something hot burned my shoulder.

The suit's knee started to rise, but I caught it with both hands and toppled him back.

He tried to re-aim the clumsy pistol but by then I had the other suit's Makarov clear of my pocket. I sent one round into his chin. Then I crawled into the Buick, and looked around the parking lot.

The police cruiser was nowhere in sight. I started the engine, lit a cigarette, then put the Buick in gear and rolled away. Tandem was not only running out of time, but also out of help.

The wind came up, whipping along the asphalt roadway. Big drops of rain spattered against the windshield. The rain hit hard at first, then slowed to a whisper before hitting hard again.

Traffic was heavy. Car tires made whooshing sounds as they passed. The multicolored neon lights fronting the shops I passed glowed like fuzzy rainbows. I caught the onramp to I-35 and headed for Jessie's apartment.

An hour later I parked in the apartment-complex lot and stared through the rain-swept windshield at the high-rise building.

It looked like a nice place to live, all twenty stories of it.

I climbed out of the Buick and dodged raindrops into the building's foyer. The mailboxes were all marked. Number 517 had Jessie Hampstead's first initial and last name under it. I pushed the buttons under each mailbox until some lonely soul buzzed the electronic lock on the door to let me in.

The elevator took me up to the fifth floor. Then I followed some nice, new carpet down a wallpapered corridor to Jessie's door.

I knocked and waited.

When a minute passed without response, I dug out my lock picks and put them to work. Ten seconds later I was inside her living room with the door shut, and the lock set.

The place was spotlessly clean, the furniture looking new.

I took out my penlight, turned it on and went exploring. There were six rooms in all: two bedrooms, bath, kitchen, front room and a den which appeared to double as an office. But there was no Jessie.

Inside the den was a recliner, a desk and chair, a bookcase loaded with romance paperbacks and a liquor cart. I helped myself to some scotch. Then I went over to the desk and sat down.

The drawers were locked. It had one of those key systems where the center draw's locking mechanism secured the other drawers. It took only a few seconds to open it. Then I set about searching drawers.

The center one contained a fat photo album.

I paged through it. There were the usual snaps from trips and gatherings. Then I came to a multi-page collection of photos with Helen Martinis as the focal point. Most were shots of Helen with Elsa. This was followed by another section that appeared to be more personal. Page after page of photos contained Jessie and Gino Picot. In each, the pair held hands like lovers. I felt a slight pang of sympathy for her and what she lost because of Jacob Tandem. Then a thought came to mind along a different vein.

With Tandem's guns keeping guard on him night and day, what were the options for Frankie Gravano to get at him? There was always gang-warfare. But with the Feds constantly lurking in the shadows, such a brazen action would likely hurt Gravano and his people more than killing Tandem was worth. Gravano could try bribing Tandem's people, of course. The locals Tandem had taken on would be easy enough to get around. But based upon the ones I had come into contact with, they were strictly second-raters. They'd never have a chance to get Tandem with his bodyguards present. The stalwarts Tandem brought from Chicago had proven their devotion to him and were untouchable.

Any other options for Frankie Gravano? Only one: Jessie Hampstead. What had Jessie said? Only she was close to Jacob Tandem.

I took out my cell-phone and dialed Leon Martin's home. If Jessie had loved Gino Picot, she might be willing to make the hit on the man responsible for his death.

When I got Leon on the line I asked if his check on Jessie and her mother turned up anything.

"Jessie's got history in Florida," he told me. "She was suspect in a shooting in Tampa a couple of years back. No charges were filed, but I spoke with the investigating officer. He says the victim was a Mafia numbers-runner from Chicago —Ignazio 'The Waiter' Terranova. It's believed that Terranova was one of the four men who backed Tandem's claims against Gino Picot when the Mob investigated that hundred million dollar embezzlement."

"What about the others who helped Tandem frame Picot?"

"According to the F.B.I. database, dead. They were Cesare 'Cheesebox' Testa, Vincent 'The Clown' Galante and Vincenzo 'Iceman' Petto. All shot. A single round fired to the back of the head—a different weapon each time. No arrests. Not one bit of evidence pointing to anybody. It was like they were whacked and then somebody came in and made a clean sweep of the scene."

"Chicago took them out?"

"Possibly. But those goons died before it got out that Tandem funds had been tapped for a hundred million—which was what cued the Chicago Mob that Tandem, not Picot, embezzled the money. Jessie Hampstead may have been an amateur when she started with Terranova. But, somebody spent a lot of time and effort to train and protect her since then."

"Somebody like Frankie 'The Wop' Gravano?"

"Gravano never believed Gino Picot was dirty. He and Picot came up through the ranks, together. Frankie knew and, according to my source, adored Jessie Hampstead. When Tandem pointed the finger at Gino Picot, Gravano refused to believe it. Even when Terranova and the others backed up Tandem's claim, he refused. But Gravano's superiors wrote off Gravano's objections as a friend trying to save a friend."

"That should've terminated Gravano's hopes of promotion."

"It would have, except shortly after the Terranova hit there was a big shakeup, within the Chicago Mafia. The Feds made some busts that eventually took out the whole upper echelon. Coincidentally, that's when Frankie Gravano made his move. A few cages were rattled and he came into power as the new *Capo de Tutti Capi*."

"It sounds like Gravano provided the evidence the Feds needed to make those busts."

"Maybe. But Gravano had the hots for Jessie. It follows he kept in touch with her. He might've had her watched. He might've figured her for that Tampa business. He might've even taken it upon himself to help Jessie take revenge on the others."

"I don't think Gravano is that love-sick, Leon."

"Maybe. Maybe not. I just wish Jessie's hit-list included my wife and mother-in-law."

"I take it your live-in loved-ones are not at home?"

"Exactly," Leon said. "Which is why I can speak freely without fear of reprisal."

Initially I had assumed Jessie's interest in the hundred million was the same as the others who looted it. Now, I changed my mind. Jessie wanted the money, sure. But the hundred million was just sauce for the main course—killing Jacob Tandem.

"Sounds like you've found the shooter Chicago sent, Leon."

"I agree. But until Jessie Hampstead makes a move, there's nothing I can do. Did you talk to Tandem about Rita?"

"He had nothing to do with Rita's disappearance," I said. "That involved Joey Fortuna and Joel Kingsley—Fortuna admitted it before Tandem had him delivered to Salvator Portello, for dipping."

"Holy shit," Leon gurgled. "You saw it?"

"I was there when Joey confessed."

"And Tandem turned you loose?"

"He thinks I have his hundred million."

There was a frantic whimper at the other end of the connection. "Where is it, Bishop? So help me God, if you have it and don't cut me in I'll hunt you down like a dog."

"Relax, Leon. I'm still having trouble finding two nickels to rub together. But should I come across Tandem's cash, I won't forget my friends."

"Where have I heard that before?"

"See ya, Leon."

"One more thing, Bishop. When was the last time you saw a Webley?"

My mind raced back to the burned-out wreck and the two losers I shot. "I don't recall, Leon. Why?"

"Remember when I told you Benny Jacobson was killed with one?"

"What's your point, Leon?"

"You're not going to believe this, but Forensics pulled a Webley .455 round from a stud in the apartment where we found Elsa Jacobson. They're pretty sure that's what was used on her. Now between you and me and the wall, what do you think the odds are of two guns like that being used in two different killings three hundred miles apart where the victims were brother and sister?"

"You're making my head hurt, Leon."

"There's more. We found a Webley in that car that went airborne off I-35."

"Are you saying that gun was the murder weapon?" I asked, trying to keep my mouth from going dry.

"Actually, Bishop, I'm asking what you know about it? Because the coroner claims those bodies in the wreck didn't die in the crash. They'd been killed by a 9mm round. Forensics found three cartridge-cases in the car. Your Mauser's a 9mm, isn't it?"

My stomach tightened unpleasantly. "That's a common caliber for pistols these days, Leon."

"You're right, Bishop. But what's not common is that somebody took out those bozos while driving that wreck to oblivion. He had to be pretty damn good behind the steering wheel and a dead shot with a gun. You see what I'm getting at?"

"Aren't your wife and mother-in-law due back soon?"

"That pair of losers were armed and would have been shooting back. Nothing personal, Bishop, but somehow you come to mind."

"Is this a formal inquiry or just a hypothetical discussion between old friends?"

"Sweet Jesus, Bishop! Was it in self-defense?"

"Close enough for police work, Leon."

"Mary Mother of God…"

"Leon, that hundred million is nearly in my hands. I'd hate for us both to lose out because of the firing-pin marks on those cartridge casings."

"And to think I used to be a good Catholic."

"You'll make a much better Captain, Leon."

I rang off, thinking about Jessie Hampstead. From what Rita told me, Jessie was part of the hundred million. I knew that Jessie had convinced Elsa and Helen to wait until the Chicago Mob assassinated Jacob Tandem before splitting the money with the men. But why? If Jessie was the one going to kill Tandem, why delay the split on that basis?

In my mind I rehashed all that Rita said about the recorded conversations and what she observed while with the three women. At the time, I had assumed Joel Kingsley was the brains behind the theft. He had the experience and the balls to take on Tandem and the Mob. I no longer thought so: Jessie Hampstead orchestrated it.

With Jessie's looks, it would have been little trouble to find out what Harold Maybe knew about the hundred million dollar embezzlement. If she gathered that information from Maybe over time in small doses, he would not realize his indiscretion.

Once Jessie knew where the money was, it was just a matter of finding people willing to risk everything.

Jessie needed someone like Joel Kingsley to play the part of the organizer. Again her looks would come into play. Once Kingsley was hooked on her, she merely had to mention that Harold Maybe knew where the embezzled hundred million was sitting to get Kingsley on her team. Kingsley, always the hero-type, would have taken Harold Maybe in hand and, through threats or physical force, gotten all the necessary details. After which, the consortium of thieves made their move.

Someone made Harold Maybe the fall-guy. It was probably Jessie. Harold would have spilled his guts hoping to save his own hide. In so doing he would have provided Tandem with the names of the other players. This information, of course, would have excluded Jessie Hampstead. Poor Harold Maybe would only remember telling Tandem's secret to Kingsley. Maybe's talking was also essential for Jessie's plan. Otherwise Tandem could not pursue his transgressors.

Jessie, of course, would have augmented what Tandem learned from Harold Maybe by telling Tandem about the Jacobson's father in Austin. Not only did this bolster Jessie's position with Jacob Tandem, it also gave the gangster a logical starting search-point. Naturally, he would want to bring his favorite bit of fluff along. Something Jessie would not resist.

For whatever reason, Elsa and Helen had the job of moving the money. I did not see Joel Kingsley agreeing to that so I assume Jessie had instigated it. She may have even convinced Elsa and Helen that cutting the men out of the money was the only way to keep themselves safe. In any event, Elsa and Helen brought the money to Austin and secured it in a public storage facility. Then, they waited—probably still following Jessie's orders.

When Jessie and Tandem arrived, Jessie connected up with the female members of her team to make sure the money was safe. By that time Kingsley and Benny had tracked down Elsa and Helen. Perhaps they knew all along where the women were headed. But I didn't think so. In any event, Jessie would have used the presence of Kingsley and Benny as justification to move the cash to Elsa's house. As part of that tactic, Jessie must have suggested they hire someone to build duplicate crates. Jessie would have explained how the new crates would be filled with the money and the original crates would be stuffed with bundles of paper In case they needed to convince someone the money was still untouched.

Then it was time for Jessie was to get rid of her cohorts.

With Jessie's experience in Tampa and in killing the others who lied about Gino-Picot, killing most of them was no problem. Kingsley, however, would not easily be taken. She had to rely upon another source of assistance: the man she intended to kill, Jacob Tandem. His men could handle Kingsley, but Tandem would make his lethal moves only after getting the money back.

How does one convince another that a missing hundred million is safely back, without actually handing it over? This was where the duplicate crates came into play. Jessie must have dumped several layers of real money in each crate so when Tandem opened them to make sure his millions were there, he would see the real thing. She probably convinced him to leave the crates where they were as bait for the thieves. With his lust for vengeance running full tilt, he would have agreed with that. Regardless, Jacob Tandem sent two men to kill Benny and those same two men to kill Elsa.

"That's the theory, at least," I mused.

There were still a couple of loose ends. For starters, why was Elsa in an apartment rented by Jessie Hampstead? An apartment Jessie did not need, and considering its crude trappings and less than luxurious location, an apartment she would not normally have rented. It made no sense. Or did it? What if Jessie offered her female partners another measure of reassurance by providing them with a place they could escape to—a safe-house, so to speak? Elsa and Helen would have received such an arrangement as a blessing. If Kingsley or Benny or even Tandem showed up, Elsa and Helen would have a place they could flee to. The reality, of course, was quite different: that little hideaway was a convenient place for murder.

I leaned back in the chair, propped my feet atop the desk, lit a cigarette and did some more thinking. Theory-wise, I had it all worked out—except for Helen. Her murder didn't fit. Tandem was convinced he had the money, I could see him killing Helen, that way. Why not? He needed take whatever revenge was available quickly because he still had Frank Gravano and the Chicago Mafia to deal with.

Deadly Turn

I tried to put Tandem's men into being the ones driving the red Dodge. But there would not have been enough time for them to get to where they ran me off the road from Lake Travis. The interval between being pulled over by Dom's men posing as Highway Patrolmen and the time of the incident was too short. Therefore it had to be someone the Patrolman talked to on the phone, after he had confirmed that Helen was in my car. That could only mean Dominic Portello.

I dropped my feet to the floor, snuffed out my cigarette in the ashtray on the desk and stood up. It was party-time. Whether I would enjoy what was to come depended entirely on Rita's safe release.

It would not be the cakewalk Jessie probably thought she could convince me to believe. Because before this night was over, she would have to kill four more people: Joel Kingsley, Rita Portello, Jacob Tandem and me.

I let my lips curl back from my teeth and headed out to the Buick.

CHAPTER SEVENTEEN

Anderson is a major thoroughfare in Austin. Number 5619 was a classy spot with a neon sign across its front proclaiming the best steaks in Texas. I did not believe it. If anyplace could make that claim, it was *Ruth's Chris*—their Rib Eye on the Bone was my idea of steak-perfection. Nevertheless, I was not there to enjoy a meal. I intended to get Rita, and with a little extra luck, her hidden hundred million to a safe place where I could work my wiles to convince Rita I deserved to be a man of leisure. It wouldn't be easy. Rita was determined to marry me and the two killers at the meeting had their own plans for that money.

I parked near the bar entrance, got out of the Buick, and went inside.

Just past the front door, I found a shadow to stand in. Then I let my eyes drift.

Jessie Hampstead sat at the bar, chatting with a guy in gray tweeds and wingtips. Jessie's hair was coiffed in a pageboy style. Her dress was equally historic in its 1930's design and peach hue. It almost looked like she was dressed for a celebration. She shifted on the stool impatiently. First, she squirmed her firm backside, then she flexed her well-muscled calves. After a moment, the process started again.

From the look on her face Jessie knew the chatty-guy was hoping to bed her. From that same look, she was trying to get rid of him.

I did not see Kingsley or Tandem or any of the Mafia-Don's men. So I strolled over and draped one arm around Jessie's shoulders.

With a start her head turned toward me. In her first moments of astonishment Jessie's face held a look that was akin to terror—her mouth gaped and she went as pink as a fresh blister. But seconds later, a gleam of defiance replaced her wide-eyed stare. Her jaw tightened. Her lips thinned.

I reached out and squeezed one of her breasts. From the angry flicker in her eyes, Jessie did not like it. But she made no resistance.

"Sorry I'm late, Hot-Stuff." I gave Jessie's cheek a kiss.

"No… no problem, Deke," she choked, in reply.

I let my hand drop from its fun and gave the guy in tweeds a dirty look.

He took that as his exit-cue and moved off.

I settled onto the stool next to hers, and lit a cigarette.

"I'd have been here sooner," I quipped, blowing smoke into her face. "But I was forced hold a couple of impromptu executions. Is Tandem still alive?"

"He's home—as far as I know." Jessie's eyes darted toward the rear of the lounge, and then back to my face.

In my dirty mind, she was no longer in the bar. I was seeing her curled up on my bed wearing nothing but an eager leer.

"I heard you've been a busy girl since Gino took his unexpected fall from grace. Four hits to your credit. Tandem will make five. Are there others planned? Such as Joel Kingsley?"

Her face wrinkled slightly and her mouth worked in silence.

"He's not going to give up that hundred million without a fight," I pressed.

She tossed the narrow corridor leading past the restrooms sign an empty look, still not speaking.

"Talk to me, Jessie. I'm one of the few people you can trust."

Her eyes returned to me and her lips settled into a thin, mean line. "I don't trust anybody, Mr. Bishop."

"What's your plan for Tandem? Do you intend to lure him out to where the money is and then pop him? Or have you got something more intimate in mind? Like a bullet to his brain while he's groaning out his last gonad-pump?"

"Go to hell!"

I took a drag on the cigarette and blew more smoke into her face. "You should've come clean to Frankie Gravano when you first pinpointed the hundred million. What you've got planned won't work. Once Tandem's dead, Frankie will realize you've got the money. Or do you plan to take him out, as well?"

One hand batted away the smoke as she forced a brittle smile. "I'll let Joel know you're here."

Jessie dug around in her purse and took out a cell-phone. After punching numbers, she told someone at the other end of the connection I was ready to deal. Then she rang off and put the phone back into its hiding place.

"How long will it take for Joel to get here?" I asked.

Jessie hesitated. "He said he'd park out back in the alley."

"Is he bringing Rita along?"

"I assume so." Her chin came up defiantly. "That was the deal."

I made a concerned sound with my lips. "If he doesn't, the deal is off."

She glanced around as if looking for rats.

"You're scared," I said. "Joel or me?"

"I think Tandem knows."

"I thought you'd put a ring through Jacob Tandem's nose. How did you convince him about the money?"

Her eyes came back to mine and she smiled slightly. "I showed it to him."

"The real-deal or the crates of paper?"

"You figured that out?"

"I knew you'd had duplicates made. The only reason would be to pull a sham. Who were the suckers? Kingsley and Benny Jacobson?"

"Tandem would not be so easily fooled. He dug down and jerked out bundles from several levels in each crate to see if all was as it should be."

"It was cold blooded of you to tip Tandem to the others."

"I didn't tell him to kill Elsa and Benny."

"What about Helen?"

"That went off, but only after a few hitches."

"Dominic Portello took care of her?"

She shrugged. "The night Helen died, he called Jacob. Jacob got real excited. He sent Joey Fortuna and several others to meet Dominic."

"No pangs of guilt over what was to happen?"

"I can't afford the luxury of emotion."

"What makes you think Tandem's figured you out?"

Another shrug. "He went out with several of his men. When they came back this afternoon he seemed very distant."

"Angry with you in particular?"

"Jacob just seemed cold, agitated. Not at all like himself."

"If Tandem's worried about your devotion I don't see him letting you wander around unwatched." I gave the place another visual going over, but I saw no familiar faces. "Did you make sure you weren't followed here?"

"Jacob thinks I'm at home nursing a headache."

"He's not that stupid, Jessie. Call Joel. Tell him to meet us at my place."

Jessie took her phone out again and repeated the number-punch. But this time there was no connection. "Joel must be on his way."

"Where's the back exit?" I asked.

Jessie tilted her blonde head toward the restrooms. "The door at the end of the hall leads out to a private-party area in the back. It's fenced in, but there's a gate to the alley."

"Let's go." I stood. "If Tandem's people are around, I want to deal with them outside—before Kingsley arrives."

She looked up at me, worry filming her eyes. "If something happens to me tonight, I want you to promise you'll kill Tandem."

"Sweetness, after what I went through today, I intend to do so in any event." I took a final draw on my cigarette, dropped it to the floor, exhaled and watched the smoke rise toward the plastered ceiling. "Are you carrying?"

"In my purse." Jessie puckered her smooth brow as she concentrated. "Are you connected in Chicago?"

"If you're asking whether I've informed on you to Frankie 'The Wop' Gravano, I haven't and I won't. But you're stupid if you think he won't come after you and the money."

"I'll be long gone by the time he figures it out."

"Mafia Don's, even second raters like Gravano, have spies everywhere."

Her eyes scanned the room again.

"Don't worry. I'll help you deal with Kingsley. Tonight you'll have the money. If you're smart you'll contact Gravano."

I took hold of her arm and pulled Jessie to her feet. "You lead. I'll follow. When we get outside, find a dark, quiet spot to hide. I'll watch the door to see who follows." I glanced at my watch. "I hope Kingsley's gets here soon."

Jessie turned toward the back of the bar and moved off on stiff legs.

I followed. As we passed the bar, I got a corner-of-the-eye glimpse of a thin man in a dark suit and light-colored fedora sitting at a table in the shadows. He rose and dug for money.

"Revenge ends when that bastard dies. You should've confided in Sal. He might've given you permission to use his dip-tank on Tandem."

"Is that what happened to Joey Fortuna?"

Deadly Turn

"It's a safe bet. Nobody touches Rita without risking a long swim in nitric acid. That goes for Kingsley, too—in case you've made long-term plans for him. No matter what happens tonight, Sal will hunt him down."

"This is strictly business."

I glanced back. The thin man still stood. He was finishing his drink with one hand while giving a hitch to his trousers with the other.

At the restrooms, I grabbed her arm and pulled Jessie to a stop. At the end of the corridor was a steel door. She turned so she faced me, her eyes narrow with concern.

"I just thought of something." I tilted my head toward the steel door. "Tandem might have men out back."

She gave a nod of agreement. "Which of us goes first?"

"Me." I jerked out the Makarov I had taken from the goon in the Double Day parking lot, and cocked it. "Give me ten seconds. Then follow if you don't hear trouble."

"You're my only lead to the money. If there's trouble, I'll be at your back."

"No too close. I tend to need swing-room."

Jessie retreated a few steps. As she moved she glanced back as if trying to lock a picture of me in her mind.

I crept over to the door and turned the knob.

Before I could react the door jerked open from the other side and two men barged in.

Jessie screamed out a warning.

I gave the Makarov a swing, catching the first man across the bridge of his nose with the weapon's butt.

He was a lumpy joker, built like a fat football player. My blow staggered him back into the second man, a moonfaced guy with spreading baldness giving his thin black hair a horseshoe styling.

The second man jerked out a pistol to fire but the barrel got caught in the first man's coat.

I pushed the Makarov against the first man's throat.

In a panic, the second man discharged his weapon. The round caught the first man in the kidneys and he dropped with a whimper.

From the café I heard screams, shouts and feet running away. But I was too busy getting my hand around the second man's throat to worry about who may have been hit after the round passed through his pal.

He tried to bring his gun into line with my head.

My knee caught his groin. Then I lashed out with the Makarov, again.

The weapon's barrel struck the side of his head. His eyes rolled back in their sockets as he crumpled. But before his knees hit the floor he squeezed off another round, sending it downward into his fallen companion.

I jerked my other knee up and caught the second man's chin.

He dropped the pistol just before sprawling onto his back.

151

I twisted toward the bar. Jessie was nowhere in sight. In the distance I heard a siren wailing. Just out back I heard car tires squeal. Thinking it was Kingsley screeching to a stop, I charged the door, bulling it off its hinges.

Outside, I saw nobody and no car. Then something cold and hard touched the side of my head.

"Drop 'em!" a voice whispered.

Off to my right, I heard the light click of a pistol-hammer cocking.

"Tandem's got business with you, Bishop," another voice chimed. "Don't get cute. He's got your girlfriend. Cough up his dough and you get her. Then the two of you will be clear of this thing. Get me?"

The second voice was the one I had heard after dragging Helen Martinis from the Buick before it exploded. He had been the one shouting orders.

I did not know if the word 'girlfriend' meant Rita or Jessie. Or if it was a complete bluff to get me to relax? I assumed it meant Tandem knew Jessie was planning to kill him. The one thing I was certain of was nobody would get clear of Tandem after being involved with his hundred million bogey—not alive, anyway.

"Do it," shouted the one on my left.

I swung my left hand, hitting his pistol. Then I twisted toward him and let the Makarov bark.

A purple-bordered hole bloomed in his white shirt.

He was one of the pair who had worked over Joey Fortuna, but he no longer looked tough or dangerous. He fell to the dirt like a bag of discarded laundry.

I twisted toward the second man intending to fire. But a second later I heard a footfall directly behind. I twisted to look over my shoulder and caught sight of a light-colored fedora. Then something hit the side of my head, shutting down my vision.

I dropped my weapons because they seemed to weigh a ton. Something hit my head, again. I whirled and reached out through a suffocating darkness only the blind know. With clawing fingers I got hold of somebody's throat. I crushed with my left hand and hung on while I swung the right. My knuckles were getting sore from bashing flesh and bone. But it was a nice pain. There was another thump to my head. My knees started to buckle. But still I hung on and still I swung my fist.

Somewhere I heard a hollow scream. Then curses. But I kept swinging, kept bashing.

Again my head took a hit. This time my arms went limp. I was tired. I needed a rest. I hit the ground as silence folded around me like a body bag.

CHAPTER EIGHTTEEN

When I opened my eyes, I tasted the murky bitterness of blood in my mouth.

I was lying on a narrow cot in a semi-dark room. There was only one window; something about two feet wide and a foot high and positioned well above human reach. Through it I saw star-pinpoints in a blue-black sky.

My hair stuck to the pillow when I lifted my head. The movement caused my skull to throb like a straining diesel, so I eased back.

I tried to raise my hands, but I was tied spread-eagle, wrists and ankles lashed to something—presumably the bed's frame.

I turned my head to look around. The room was squarish, a place I had visited before, but I could not recall when or where. Near the wall below the window was a straight-back chair. I let my eyes drift until I saw the dark outline of a door. It looked to be about four yards from the bed.

I twisted my wrists hoping to wrench free. But whoever tied me knew the business. There was not a quarter-inch of play in the ropes.

I held my breath and listened for sounds. Outside I heard the chirping of a lovelorn cricket but nothing else.

I let go my breath and filled my lungs, again listening.

This time I detected the sound of footsteps. I cocked my ears toward the sound as best I could. The footfalls were from more than one person, heavy and coming closer.

I let go my breath.

A moment later there was the grating of a key in the door-lock. Then the door-outline swung inward, chased by beams of a yellow light.

Two men, one behind the other, stood in the doorway. From behind them was the light-source. The light flickered around their forms gave the men the appearance of ghostly apparitions.

"He's awake," one of them said.

The pair came over and stood side-by-side; staring down at me.

"How's tricks, Bishop?"

Their faces were lumps and hollows in the backlighting through the door.

"Cut me loose and I'll show you," I said.

One grunted out a laugh, the light through the open door reflecting off the hard edges of his teeth.

"Tough-talker," said the other one. He stuffed a cigarette in a corner of his mouth, letting it dangle from his lower lip.

"Yeah," Laughing-boy chimed. He kept his lips pulled back from his teeth and talked through them. "But that won't last long. You'll be beggin' to die by the time we're done."

Using the drawled, over-polite voice of deliberate insolence Cigarette said, "You want to tell us where the money is and save yourself a lot of pain?"

"Sure," I replied. "It's where none of you will ever find it. Tell Tandem that. I want him to understand what he's risking."

Laughing-boy cocked his head sideways. "We'll tell him, tough-talker. In the meantime, you count your breaths. Enjoy each one."

"Because you're working your way to the last one," Cigarette chimed, causing the weed-stick to jiggle in his mouth.

Then they turned and strolled out, closing off the light and locking the door after themselves.

As I listened, their steps died along the corridor.

I took their threat to heart. If I was to get out of there alive, I had to get free of my binds.

I began a sideways shift on the bed, rocking it back and forth.

After a few seconds, it began to tilt with the inertia from my weight.

I increased the heaving of body against air until the bed began to dance on its legs. Thump-ditty-thump. Thump-ditty-thump. Thump-ditty-thump.

I thrust my hips from side to side, adding to the inertia.

Finally, I felt a sense of flight. It was momentary. A second later the side of my right wrist hit the hard floor as the bed toppled.

It did not get me free. But the change in position folded the cot's legs. This, in turn, created slack in the loops around my wrists.

It took several more minutes of squirming against rope before I got one hand free. Minutes more of struggling got me to my feet. There was no relief from the pain in my skull, but I did my best to ignore it. I was unarmed and there were at least two of them beyond my makeshift prison. Free of my binds or not, I was still a long way from being out of danger.

I put the cot back into its upright position, then moved about the room, getting the circulation going in my limbs. When they returned, I would have seconds to gain control of the situation. Mere seconds to do or die against men who were probably as skilled as I in the art of killing. I did not relish the coming struggle, but there was no alternative.

From beyond the door came the sound of approaching footsteps.

This time the footfalls were hurried, eager with anticipation.

I crept over to the wall adjacent to the doorknob and waited.

When the steps stopped just outside the door, I cocked my arm and dropped back a step putting all my weight on my splayed legs. I had to make the first swing connect with all my weight behind it.

The door swung open, letting in a flash of light. The first man swaggered in tipsily, his hands cockily akimbo at his hips.

I swung a perfect left hook that connected with his liver.

He let out a gasping, hiss of a scream. As his knees buckled, I reached inside his suitcoat and grabbed the pistol holstered there.

It took me two jerks to get it free because there was a silencer threaded to the barrel.

The second character led a sucker right. It was a feint and his left banged the side of my face.

I brought the silenced pistol to bear, and fired. The bullet went into his mouth.

Chunks of teeth sprayed out, mixed with pieces of bone and bloody flesh. Like marionette whose strings had been cut, he collapsed at my feet, flopping over on his face. From the gaping hole in the back of skull a thin stream of brains trickled down.

I turned to the first man and squeezed off two rounds, one into each of his lungs. His throat rattled for two or three seconds before falling silent.

"How's that for begging?" I asked their corpses.

Then I squatted beside each man and went through pockets. One had the Mauser they'd taken from me. I holstered it. Then I took the second man's pistol and cocked it.

With one of their guns in each hand, I straightened and crept out of the room into a long unlit hallway.

The bright light I had seen through the doorway originated from another room, three doors down. I moved toward it, not knowing what or who might be waiting.

When I reached the doorway I peeked into a red room.

The light was provided by a floodlight mounted to the top of a pipe stand and positioned head-high. With its mahogany roll-top desk, a triptych of horse-photos in gilt frames, and a large ebony and ivory crucifixion, the room looked like the reception room in a Victorian-Era brothel. It contained a horseshoe sofa covered in red velvet, chairs of carved mahogany with seats and antimacassars of red lace. There was a gilt clock on a pink, marble mantel, a grandfather clock ticking lazily in one corner, and red silk flowers stood in a crystal vase upon an oval table with a pink marble top, and curved legs. The carpet was thick and gray splotched with sprays of red flowers. There was even a mahogany cabinet for obscene bric-a-brac—with plenty of obscenity in it, dildos, vibrators and other toys for the lonely or so inclined. Long red lace curtains hung across both windows. I was back in Henrico's lake home.

There was one other piece of furniture: a wooden armchair.

Leather straps decorated each of the chair-arms. More straps dangled from chair legs. Each strap was designed to hold limbs at bay while undeterred fists worked upon flesh, and bone. A setup like that might make a man talk—assuming he had something to say. In this case, a blonde woman was strapped in it. She was naked. Her chin rested on her chest. Her arms and legs were limp within their bonds.

I hurried over, grabbed her by the hair and pulled her head up. It was Jessie Hampstead—or what was left of her.

Her eye-sockets were empty. Blood had left a trail from each of her ears. Her open mouth showed her gums and the sockets for each of her jerked-out teeth.

She wasn't breathing.

I let go and went back to the hallway. A sickness was forming in my belly. Jessie had talked—I had no doubt about that. She had told Tandem everything

—including the setup with Kingsley. She must also have told him about Joel holding Rita.

I moved down the hallway.

At a staircase landing, I looked downward through darkness.

Then I caught the scent of burning tobacco. My nose twitched at the enticing smell and my body shivered with anticipation.

I tiptoed down the stairs, following my nose.

At the first-floor landing, I noticed dim light coming from a room with a partially closed door. I sniffed.

The smoke came from that same direction.

For a moment, I let my nicotine-drained spirit savor what was to come if all went well. Then I made sure the safety on each weapon was off, the hammers were cocked and a round was in each chamber and crept forward.

Just outside the door, I paused to listen.

From inside I heard labored breathing from at least one person.

There could be others. Unfortunately, there was only one way to find out.

I took a deep breath. With guns at the ready, I nudged the door aside with an elbow and stepped into the room.

Tandem sat behind a desk, alone. He had a glass of liquor in one hand and a cigarette in the other. A half-eaten bologna sandwich rested on the desk in front of him. His lips moved like he was talking to himself. His face was wet with sweat, the kind pumped out of a guy with untreated high blood pressure. The shadows under his eyes were like pits.

When he looked up at me his mouth sagged slightly. Then the glass crashed to the floor. A moment later the petulant expression of a man used to getting his own way returned. The Mafia-Don's eyes went hostile and he rose to his feet.

I grinned. "Surprise, surprise."

His eyes focused upon the guns for a moment, then rose back to my face. "I keep underestimating you, Mr. Bishop."

"It happens a lot," I said. "I'm still looking for Rita. I've still got your money."

"Then we can do business." He dragged out a crumpled handkerchief and wiped it over his sweaty face. "I have her in a safe place."

"I saw what you people did to Jessie. If so much as a hair on Rita is out of place, I'll see that Sal dips you for my enjoyment."

"Rita's not been harmed be me or my people." He returned the handkerchief to its keep. "I can't attest to what went on while she was in Kingsley's hands. As for Jessie… She was sent to kill me. I could hardly let her actions go unpunished."

"Kingsley told you?"

He nodded, studying me through half-shut eyes. "Even the bravest of men will talk when they are bargaining for life."

"I find it hard to believe you let Kingsley go after he talked. He was as deeply involved in the theft of the hundred million as Jessie and the others."

156

"I didn't let him go." He dragged a hand wearily across his head. He was trying to give the impression of being calm and in control. But his shaking fingers betrayed him. "One of my men got careless. He won't get careless, again."

"Good help is so hard to find." I waggled the Mauser. "Take me to Rita."

He tried to grin, but all he managed was to curl up one side of his mouth.

His eyes had almost disappeared into their sockets. They were doomed eyes: the eyes you see when a man realizes there is no turning back, no starting over, no place to hide—unless a miracle occurs.

"You hand over my money and I will." His voice now quaked.

I chewed my lower lip realizing he was not going to budge under threat alone. Finally I said, "Did you ever meet Old Frank Portello?"

He just stared at me.

"Frank was an expert at interrogations. The trick, or so he explained it, was to understand a man's limitations. Some men are willing to die for their principles: God, family and so on. These you kill and move on because torture is just a waste of time. Others will try to bluff their way through. By nature, they are cowards. Nothing is more terrifying to them than dying. They are willing to sell their dignity, their country, the things they love most—so they can continue to live. I think you're that type, Tandem. I think you rode your way to the top on the coattails of other men. Men with balls. Men like Gino Picot."

"Rita will die unless you accept my demand, Bishop," he warned.

"Old Frank's favorite game was called Truth or Pain. He would ask a question. If he got the right answer, he would go onto the next question. If he heard a lie, the one being questioned felt a great deal of pain. In this instance that pain will be the result of my blowing a hole in one of your joints. The pain is excruciating. The force of the round not only shatters the bones on either side, it tears the ligaments loose. Shall we begin?" I took aim at his right shoulder with the silencer-equipped pistol. "Where's Rita?"

"I've got men outside, Bishop. One shout from me and you're history."

"Not by my body-count. You and I are all that's left. Where is Rita?"

His eyes fell to the floor as he said, "Where's my money?"

I squeezed the silenced pistol's trigger. The weapon jerked with a popping sound, as the round whined to its target.

"Jesus!" Tandem's left hand clutched his shattered shoulder; blood streaming between the fingers. "Dear God!"

I took aim at his left shoulder. "Where is Rita?"

"In the mudroom at the back of this place. Just down the hall." He forced a twisted grin. "I didn't think you were the type to get serious over a slut like her."

His innuendo put me over the edge. I sent a round into his left shoulder, then through each wrist, separating hand from arm.

He collapsed to the floor squealing like a pig as blood spurted from the stumps at the ends of his shirtsleeves.

"Where's Kingsley?" I asked.

"I don't know," he shrieked, in agony.

I fired twice more, putting a round into each of his kneecaps. At that point, his voice reached notes I had not heard since my grade-school violin lessons.

"If Rita's not as you claim, Tandem, I'll come back and finish the game."

He sagged back, his eyes rolling like white ball-bearings in their sockets. "She is."

I backed out of the room.

Once in the hallway I headed for the rear of the house. I opened each door and looked beyond only to find another uninhabited room.

Finally in the tiny room at the very back, I found her.

Rita was barefoot in thin blue Chinese pants and a loose crimson pullover —a combination that showed each and every one of her beautiful curves. She was lying on a mattress set on the floor; bound-up like a hog waiting for slaughter.

When Rita spotted me she started mumbling what I took to be blue curses. I tore the gag off to discover I was correct.

"Where in hell have you been, Bishop?" she squawked.

I dumped the pistols into my suit pockets. "I love you too, Rita." Then, I cut her loose.

Immediately she jumped up and made a beeline over to a sink mounted on the wall, dropped her pants, and perched on its rim.

"This is no time to get kinky on me," I warned. "It's been a long, tough day. I'd like to pick up our hundred million and go home."

"I have to pee, damn you."

I lit a cigarette. Many seconds later. Rita dropped to the floor. With a sigh of relief, she pulled up her clothes. With each jerk, the red shirt and what was underneath did a rumba.

"I damn near pissed my pants," she complained.

"Glad I got here in time. What brought you to Romero's place?"

"Kingsley brought me here. Then Tandem's men showed up. They caught him by surprise."

"Are you okay?"

"Now I am."

"Kingsley's dead?"

Rita opened her mouth and put a funny little confiding smile on her face. Then her eyes darted past me. The smile abruptly folded and her throat bobbed. Rita made a frightened croaking noise. Her teeth actually rattled with it.

A second later I heard a noise from behind. I whirled around.

Joel Kingsley stood in the doorway pointing a gun at us. One of his eyes was swollen shut. His lips were split and puffy. He held his left arm up with his tie as a sling, as if it had been broken.

"Looks like you've had a tough day, too," I quipped.

"Shoot the crazy bastard, Bishop," Rita shouted.

Calm determination came into Joel face as he cocked the pistol. "All I want is the money, Bishop. Just the money."

"Sure. No problem," I told him. "Rita walks out of here. Then I take you to the crates."

He moved his broad shoulders in a deprecatory shrug.

"If you think I'm going to tell you where that damn money is, Bishop, so you can give it to his bastard..." Rita blurted.

Kingsley's eyes bugged as realization hit him on the chin. Without knowing it, he'd kidnapped the one person who knew where the hundred million was. I grabbed for the Mauser. A split second later, the pistol he held belched a wad of flame.

I felt the round burn through my belly. I was raising the Mauser to fire when his second slug ripped through my right arm. My hand went numb and I heard my pistol hit the floor.

I was in motion towards him when the third round punched through my ribs.

I was still moving when the fourth burned my cheek.

By the time the fifth bore through my guts, I had him by the throat with my left hand and my knees were giving his groin a workout.

He managed to get his gun against my head, but before he could fire, another shot rang out, behind me.

Blood and brains sprayed my face, then Kingsley dropped to the floor dead.

I staggered around to see Rita holding the Mauser.

"Nice shootin', Tex." I stumbled toward her. By the third step, my legs went numb. Instantly, I hit the floor.

"Bishop?" Rita rushed over to me.

"Get out of here before somebody else shows up," I told her. "On your way out, stop by the room near the steps and put a round into Tandem's head. I want to die knowing that bastard did before me."

"Like hell you're going to die!"

"Tell Momma I'm sorry I took so long to find you," I mumbled.

"Don't you die on me, you bastard!" Rita shouted.

I chuckled as my body started growing cold. "I don't have a choice. If only I had pissed my pants."

Her hands touched my face and I saw tears streaming down her cheeks.

"You have to tell me one thing, Rita. The truth, before I die."

"Anything, Bishop," she sobbed.

"Where in hell is that damn money?"

CHAPTER NINETEEN

It was six long weeks of hospitalization before I could get around without falling, fainting, or generally oozing a bloody trail. During the last three days, my flop's landlord telephoned my hospital room each morning asking when I would be released.

Being late on the rent was nothing new in our relationship, so I offered up the usual assurances. From Horace's quivering voice, I realized there was something far more serious at issue.

"They want to keep me for another week," I told him. "Can't this wait?"

His words became babblings about corpses, the cost of renovations due to body-fluid leakage and a general fear of being boxed in cement for failing to cooperate.

"Horace," I pleaded, "what corpses? What cement?"

He broke down in tears and begged me to return as soon as possible. So against my doctor's wishes, I checked myself out of the hospital and caught a taxi for home.

It would be several more weeks before I could actually do any work. My pension was enough to handle apartment-rent and daily needs. But my office lease was another matter. I would have to put the furniture into storage and hope I could find another spot that was just as cheap after my strength returned.

"Why bother?" I muttered, as the taxi chased every pothole along I-35. "You're too damn old for this abuse. No matter which way you turn, you end up with your ass kicked. What you need is a dog, a pipe, a pair of slippers—and your head examined."

"Amen to that, brother," chimed the hack-driver. "I can dig where you're coming from."

"You used to be a Private Detective?"

He gave his head a shake. "But I used to be married."

"Redhead?"

"Meanest bitch I ever knew."

"I think it's the hair-color."

"Amen to that, too."

When I got to my apartment building, I paid the driver and made my way inside. I toyed with visiting Horace to get the lowdown on his worries, but I was too exhausted.

I made my way down the hall to my flop as quietly as I could. I would deal with Horace in the morning—assuming those little red drips running down my legs did not become a flood.

After unlocking my door, I stumbled into the kitchen. At the table, I paused to light a cigarette.

Deadly Turn

As I took a deep draw to fill my lungs with the addiction hospital-rules had denied me for the past many weeks, I noticed several new additions to my living room: five huge, wooden crates.

I blinked several times in disbelief, wondering if I was hallucinating or if this was some terrible, taunting dream. But the crates were there, all right. Five of them huddled between the recliner and the Murphy bed.

My mind raced with possibilities. But I only knew about five crates the size of steamer trunks: those containing Tandem's hundred million! I stuck the cigarette into my mouth and staggered into the living room, my arms reaching; my fingers clawing.

I reached the nearest crate and lifted its hinged top.

My breathing stopped. Piled neatly inside were bundles and bundles and bundles of hundred dollar bills. Hundreds and hundreds of bundles! For a man of my jaded interests this was more than a dream come true. It was a future filled with all that womankind, racetracks and casinos could offer.

"Well, fuck me gently…" I gasped.

"That's not my style."

I did a robotic turn toward the voice.

Sitting on the floor in the far corner was Rita Portello. She stood up, unsmiling.

"Rita," I grinned. "You've made me the happiest man in the world."

She looked at her fingernails and frowned. "By being here when you got home?"

"That's nice too." I did another stiff turn to look at the crates; my face in a permanent grin, my tongue hanging out, my eyes bulging. "Is all the money there? The entire hundred million?"

"The money isn't important, Bishop." Rita lifted her eyes slowly as if they were very heavy, and stared into mine.

"Like hell, it isn't!" Then I reached into the open crate and lifted out a couple of bundles. "What say we strip off and roll around in all this green?"

She smiled sadly. "No time."

"A sorry sense of devotion that is." I dropped the bundles back into the crate and returning my attention to her. "I don't see you for a month and a half and when I finally do, you give me a cold goodbye?"

Rita came over and gently kissed my cheek. "The emergency room doctor said you were beyond hope."

"He probably had trouble finding my pulse."

"I think it was not being able to find your insurance card."

"I had a similar reception the first time I was there."

Her silvered fingernails toyed with a lock of the hair near her left ear. "I told that doctor if you died, so would he."

"That's what I've always loved about you, Rita." I reached out with both hands patted her shoulders. "Your delicate way with people."

"Six hours later Sal and Dom showed up there." Rita looked at me emptily. "Sal was ranting and raving about how you might make it—unless his luck held. Dom was trying to convince him they should unplug your I.V. machine."

I hobbled over to the recliner and snuffed out my cigarette butt in the ashtray on the adjacent table. "I'm glad your brothers haven't lost their sense of fair play."

"I didn't dare visit you after that." She took a deep draw on her cigarette. "I loved you too much. So much, I was afraid my showing up might somehow turn your luck against you. So, Momma went instead."

I pointed at the crates. "Why the money?"

Rita gave the crates a disinterested glance. "I had those delivered a few days ago."

"I'm surprised Sal didn't force you to send Tandem's millions back to Chicago."

"I hoped the money would convince you to marry me."

"Marriage?" I gave the crates another greedy look. "Why ruin the good thing we've got?"

"That's what I thought you'd say." She walked over and gave me a light tap on one cheek. "You're never going to change, are you?"

I grinned at her. "Like I said, why ruin a good thing?"

Rita backed away, chuckling softly. "Why, indeed?" Then she turned away offering me her back. "I went to the doctor this morning. He… Never mind. I just thank God you're going to make it."

"Are you ill?"

"No." She turned to face me. Her eyes tried to focus on my face, but I could see they were vague and empty, as if the love behind them had died. "The Doc says I'm as fit as they come."

I walked over to the second crate and tilted up its top. More piles of green came into view. "What about something to drink? We'll celebrate while deciding how to split this."

"I gave up the booze." She held up the hand holding her cigarette. "My last one—at least for the next eight months."

I moved to the third crate and looked inside at more bundled bills. "Momma's been preaching virtue again, I take it?"

"No." Rita snuffed her cigarette out in the ashtray on the table next to the recliner. "Things have changed in my life. While you were at the hospital I did some real soul-searching. I decided it was time I grew up. I decided it was time I took responsibility for myself—and mine."

I reached inside the crate and dusted my fingers across the cash. "My landlord didn't ask any questions when you had these crates dumped here?"

Rita nodded. "He was very curious—until I told Horace they were full of bodies my brother needed to store until you got back home. He didn't want to hear anything after that."

"That explains his phone calls." I looked over at her my brows furrowing in puzzlement. "What possessed you tell Horace a lie like that?"

She folded her hands and tried to smile. "I figured it was the only sure way to keep him from nosing around."

I went over to the fourth crate and lifted its top. Inside, were more bundles. I moved my jaw with the idea of saying something. But the sight of all that green left me dumb.

She swayed back over to me. "I paid your back rent—apartment and office."

I gave Rita a smile of appreciation. "I'll pay you back."

"Forget it."

"Leon Martin came by the house. He wanted to question Dom about Helen Martinis. Before he left, he gave me empty cartridge cases. He said they belonged to you. I put in one of the kitchen drawers."

"Dom was driving the red Dodge, wasn't he?" I said.

Her eyes dipped to the floor. "He wasn't driving it. Joey Fortuna was."

"Dom's lie or fact? Not that Fortuna will be able to refute it."

Her eyes flashed over at me. Then her voice snapped, as if she was aching to turn it loose on me. "My brother had nothing to do with what happened to Helen."

"No? Dom called Tandem because he was trying to give Helen a helping hand."

"When Dom realized she had gotten away after the accident, he panicked." Her hands clenched. "The store isn't doing well. In fact it's a bust. He thought settling for the five million Tandem originally offered would be better than ending up with nothing. So Dom asked for any men Tandem could spare." She paused to take a deep breath. "I'll deny all of this if you take it to the cops."

"I assume it was Dom's idea to frame me for Helen's death?"

Her head nodded ever so slightly.

I was then my eyes noted her wan countenance. Rita looked like she had aged ten years since last I saw her.

"You look tired," I remarked.

"Lately my morning-stomach disagrees with me." Rita came over and gently wrapped her arms about my neck. "I'm going to miss you, Bishop." She gave me a light kiss on the lips, turned and headed for the kitchen.

"Where are you going?" I called to her back. "I thought we'd sit around, get drunk and while you were putting a smile on my face I'd be counting out the money-split."

"There's fifty grand in your checking account," she said, still moving. "That should take care of you until you're strong enough to work."

"A hundred million in mob-money? You think I'm going to work?"

Rita paused at the doorway into the kitchen to look back at me. "Ninety million."

"Not that I'm looking a gift horse in, but won't Frankie Gravano wonder what happened to all Tandem's green?"

"As far as Sal, Dom and Chicago are concerned that money burned up with Tandem."

"Burned?" I echoed. "You burned down Romero's lake home?"

"Sal did. You know how he likes everything nice and tidy. I think it's his feminine side."

"More likely a fear of leaving fingerprints. What's Romero going to do? He'd planned to retire there."

"I made him whole on the deal."

"Whole, how?" I asked, glancing over at the crates.

"Don't worry. It came out of my end."

"Tell me something," I said. "How did you get me to the hospital?"

"Sal was tailing Joel Kingsley hoping Kingsley would lead him to me. When Kingsley started shooting, he and Dom and the Sicilian Brothers came in."

"Your brothers actually wanted to help me?"

"Not exactly. I put your gun to Sal's head and told the Sicilian Brothers to get you to the hospital if they valued their continued employment. They did, surprisingly enough. Or maybe they would've done it anyway. For some odd reason they like you."

"That must've put you on his black list."

Rita backed away smoothly, lightly. "He'll get over it—in another eight months."

My brows furrowed in confusion. "You've got it down to a calendar date?"

"To the day—if I'm not late."

I went to the last crate and pushed up its top. It was filled like the others. "I'm thinking a fifty-fifty split. Fair enough?" I said, still gaping at the bundles like a young sailor at his first strip-show.

"What's there is yours, Bishop. I already took my cut."

I reached in and picked up several of the bundles. "When are you coming back?"

"Never."

I dropped the bundles back into the crate. "I know I'm a little on the soggy side in spots. But I think if you do most of the work I can manage a bow, or two."

Her lower lip went in under her teeth and her eyebrows dipped at the corners. "I'm not in the mood."

"Wait!" I called. "We've got things to discuss."

"Nothing more to be said, Bishop."

"But I barely leak." I hobbled after her. "We'll put towels on the sheets. You can be on top just in case I need artificial respiration at the critical juncture."

Rita opened the door and looked back. "Enjoy your life, Bishop."

I felt a terrible pain in my heart. "You can't walk out on me, Rita."

She drew a long breath and let it out silently. "I won't forget you, Bishop."

I watched her walk out and close the door. "She'll come back," I told myself. "How can she not? I'm a dirty old man with nearly a hundred million in cash. A young man of low moral character would be dead within a month, having this much money. In my current physical state, I'll barely last a week—

unless Rita curbs my natural cupidity. If nothing else, she'll come back to keep me alive, and in misery."

I went back to the crates, drooling. "It's all mine. Ninety million!"

I grabbed up one of the bundles and tore the binding off.

A pile of blank paper littered the floor at my feet, along with two one-hundred dollar bills: one from the top and one from the bottom of the bundle.

"Shit!"

I grabbed up several more bundles ripping each open with the same result.

"That conniving little bitch!" I turned and hobbled after her. "She took her cut, all right. Rita! Rita, you get back here. You're not running out on me with all the money. Rita? Rita!"

The End

We hope you've enjoyed DEADLY TURN.
Please check with BooksForABuck.com or our fine distributors
for more books in the
Deacon Bishop: Private Detective series.